I0701300

Old Friends

A Novel

Thomas I. Nygren

ISBN 979-8-9880031-0-6

Copyright © 2023 by Thomas I. Nygren
www.tinygren.com

All rights reserved. No part of this book may be reproduced, scanned, or distrib-uted in any printed or electronic form without permission.

This is a work of fiction. Names, characters, businesses, places, events, locales, and incidents are either the products of the author's imagination or used in a fictitious manner. Any resemblance to actual persons, living or dead, or actual events is purely coincidental.

Cover photo taken by the author at Hanging Rock State Park, North Carolina. Cover design by Vini Libassi.

Published June 2023

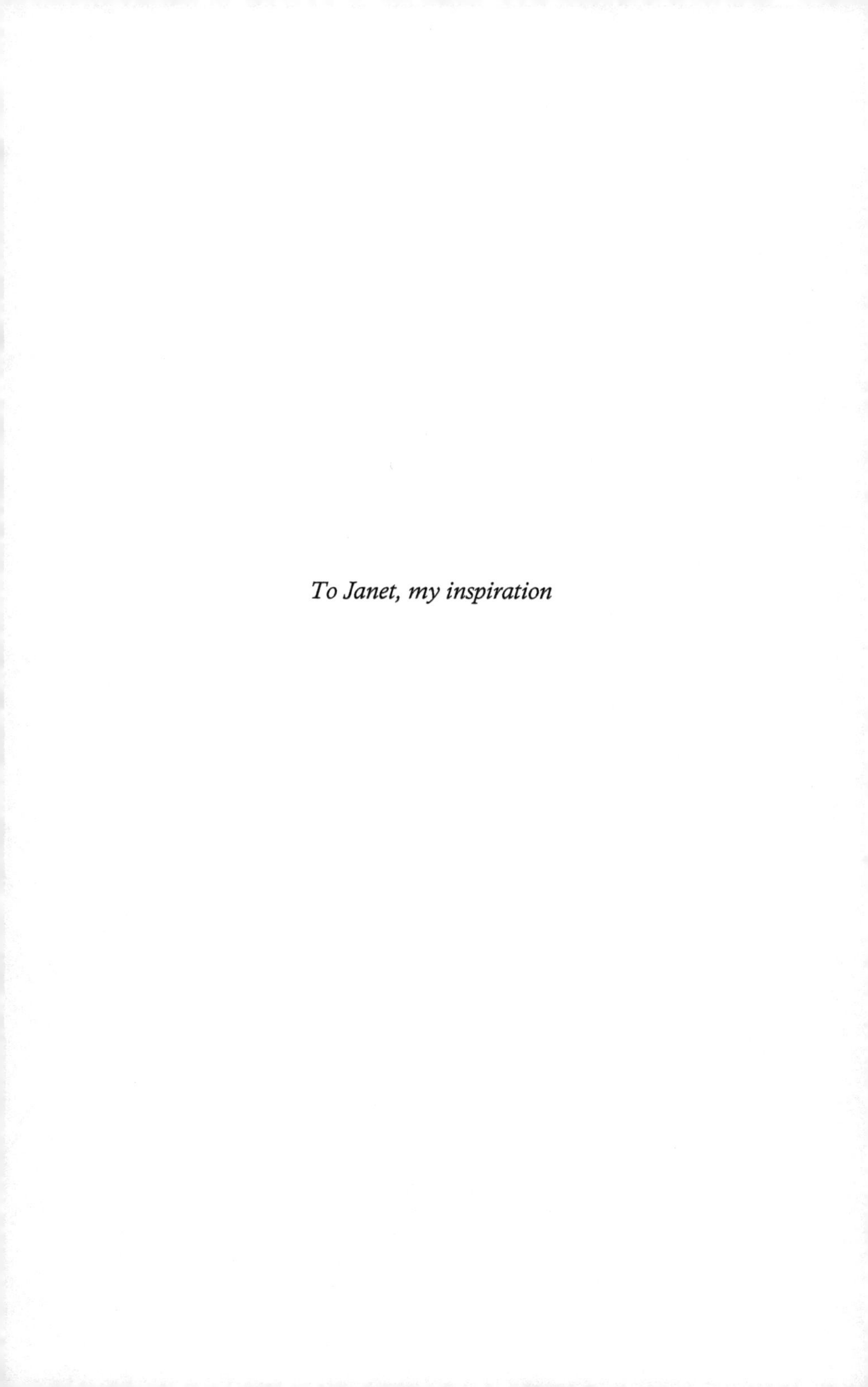

To Janet, my inspiration

ONE

We need to prank him," said Buddy to Bunny as she walked through the den on her way to the kitchen. "Frank's moping around like a dead dog, what with Becky out of the nest and a dead-end job that's as boring as hell." Buddy was in his usual spot, half watching a golf game from his favorite recliner.

Bunny stopped and looked at her husband. In the shadows, the light from the TV reflecting on his balding head, just visible over the back of the couch, created an odd effect, like a gibbous moon resting on the horizon. "I don't think the dead are much good at moping, or anything else." Bunny never missed a chance to skewer Buddy's mangled metaphors. "And who said hell was boring?"

"You know what I mean. We need to do something to get him out of his funk. I swear it's worse every time I see him."

"How's Cathy doing?" asked Bunny, her voice softening. "You never say anything about her."

"Oh, she seems fine, I guess," replied Buddy. "But what Frank needs is some kind of shock treatment. Wake up the old Frank. You know, like that epic prank I pulled at the U of O that set the two of them up in the first place."

"Not this again." Bunny rolled her eyes. She had heard Buddy wax fondly over this hallowed incident so many times she could recite it from memory. "How exactly are you going to recreate something that took place on a college campus thirty years ago? And aren't you forgetting some of the details? You didn't exactly set them up. Whatever—just leave me out of your harebrained schemes. Meanwhile, I think I'll go do something useful." She stalked into the kitchen.

Buddy slouched back in his leather recliner. Bunny was right. It would be hard to recreate that moment of inspiration back at the old U of O. His mind drifted back to those golden-hued days—yes, he didn't mind the cliché—the good old days. Life was simpler then. More fun. You knew what was what. In spite of his gloomy mood, a shadow of a smile crossed his face.

Why *had* Frank left his final paper for Poli-Sci 325 lying on his desk in plain view that day? It wasn't like him, Buddy mused. They were both juniors, both majoring in political science, often taking the same classes at the same time. Frank always got better grades, but he didn't like talking about it. He was funny that way. Very private. Buddy had never even glimpsed one of his graded assignments before. Did Frank *want* him to see that particular paper? It wasn't like him to be careless. Maybe he was mad at him about something—wouldn't be the first time. *And to be honest, I was a little peeved myself that day*, Buddy admitted to himself.

The night before, in the cafeteria, Frank had cracked a joke about Buddy that managed to penetrate even Buddy's thick skin. That was also not Frank's style. The usual gang had been sitting around the table as Buddy approached with his plate and pulled up a chair. "Where's Bunny?" Frank had said. "Still waiting for you at the library?" This was a reference to a well-publicized incident the previous weekend when Buddy had completely forgotten he was supposed to take Bunny out to dinner. She had fumed for an hour, until eventually she found him playing pool in the student center, literally a stone's throw from their planned meeting point at the library entrance. In truth, Bunny *was* still pissed, and that was, in fact, why Buddy was by himself in the cafeteria on a Friday night. Buddy had laughed with the rest of them, but it had stung all the same.

And so, he had picked up the paper off Frank's desk ("The Implications of Republican Gerrymandering on Voting Patterns in Essex County") and seen the professor's comment scrawled in red pencil under the A+. "Great job, Frank—one of the best analyses I've seen since I started teaching this class eight years ago. Definitely a strong candidate for the SP." The SP was the coveted Spencer Prize, awarded annually by the Political Science Department for the best undergraduate research paper. It was a big deal—not only for the prestige, but it came with $1,000 in cash. Buddy could never dream of coming close to such a prize, but he wasn't surprised to learn Frank was in the running. Buddy carefully put the paper down exactly as he had found it. An idea was beginning to germinate deep in his brain.

That Monday, he strolled into the office of the Political Science Department. He knew the dates of upcoming faculty meetings would be posted on the bulletin board. He was in luck. The next meeting was in exactly one week: next Monday from two to four in the Faculty Senate Room. The department chair was Professor Henry F. Jackson, a formidable and imposing personality, famous for once being listed on Ronald Reagan's so-called "Black List" of subversive academics. Buddy had never met him, and he doubted Frank had either. Old Jackson was not the type to hang out with lowly undergraduates.

Now Buddy just needed an accomplice, and he knew exactly who to ask.

Later that day, Buddy waited outside the football stadium, watching the shadows lengthen across the carefully manicured grounds surrounding the sports complex. He wondered if Frank had ever been on this part of the campus—doubtful, he thought. He had been waiting for close to an hour, sitting on a low wall under the protective glare of a huge bronze eagle whose claws and beak menacingly guarded the entrance to the sacred grounds of the stadium. Dozens of players trickled out in twos and threes, looking tired and hungry as they headed for their dorms, luxuriously constructed adjacent to the complex.

Where could Mouse be? They had been roommates their freshman year, and although Buddy had not seen much of him lately, he knew Mouse should be at football practice at this time of day. Had he missed him somehow? For the hundredth time, he craned his neck to peer into the entrance. He was starting to feel anxious; without Mouse, the prank would be a lot harder to pull off.

Finally, when he was about to give up, he saw a familiar shape looming up out of the shadows. As sometimes happens in the world of sports, his former roommate's nickname reflected the exact opposite of his actual appearance. Mouse was a mountain of a man, six foot six, weighing in at just over three hundred pounds. But Buddy was not interested in his size. It was his voice he wanted. Mouse, who was the sweetest and gentlest person Buddy had ever met, had a voice that could rouse a sleeping army, lull a charging tiger to sleep, and, more importantly, fool Frank.

Buddy jumped up and stepped directly into the path of the oncoming figure, imagining for a second what it must feel like to be a running back about to be hit by a human locomotive. "Hey Mouse! What's up? Why are you the last one out?"

Mouse looked startled, and then stopped in his tracks, almost losing his balance. When he saw it was Buddy, a broad smile lit up his face. "Coach made me do ten extra laps. I was late to practice," he answered. His deep, powerful voice, barely above a whisper, still gave Buddy goosebumps. "Long time no see, Buddy."

"Yeah, I know, I've been going crazy with assignments. How's the team looking this year? I haven't been able to make it to a single game yet." Buddy sounded like a squeaky chipmunk in comparison.

"So-so, I guess. I finally get to start, so that's good." Buddy caught a whiff of dried sweat, instantly bringing back vivid memories of their freshman room. "But I'm not expecting any championship rings," Mouse added, glancing longingly over Buddy's head at the lighted cafeteria windows across the grass.

"Hey Mouse, I know you want to eat, so I won't beat around the bush. I need your help to prank Frank." He smiled at his accidental rhyme. "You just have to make one phone call. No sweat, right?" Buddy made his voice sound nonchalant, but he was mentally crossing his fingers; Mouse could be unpredictable, and he didn't have a lot of time to come up with a Plan B.

"Buddy, you know how I feel about pranking people. Somebody always gets their feelings hurt. I don't like it. I thought Frank was your friend; why are you messin' with him?"

"Don't worry, Mouse, no one's going to get hurt. It'll be funny. Frank'll probably die laughing, that's all—it's going to be great. And remember, you still owe me one. I saved your ass in that math class." Buddy hated bringing up the math class, but he was getting hungry himself and didn't feel like a long, drawn-out conversation. "What do you say? Will you do it? Just one simple phone call, that's all. You've never talked to Frank before, have you?"

Mouse frowned and lowered his head, looking Buddy right in the eyes. "Okay, Buddy, for you, I'll do it. No, I've never met Frank. But please stop asking me for this kind of stuff." As he spoke, Mouse turned up the dial on his voice a couple of notches and Buddy could almost feel the vibration in his skull. It was not the volume—Mouse had barely raised his voice. But there was some quality of strength, authority, and intensity that was hard to describe and impossible to ignore. When Mouse spoke, which he rarely did, people paid attention.

Buddy let out his breath in relief. "Mouse, you're the best. I swear, this is the last time. Mouse, forget about football—you've got to take up acting or broadcasting, or something. Maybe opera. Hell, you should run for president. With that voice, the world is your oyster. Okay, here, I wrote down exactly what you have to say." Buddy handed him a sheet of paper. "You have to make Frank believe you're Old Jackson from poli-sci—no problem, right? Can you do it at exactly three p.m. tomorrow? I told him I was expecting a package, and he said he would be in the room. Actually, we should practice first. Call me tonight—Frank will be at the library; if he's in the room, I'll pretend you're my mom."

"Okay, Buddy, you got it. But remember, this is the last time." Mouse started walking and Buddy quickly leaped out of the way, lifting his hand in a quick wave at Mouse's massive back receding across the grass.

* * *

FRANK WAS READING IN his room the next day when the phone rang at exactly three o'clock. He grabbed the receiver and, without pausing, said, "Second floor, third door on the right," assuming it was the call about Buddy's package.

6

"Excuse me, I'm trying to reach Frank O'Donnell. This is Professor Henry Jackson." The voice was powerful, commanding, terrifying.

"Oops, sorry, sir, speaking, that's me," gulped Frank.

"I'm glad I reached you, Frank. I have some good news for you. Your recent paper in PS three twenty-five has been awarded a departmental prize. Congratulations, Frank."

"Wow, thank you, sir, that's extremely awesome, I mean, yes, sir." Frank was starting to sweat. He mentally kicked himself: *Get hold of yourself, you idiot.*

"Frank, as you know, there are multiple prizes awarded every year, not just the Spencer Prize. It is our tradition to invite all the winners to a faculty meeting, at which time the individual prize winners are announced."

"Yes, sir, very exciting, sir. A great honor, sir. Thank you very much." *I'm babbling*, thought Frank.

"The faculty meeting is next Monday in the Faculty Senate Room. Please come at precisely three p.m. The meeting will be in progress. Just knock on the door and come in."

"Yes, sir, thank you, sir. I will be there. Promptly, sir. At three p.m., sir." Still babbling, Frank cursed himself.

"And Frank."

"Yes, sir."

"Don't wear jeans."

"No, sir."

"Goodbye, Frank. We'll see you on Monday at three p.m. Don't be late."

"Yes, sir, no, sir, thank you, sir. Goodbye." Frank gasped with relief as he heard the click of the phone hanging up. He shakily dropped the handset back in its cradle. Old Jackson himself—possibly the Spencer Prize. He couldn't believe it.

That night, when Buddy walked into their room, Frank greeted him excitedly. "Buddy, guess what, my paper won a prize!"

"Wow, that's awesome, Frank! You won the Spencer Prize?" Buddy had a huge smile on his face.

"I might have, I'm not sure. There's more than one prize. Can you believe it? Old Jackson himself called me—it's lucky I was here when he called. I have to go to the faculty meeting next week to find out which prize it is. But I definitely won something. Buddy, have you ever talked to Old Jackson? I almost wet my pants I was so scared. His voice is incredible. Like listening to, to . . . I don't know how to describe it . . . like, like, when the room vibrates from some guy's speakers turned up too loud out in the street . . ." Frank's voice petered out. He shook his head and shivered.

"But Buddy, you have to help me. He told me not to wear jeans. What am I going to wear? I don't even have a suit. Will I have to make a speech?"

Buddy looked surprised. "Don't worry, Frankie boy. We'll get you a suit and tie somehow. Congratulations, you deserve to win. Yes, I think you should definitely have a speech ready, just in case. Maybe more than one, to cover any eventuality." Frank didn't notice that Buddy's smile was even wider than before.

Monday rolled around. Frank had spent most of Sunday afternoon agonizing over what to say if he was asked to speak. After hours of effort, he had a two-minute speech memorized; there would be no sweating and babbling this time. At two o'clock, Buddy helped him struggle into a suit they had borrowed from someone down the hall who was closer to Frank's size—Buddy owned two rather elegant suits, but he was a good four inches taller than

Frank. Even so, the suit did not fit particularly well, and Frank was feeling more and more self-conscious.

"I hate dressing up. I hate ties. Why do I have to wear this?" he complained, standing in front of the mirror and trying to scrunch his arms up inside his sleeves so his wrists wouldn't stick out. The jacket felt tight across his shoulders. Behind him, he heard something that sounded like a snort.

"Hey, what are you laughing at? Do you think I *want* to wear this stupid suit?" Frank turned around and saw that Buddy had buried his face in his elbow and seemed to be having difficulty breathing.

"Sorry, can't breathe, must be my allergies," he said in a strangled voice. "You look great. I'm sorry I can't walk over to the department with you. I have a, uh, a study date. But I'll walk you outside."

In the hallway, their next-door neighbor Billy smirked at the sight of Frank. "Nice suit, Frankie. Got a hot date? Kind of early, isn't it?"

"Shut up, Billy," growled Frank. "Get back in your cave."

As soon as they were outside, Buddy turned in the direction of the library. "Sorry, Frank, gotta run. Good luck! Give 'em hell! You can do this!" He strode briskly away, coughing and apparently having trouble breathing again, his shoulders shaking.

At the political science building, Frank walked slowly down the corridor, his feet echoing in the near-empty hall. The receptionist had glanced at him curiously. *Probably this ridiculous suit*, Frank groused to himself. He was ten minutes early. The door to the Faculty Senate Room was closed. He stood awkwardly, rocking back and forth from one foot to the other. A group of students strolled by, staring at him. Two girls glanced at each other and giggled. Frank swore under his breath and pretended to read the notices on the bulletin board.

He could feel sweat trickling down his back. He stared at his watch—the second hand dragged slowly around, pausing pregnantly at each number. With excruciating slowness, the minute hand touched twelve. He stepped up to the door, raised his hand, and knocked. Silence. *Urgh*, he thought, *why did I knock so softly*. Old Jackson had said to knock and walk in, but he couldn't bring himself to just open the door. He tried again, this time rapping his knuckles sharply on the polished wooden door. He thought he heard a faraway voice, so he took a deep breath, straightened his shoulders, and pushed the heavy door open.

The room was empty. No, not completely. A solitary figure sat at one end of the long, polished table, surrounded by books and papers and illuminated by a single row of lights directly overhead. Frank blinked, adjusting to the dim light, and perceived that the figure was female, looking up at him in surprise.

"Hi, can I help you with something?" she said politely.

"What . . . the faculty meeting . . . isn't this the . . . did I miss it?" Frank stammered in confusion.

"Did you say the faculty meeting?" she asked. "Oh, that was cancelled, or maybe rescheduled. Old Jackson is in the hospital. He slipped in the bathroom last week and broke his hip."

"His hip? In the hospital? Last week? Cancelled?" The wheels began to turn in Frank's head. "Damn." He smashed his fist on the table, threads popping somewhere in a seam of the too-tight jacket. "Damn, damn, damn. He got me good this time. I can't believe it. Damn."

"Um, would you care to tell me what's going on?"

Frank had almost forgotten about the girl.

"Oh. My roommate. I think I've been pranked big time. Damn, damn, damn. Just out of curiosity, have you ever talked to Old Jackson? What does his voice sound like?"

"Sure, lots of times. What does his voice sound like? Kind of southern I guess, sort of ordinary professor-ish. He's a sweet guy, actually."

"A sweet guy? How do you know him? I thought he ate students for lunch."

"That's what everyone thinks, but it's not true. I work part-time in the poli-sci office, so I see him all the time. They let me study in here when no one's using the room— that's why I'm in here. I don't suppose you want to tell me about the prank? My name's Catherine, by the way. Although my friends call me Cathy. Which I don't like."

Frank belatedly remembered his manners. "Frank, I'm Frank. Nice to meet you, Cathy, I mean Catherine. Sorry to disturb you. My roommate tricked me into thinking I was going to get an award today. He got some friend of his to call me and tell me to be here at exactly three p.m. during the faculty meeting, and just to knock and come in. Damn. I guess I've been saved by a slippery bathroom floor. Can you imagine if I had come bursting into the faculty meeting?" Frank shuddered. "Plus, he got me to wear this stupid suit. Damn, damn, damn."

Catherine tried unsuccessfully to hide a smile. "So, I guess your roommate doesn't know the meeting was cancelled either?"

"No, I guess not, but what difference does that make? What I need to do now is plot my revenge."

"Exactly," replied Catherine. "Suppose you tell him that his prank worked perfectly. Maybe throw in a few 'damns' for effect . . . but then maybe let on that Old Jackson didn't take it too well."

"Wait," said Frank, "you mean a prank within the prank? Interesting. I like the way you're thinking, but how would he ever believe me?"

"It just so happens," said Catherine with a glitter in her eye, "that I might be able to get my hands on some department letterhead . . ."

That night, Buddy was waiting on his bed when Frank walked into their room. "How did the award ceremony go? Did you give 'em hell?" he asked with an innocent look on his face.

"You are going to die a slow and painful death." Frank grabbed a pillow and began mercilessly pounding Buddy on the head. Buddy rolled onto the floor, laughing uproariously.

"Stop, stop, seriously, what did they say?" Buddy gasped. "Was Old Jackson there?"

"In a wheelchair," replied Frank. "He broke his hip last week. He was not a happy camper. I was standing in the door like an idiot, everyone staring at me, and Old Jackson says, 'Yes?' So I say something stupid like, 'I'm here about the award.' There's a dead silence and Old Jackson goes, 'What award? What is this all about young man?' By now I had figured out something was not right. For one thing, it was a completely different voice than on the phone. And Buddy, I think I did a bad thing, although it serves you right, damn you."

"What?" said Buddy from the floor, still wiping tears from his eyes.

"I told them my roommate must be behind this. Someone started to laugh, I think it was Atkinson. But then Jackson goes, 'Young man, this is not a laughing matter. You cannot simply barge in here and interrupt our meeting. Please leave immediately.' So I said 'Yes, sir, very sorry, sir' and jetted out of there as fast as I could. And now I am going to kill you." Frank jumped on

Buddy, trying to crush him in a vice grip around his chest, but Buddy, though weakened by laughter, was bigger and stronger and pushed him away.

"Who cares if they know it was your roommate. They don't know my name, and besides it was worth it." Buddy started laughing again. This time, Frank joined in—although not for quite the same reason.

The letters arrived two days later, looking very official on department letterhead and signed by Old Jackson himself. The letter for Buddy read:

```
Dear Mr. Kowalski:

On Tuesday, November 7, the faculty meeting
was    rudely    interrupted    by    Mr.    Frank
O'Donnell as part of a prank instigated by
you. It is a serious matter to disrupt the
dignity and decorum of our proceedings. This
kind   of   juvenile   behavior   will   not   be
tolerated.    The    faculty    has    unanimously
voted   to   formally   reprimand   you   for   your
role in this incident.

Furthermore, to underscore the seriousness
of this offense, the faculty is requiring
you  to  publicly  apologize  by  means  of  an
announcement published on the front page of
the   Daily   O.   This   announcement   must   be
published during the week of November 14,
at your expense.

A copy of this reprimand will be placed in
your student file.

It is the sincere hope of the entire faculty
that you will reflect upon your actions and
learn   a   positive   lesson   from   this
experience.

Sincerely,

Henry F. Jackson

Faculty Chair
```

"What! This is ridiculous!" moaned Buddy. "They can't do this to me! What kind of crap is this, 'dignity and decorum' my ass. Old Jackson has never liked me ever since we TP-ed his house last Halloween. Don't I even get a fair trial? And how come they're not making *you* put an announcement in the *Daily O?* Is this even legal? How did they find out it was me?"

Frank did his best to sound shocked. "Damn, this is going in my file too. I tried to warn you—I don't think it's a state secret that we've been roommates for the past two years. How should I know why I don't have to put something in the *Daily O?* Maybe because I already apologized in front of all of them at the meeting, which was not the most pleasant experience, I can tell you. This really sucks. Just do what they say, or else you'll make things worse. This is all your fault anyway. You know students have zero rights at this place."

Frank held his breath. It had been Catherine's idea to write letters to both of them, to allay any suspicion Buddy might have. He seemed to be buying it. It was a common practice for students to place personal ads on the front page of the student newspaper; the bottom inch of the page was reserved for that purpose. Students had even been known to propose marriage. But Frank suspected this ad would break new ground if Buddy fell for it.

And, in fact, Buddy did fall for it. The ad appeared the following Tuesday:

```
I, Rudolph Kowalski, hereby humbly apologize
for instigating my roommate to disrupt the
Political Science faculty meeting on November 7
on false pretenses.
```

That Wednesday, as students were collecting their books and notes at the end of the Poli-Sci 325 lecture, Professor Atkinson spoke up over the murmur of voices.

"Ah yes, there is one more announcement I neglected to mention. The faculty meeting originally scheduled for November seventh will take place next Monday, now that Professor Jackson is out of the hospital." As he spoke, he looked directly at Buddy, a hint of a smile in his eyes.

Buddy turned to Frank. "Now why the heck is he telling us that . . ." A look of comprehension dawned in his eyes, and then chagrin, as a faint pink blossomed on his cheeks. "Golly gee whillikers," he said slowly, "I think I've been pranked."

* * *

IN A WAY, reflected Buddy with the hindsight of thirty years, the fact that he had fallen for Frank's prank-within-a-prank evened things out, cleared the air. Otherwise, it might have turned into something else. Frank *had* won the Spencer Prize that year, which hadn't hurt, either.

Buddy sighed and gazed dreamingly at the bright rectangle of the TV in the dim light. The memories were surprisingly vivid: the look on Frank's face after the phone call from Mouse; Frank's skinny wrists sticking out of his jacket sleeves (the whole no-jeans thing had been ad-libbed by Mouse—*What a genius.* Buddy smiled to himself. *So wasted on football . . . I wonder what ever happened to him?*); the rib-splitting laughter after all had been revealed; even the musty smell of their dorm room. *What I wouldn't give to have those days back again,* he thought wistfully.

Bunny reappeared from the kitchen. "You're still here? It was so quiet I thought you must have left. What have you been doing all this time? It looks like the golf game is over."

"Oh, just thinking about how I can prank Frank again," said Buddy. "And I think I just might have an idea."

Bunny rolled her eyes again.

15

TWO

Frank sat in his car in the driveway and regarded his house. "Nondescript," he thought. "A nondescript house for a nondescript person in a nondescript life."

The house, a modest split-level ranch in a quiet neighborhood, was identical to the other houses lining the street, except that every alternating house was a mirror image of its neighbor. Spring was a few weeks away, the grass still brown and, Frank knew, full of weeds lurking and plotting for warm weather. In an earlier phase of homeownership, Frank had tried for several years to get rid of the weeds in the grass so his lawn would match the perfection of the neighbors on either side, who were known to get up early on summer mornings to carefully spritz with weed killer any lone dandelions that had popped up overnight. Frank's lawn seemed to need gallons of the stuff, but no matter how hard he tried, the dandelions spread like wildfire. He was sure his neighbors hated him for the seeds that blew across the property line. Whenever Frank finished mowing, he would stomp into the house cursing the lawn, cursing the weeds, and, sometimes, cursing God and the universe. Eventually, Catherine had quietly taken over the weekly job of mowing. She had decided it was better to focus him on other projects.

He grabbed his briefcase, got out of his car, and slammed the door behind him. Although they had a garage, it was impossible to use it. For Frank, it was another metaphor for his life. "Full of useless crap," he grumbled. "I swear, this is the year it gets cleaned out, even if I have to burn it." For a moment, he fantasized about smoke pouring out of the garage door, boxes of old bills exploding in flames, and bags of abandoned stuffed animals melting in puddles of plastic.

Frank opened the front door and paused, listening for Catherine. If classical music was playing, he knew she would be on the couch in the den, red pen in hand, grading piles of assignments. The work of a teacher never ended at the door of the classroom. For that matter, neither did the work of a senior accountant.

Frank sighed as he glanced at the briefcase weighing down his left arm like a sack of cement. He heaved it to the floor, harder than he needed to, next to the pile of shoes and umbrellas cluttering up the entryway. An umbrella toppled over, striking the stack of newspapers waiting to be recycled, tumbling them into the open doorway and preventing the front door from closing. Frank cursed, carefully restacked the papers, and stood the umbrella up. It promptly fell over again. He knew for a fact that this particular umbrella was non-functional. "More fuel for the garage apocalypse," he grumbled.

No music, so she must be in the kitchen. Frank took a detour through the dining room. He knew that Fred would be sleeping on the chair at the head of the table, partially hidden by the edge of the tablecloth. Growing up, his family had always had a cat, and the cat had always been named Fred. Frank had continued the tradition, much to the annoyance of Becky, who had just entered middle school when this particular Fred arrived. In protest, she had named the kitten Bubbles and defiantly sworn that the name Fred would never cross her lips again. But her protest had been short-lived, and it wasn't long before Bubbles was forgotten and Fred was just Fred. Frank scratched Fred between the ears and continued into the kitchen. A moment later, he heard a quiet thud as the cat jumped to the floor and followed him, knowing that Frank's arrival meant dinner.

"What was all that noise, honey?" asked Catherine, looking up from the kitchen counter where she was assembling two salads in carved wooden bowls.

"The usual stupid umbrellas, stupid newspapers, and stupid crap that my life is full of," he groused. "Why can't we get rid of some of the junk in this place?" Immediately, he felt guilty. Catherine was the one who kept the house together, quietly doing most of the household chores with never a word of complaint, despite the fact that she too had a full-time job. Why did he always snap at her these days? The tiniest things seemed to set him off, like pricking a balloon with a pin. "Sorry," he muttered. "Is Becky here?"

Fred purred and rubbed against his legs. Frank dumped a spoon of tuna-flavored Purina Cat Chow in his bowl (Fred turned up his nose at any other brand or flavor).

"No, I haven't seen her since I got home. It's Friday— she's probably out with her friends."

Frank was about to make a comment about Becky's absence, but then held his tongue, knowing it would probably just upset Catherine. He knew she had been hoping Becky would eat dinner with them regularly, now that she had graduated from college and was back home again. Being an empty nester had been hard on Catherine—on both of them, really. At first, Becky had made a point of eating with them, and Frank had seen Catherine start to come to life, like one of those bulbs that suddenly shoots up in the spring. For a few brief weeks, it had seemed just like old times. When Becky was young, and even through most of high school, Catherine had always made it a priority to have dinner together as a family. But lately it seemed like Becky was always out. Where she went, or what she did, was a mystery. From time to time, some of her friends would appear at the house. But they rarely stayed long and Frank did not have a clear sense of who was in Becky's world.

"Do you have a lot of work this weekend?" asked Catherine, her back still toward him as she chopped vegetables. "I was thinking we could do something fun tomorrow. It's supposed to be a pretty nice day. I saw some snowdrops blooming by the school; maybe we could go to the park and see if anything else is blooming." Frank heard the microwave beeping behind her.

"The usual. No, not the usual, worse than the usual. That idiot Rupert, who is the most obsequious slimebag I have ever had the privilege of working for, is obsessed with getting the monthly reports done two days before they're required, just to make him look good. I know for a fact that the real deadline is Wednesday—I even asked the department secretary. There is absolutely no reason I couldn't do them on Monday, or even Tuesday, but no, I have to have them done by Monday morning so he can print it out and put a little plastic cover on it for his boss, just like a fifth grader sucking up to his teacher. This happens every month and I'm getting sick of it."

Frank often ranted about his latest boss. A pattern had emerged over the years: his supervisor would be promoted, Frank would apply for the position, someone else would get the job, Frank's hopes would be dashed, and the process would repeat itself three or four years later. Lately, his new bosses had all been significantly younger and less experienced than Frank. His cynicism had slowly grown, and with it, his rants and sarcasm.

"Well, maybe we can at least go on a walk around the neighborhood." Catherine set two plates of warmed up meatloaf and microwaved potatoes on the kitchen table, grabbed some salad dressing from the fridge, and sat down to eat. "There's cold beer in the fridge."

"No thanks, not for me. I just had a beer, on the way home. Buddy and I finally got together after work today. We've been trying to find a time for weeks. I don't think we've seen each other since last November."

"Oh good, I'm glad you got together—how's he doing? Are you guys going to be able to make it to the first Phillies home game this year like you usually do?"

"Yep, got it on the calendar. He's fine, I guess. Things seem to be going along about the same as usual. If anything, he seems a bit restless. We were both remarking on how long we've been in the same jobs." Frank pulled up a chair opposite Catherine.

"How's Bunny?" Catherine asked.

"He didn't say much about her, although I guess he did mention that her real estate business has really taken off this past year. So I suppose she's pretty busy."

Frank stabbed his fork into the meatloaf and took a big bite. Silence descended, and the clink of their forks and knives was the only sound to be heard. He knew Catherine wished he would tell her more about his day and what he was thinking, but he just didn't have the energy. Nothing ever changed, so what was there to talk about? Anyway, telling her what he really thought about his life would probably just make her feel bad. If he waited long enough, he knew she would eventually break the silence. In the stillness, he could hear himself crunching on his salad, and focused on chewing as quietly as he could. For some reason, Catherine never made any noise when she chewed.

Catherine said, "Today is the end of the third marking period, so I actually have nothing at all to grade this weekend, if you can believe that." Catherine taught fifth grade at the local elementary school. She loved her job and was good at it. "I picked up a couple of DVDs at Blockbuster on my way home—want to watch one with me tonight?"

Frank grunted, which Catherine took for a yes, but they both knew he would probably not make it through a whole movie. He was usually out of the house by six thirty in the morning, and it was a rare movie that could keep him awake after a beer. But Friday night movies were a tradition, going way back to when they would watch Barney the dinosaur with Becky when she was a preschooler (Frank shuddered, remembering the insidious Barney song that even now sometimes surfaced from the hidden recesses of his brain), and he knew spending time with Catherine was important. At least a movie would be easier than trying to carry on a conversation.

After they had stacked the dishes in the sink, Frank found his favorite spot on the couch and Fred promptly jumped up on his lap, purring and curling into a ball, the tip of his tail covering his nose. Catherine settled on the couch next to him. Sure enough, it wasn't long before Frank felt his head jerking and flopping sideways. He yawned loudly, causing Fred to open one eye and twitch his tail. "Sorry love, I think I'd better hit the hay. Maybe we can finish the movie tomorrow night."

Catherine smiled. "Sure honey, I'm tired too—I'll be up in a few minutes." With that, Frank stumbled upstairs and was sound asleep minutes after his head hit the pillow.

"FRANK, FRANK, ARE YOU awake?" Frank grunted and rolled over to the far side of the bed. Catherine was sitting up, her brow furrowed. "I don't think I heard Becky come in last night. Did you?"

"Is it morning? What time is it?" Frank tried to see the numbers on the digital clock on his bedside table. The clock read 6:37. "Catherine, can't you let me sleep at least one morning of the week? You know how I feel about that." He pulled the covers over his head and closed his eyes again.

"I'm sorry, honey. I just realized I never heard her come in." Catherine was a light sleeper. Becky's room was at the far end of the hallway on the second floor, and to reach her room Becky had to walk by Catherine and Frank's door. The steps and floor had creaky spots that were hard to avoid (although Becky was quite good at it).

It was funny—when Becky had been away at college, doing whatever she wanted at all hours of the night, they had never worried about her at all. But having her back in the house had brought back all the anxiety of the parents of a teenager, especially for Catherine. She was still trying to figure out what it meant to have an adult child back in the nest.

"I'm going to check if her door is closed."

Frank closed his eyes again. But seconds later Catherine was back. "Frank, wake up, something's wrong! She's not here. Her bed hasn't been slept in!" He bolted upright, his heart pounding. Visions of mangled cars and flashing ambulance lights popped into his mind. Like every parent, Frank had always lived in dread of phone calls in the middle of the night. Something terrible must have happened. They both ran down the hall. Frank switched the light on. Catherine went back out and checked the bathroom, and then came back and looked in Becky's closet. "Her toiletries are gone, and a lot of her clothes are missing. I don't see her suitcase either."

Frank's heart was still pounding, and the room seemed to be revolving in slow motion. Tiny details jumped out in sharp outline, as if a camera were taking freeze-frame shots. The high heel of a shoe sticking out from under the unslept-in bed. A framed childhood drawing of the three of them, slightly askew on the wall above her bed. A dresser drawer partly open, with a brightly colored piece of fabric sticking out.

"Something's happened. I'm calling 9-1-1." Frank started to run out the door.

"Wait, Frank, stop, calm down. What are you going to tell the police? That our twenty-two-year-old daughter missed her curfew? Could she have just gone away for the weekend with friends and forgotten to tell us? I can believe she might stay out all night, but pack a suitcase and leave without telling us?" Catherine walked over to the dresser. "It looks like her jewelry box is gone too. Wait, Frank, what's this?"

With shaking hands, Catherine unfolded a small square of paper that had been propped up against the mirror. She read it and handed it to Frank. It didn't take long to read, scrawled in Becky's loopy, still oddly childlike handwriting.

> *Mom, Dad—I know this will be a shock, but I'm in San Francisco with Ricky. Don't worry, we're staying with some friends of his. I'll call and explain tomorrow. Please don't freak out. Love, Becky*

Frank looked at Catherine. Her face was frozen in shock. Frank's heart began to slow down. Images of mangled steel and shattered glass faded, replaced with a flood of questions. "San Francisco? Ricky? Who is Ricky? What is she doing? Why didn't she tell us? I'm calling her cell phone right now." His initial feeling of relief that

Becky was not in jail or about to die was quickly turning to anger.

"Frank, you can't call her now—it's four in the morning on the West Coast." Catherine's eyes began to fill with tears. She put her arms around Frank; he could feel her trembling. "Frank, I don't understand."

"I don't either. What's going on? Why San Francisco? Why did she run off without telling us? And who the hell is Ricky?"

"One of her friends. You've met him. He's been here a few times. I think you even talked to him once—a skinny black guy, glasses, scruffy clothes. He seemed pretty nice. I think he was some kind of computer guy. Maybe that explains San Francisco—you know, Silicon Valley and all that." Catherine pulled away from Frank and took several deep breaths, wiping her eyes with the back of her hand.

Frank made an effort to remember. "Okay, yes, now I know who you're talking about. We did have a conversation once—something about hacking, identity theft, that kind of thing. He seemed really into it. But I don't know about nice. More like young and full of himself, the kind of guy who thinks he knows everything just because he studied computers. She's with *him*? A black guy? In San Francisco? I can't believe this is happening." He pulled himself free from Catherine's arms and said abruptly, "Let's go downstairs. I need some coffee."

In the kitchen, he switched into autopilot. He had once calculated that he had made coffee in that kitchen over ten thousand times: six cups of cold water poured from the carafe into the top of Mr. Coffee, a fresh filter from the drawer below the counter, six rounded scoops of coffee from the can, the satisfying click as he flipped the brew switch and the green light blinked on, the comforting gurgle as water began to trickle into the filter.

The smell of the fresh coffee began to calm his nerves. Fred appeared and wound around his legs, purring furiously and meowing for breakfast. Getting up early suited him just fine.

"Why would she do this to us? She literally ran off with some strange guy without telling us. She's never done anything like that before. I don't trust that Ricky person any farther than I can spit. He must be behind this. What do we do now?" Frank could feel his rage growing. "I don't care what you say, I'm calling her right now."

He grabbed the kitchen phone from the wall and dialed Becky's cell number from memory. It went directly to voicemail. Frank had not thought about what to say on a message. He blurted out, "Becky, we got your note, how could you do this to us? . . . uh, we hope you're okay, please call as soon as you can." He hung up and cursed.

"Ugh, that was awful. I sounded mad. That's not going to make her want to call us."

Catherine, calmer now, said, "She said she would call. I think we just have to wait. What else can we do? She'll probably call after she wakes up, and if they were flying all night, who knows when that might be."

"I can call the cops about that Ricky slimebag, that's what I can do," muttered Frank, but he knew Catherine was right. "I guess I'll try to get some work done in the meantime, if I can concentrate, that is." He took a sip of scalding black coffee and popped a frozen bagel into the toaster. "Do you want a bagel?" Catherine shook her head.

The morning hours ticked slowly by. Frank opened his laptop and made a half-hearted attempt to pull together the monthly sales figures, but his mind had trouble focusing. Once, the phone rang, sounding twice as loud as usual in the eerily quiet house. They both jumped, but Catherine got there first. It was the local fire department making its annual fundraising call. Finally, Frank couldn't sit still any longer and called out to Catherine. "I'm going on a walk—want to come?"

"No," she answered, "I want to stay near the phone. I don't know if she'll try the landline or one of our cells. Anyway, the cell coverage around here is lousy."

Frank went out the front door, turned left, and then right at the first side street, toward a small park a few blocks away on the other side of their neighborhood. The maple trees along the street were starting to get that deep red color that meant buds were starting to form. Frank always looked forward to spring. The winters in New Jersey weren't too bad, but the cool, damp weather seemed to drag on forever as March turned into April. Today, the breeze in his face was mild, and, just as Catherine had predicted, he saw clumps of snowdrops already starting to bloom in south-facing gardens where the sun had warmed the soil. The mild weather seemed incongruous with the unsettled thoughts and emotions swirling in his head.

Unbidden, a memory flashed into his mind. Becky was in middle school. Frank had come home late as usual, angry with his boss as usual, disgruntled with life. When he had walked in, Becky was in tears on the couch. Unlike her father, she had hated math with a passion. "I just don't get it," she said. "I never get it. And it's stupid and point-less."

Frank sat down next to her and looked at the problems she was working on. "Becky, these are the same as what we worked on last night. You know how to do these! You're just not trying." He had sensed her stiffen next to him.

"No, I hate math, I hate it, and I can't do it!" she had burst out, "I'm not doing this. I'm just stupid and I give up." She jumped up and stormed out of the room, tears of anger and frustration streaming down her face. Frank had felt his own frustration boiling up inside of him and shouted after her, "Well I guess you *are* stupid if you won't even try." He heard her door slam upstairs. Then he too had stomped out, going outside and slamming the front door behind him.

It occurred to him that he had walked this exact same route that night. *Why, why did I call her stupid? How many times did I say things like that? What does she think about me? What kind of a dad am I? Why do I always seem to be angry at someone?* He could feel the tension inside him, like a tightly wound spring. He looked up at the pale blue sky, framed by gently waving maple branches silhouetted against the light. An old robin's nest from the previous summer was wedged in the crook of a branch. *I guess we really are empty nesters now*, he thought. *Where has our little bird flown?*

THREE

After Frank left to go on his walk, Catherine sat at the kitchen table watching the phone, pretending to read the newspaper spread out before her. She knew she was overreacting; kids in their twenties did this kind of thing all the time. Becky was not dying in an emergency room, she had not overdosed on drugs, she was not in jail, she had not been kidnapped. She was in California with a friend. She had probably just decided to go on the spur of the moment. The phone was going to ring any minute.

The phone was an ugly beige color that clashed with the white appliances and pastel colors of the kitchen. It was mounted prominently on the wall next to the door into the garage, the long, twisted cord dangling below it. When Fred was a kitten, he had loved pouncing on the cord, once actually pulling the handset off the cradle and nearly being hit as it crashed to the floor. She hated that phone. Why did Frank refuse to get a new one? He could at least get a wireless handset—who else still had landline phones connected to the wall with old-fashioned spiral cords? Frank had this theory that the neighbors would be able to listen in if they used a cordless phone—as if anyone would care about their boring lives.

She looked at her watch: ten thirty on the East Coast, seven thirty on the West Coast. Becky wouldn't wake up that early, would she? What about jet lag? Would that make her wake up earlier or later? The image of Becky's unslept-in bed upstairs popped into her mind, the bedspread smooth and neatly tucked under the edge of her pillow, just the way Catherine had taught Becky to do it when she was in second grade. In fact, it was still the same bedspread, a profusion of spring flowers in her favorite colors, faded now but still brightening the room.

Maybe it was the unslept-in bed that triggered the still raw memories, never fully healed even after twenty-five years. It wasn't the note, because Frank hadn't left a note when he disappeared. When Catherine had returned from the hospital that Saturday afternoon almost exactly twenty-five years ago—driven by a friend, because Frank was nowhere to be found—their bed had looked just like Becky's: untouched, the bedspread tucked neatly in under the pillows. The house had been deathly still, no lights on, the air slightly stale. But it was the neatly tucked-in bedspread that had convinced her Frank hadn't slept there and was really gone. When left on his own, Frank never made the bed at all—a waste of time he always said; why make the bed when you're just going to sleep in it again in a few hours?

The memory was surprisingly vivid, even this many years later. That Friday she had noticed a few spots in the morning. Her three-month checkup was coming up on Monday. Everything had been normal with the pregnancy up to that point, so she decided she would wait until Monday and ask her doctor about it then. As Frank ran out the door, she waved goodbye and finished getting herself ready for work. There were more spots after lunch. She decided to call her doctor after all. Maybe her doctor could squeeze in an appointment after school was out.

Dr. Abram had called back right away. "Yes, come in as soon as you can," he said calmly in a no-nonsense tone.

"I need to wait until the kids leave; I'm on bus duty today," she replied, still not feeling overly concerned.

Getting the last kid on the last bus seemed to take forever. The first cramp came right after she pulled out of the school parking lot. It was not too bad, but moments later there was a second one—this one like a sudden stab of a knife in her gut that took her breath away and made her gasp. She decided to go directly to the ER, abruptly swerving into the left lane and making a U-turn at the next intersection. She heard a screech of tires and a horn from somewhere behind her.

A knot of fear started to form in her stomach as she merged onto the main highway. She tensed, waiting for the next cramp. When it came, she grunted and couldn't help squeezing her eyes shut. She heard the thump, thump, thump of her tires hitting the rumble strip on the edge of the road and swerved back into her lane. "Oh God, help me make it," she whispered.

For as long as she could remember, Catherine had wanted to have three children. Growing up in a family with four kids had sometimes seemed chaotic—especially with three older brothers. So she had decided three would be perfect, with gaps of two years, or three at most. That was the way it would be. Although they had been married just over two years, Catherine knew that motherhood was her calling and she had convinced Frank to start a family as soon as he had finished his master's in accounting. The timing of the pregnancy was perfect; Catherine would be able to keep teaching right up to the end of the school year and have the baby in July. She was hoping to stay at home the first few years, maybe longer, assuming Frank had a decent job.

And now, what was happening? Fear began to morph into terror as Catherine swung into the ER drop-off. How could she park? She needed to call Frank—but how? She dumped out her purse on the floor of the passenger seat, looking for a pen and something to write on. An orderly came up to her window. "Ma'am, do you need help?"

Another cramp gripped her in its vice. She felt dizzy with the pain. "Yes, please, can you call my husband." As the pain receded, she finally found a pen at the bottom of her purse and scribbled Frank's number on the back of a grocery store receipt. "His name is Frank—please, tell him I'm here and to come as fast as he can." She thrust the crumpled piece of paper out the window.

The orderly took the paper and helped her out of the car, holding her arm as she stumbled through the automatic doors. "What about my car," she gasped, "I'm sorry, can you tell him to move the car too." She could feel something warm and wet between her legs. The next few minutes were a blur as she was sucked into the impersonal efficiency of the emergency room. A doctor asked her about her pregnancy. Time must have passed, because she thought she heard Dr. Abram's voice. She heard disjointed phrases between the waves of pain, *heavy bleeding . . . looks like inevitable . . . d and c.* The voices faded.

More time must have passed. Now she could hear Frank's voice, surprisingly distinct, yet sounding distant at the same time, as if he were shouting across a great chasm. "I don't know where her insurance card is. It should be in her purse, but her purse is empty."

She drifted back into unconsciousness. Later she awoke again with no sense of how much time had passed. "What time is it?" she asked groggily. She heard footsteps and then Frank came into view.

"It's just after nine p.m." Frank sounded weary.

"Honey, what's happening, is the baby okay?" Terror flooded into her heart.

Frank took her hand. "Oh Catherine, I'm so sorry. There was nothing the doctors could do." Even in her grogginess, Catherine could sense the agony in his voice. As the truth sank in, tears welled up in her eyes and she began to sob, great heaving sobs; she couldn't breathe. She heard Frank call for a nurse, and heard footsteps. "We're going to give her a mild sedative to help her relax and sleep," said a voice. She felt Frank squeeze her hand and heard him whisper, "Just try to sleep right now, my love. You've been through a lot."

With the help of the sedative, and exhausted by grief and pain, she slept deeply all night. And then, the next morning, when she awoke, Frank was nowhere to be found. The nursing staff was a different shift and had never even seen him. Her purse was on her bedside table, everything neatly in place, with a ticket for the parking garage prominently visible in the front pocket—Frank must have discovered the contents on the floor of the car. Using the phone beside her bed, she called their home number, his office number, Buddy, everyone she could think of. Nothing—one knew anything.

After another visit from the doctor, the hospital discharged her about midday, warning her that she was not in a condition to drive. Not knowing what else to do, Catherine called a friend from church. She left her car in the parking garage, a problem to be solved later. She did not tell her friend about the miscarriage. "The doctor just wanted to do some tests and observe me overnight," she lied. When her friend asked where Frank was, she told her he was traveling.

At home, when she unlocked the door, she was greeted by angry complaints from Fred about his empty food dish. She fed him and was rewarded by loud purrs that seemed to echo in the quiet house. She wandered dully into the bedroom, pulled back the untouched bedspread, and crawled under the covers. *I'm so tired*, she thought. A wave of grief rose up inside her, but she pushed it down. She felt Fred jump up on the bed by her feet.

It was Fred who woke her up later in the afternoon, meowing inches from her ear and batting her cheek with his paw. Catherine could tell he was still not pleased that his dinner had been skipped the night before and wanted to make sure it didn't happen again. She fed him and sat down at the kitchen table, feeling drained. The ugly phone leered at her. She tried to convince herself to eat something, and finally made herself a piece of toast. The hours inched by, the world seemed flat and dull. *Where is he*, thought Catherine? *Where is he?* She stared at the phone on the wall, willing it to ring. *Where is he? Where is he?*

That night, lying in bed in the empty house and trying to sleep, Catherine heard the front door click. She sat up and listened. Yes, she could hear steps on the stairs. The bedroom door swung open, and there stood Frank, his clothes rumpled, his hair disheveled, dark circles under his eyes. Catherine stared at him.

"Hi, I'm home." Frank's voice was flat.

"What happened? Where have you been? You didn't call, I've been sick with worry!"

"I went on a walk. I'm sorry." Frank kept his eyes on Fred, who was happily winding around his legs and purring.

"That's it? You went on a walk? You couldn't be there when I woke up in the hospital? I don't understand. You couldn't even call me? You couldn't leave me a message?" Catherine could hear her voice starting to rise and become shrill. "What is wrong with you? What kind of a husband are you?"

"I came back, I'm sorry," said Frank in a low, tired voice, still avoiding her eyes.

Now Catherine was screaming. "You came back? That's all you can say? Don't you understand? Our baby is dead. I needed you. You weren't there. How could you not be there when I needed you? Don't you even care? What is wrong with you?" Her anger shocked her. She had never screamed at anyone before.

Frank finally looked her in the eyes. "Yes," he whispered. "I do care. I didn't know what to do." A single tear trickled down his cheek.

And that was that. Catherine never found out exactly where he had gone, or what he had done while he was gone. At first, she had tried to talk to him about it, but he always clammed up, hiding inside some private world of his own pain. Some part of him deep inside was hidden from her. Even now, it was hard to get him to share anything about what he was really thinking. Last night at the dinner table had been typical: a few sentences about his day, and then either long silences or her doing most of the talking. Whenever she tried to share her own feelings, he seemed to clam up even more.

At times, she worried they were slowly drifting apart. It had been worse after Becky left for college. Now that Becky was back home, Catherine had hoped he might open up more, be more like he was when they first got married. Memories of the old U of O days and the first few years of marriage flitted through her mind. She would give anything to bring back the Frank she had fallen in love with in college, the easygoing, funny, smart, sweet Frank, the Frank she had married the day after graduation, nearly twenty-seven years ago. She knew *that* Frank was still there—even now, on good days, she could catch glimpses of him—if only she could find a way to break open the shell that seemed to have slowly hardened over the years.

After the miscarriage, life had returned to normal, more or less, at least on the outside. The doctors said there was no reason not to try getting pregnant again, and two years later Becky was born after a pregnancy that was uneventful, but haunted by fear every day. The birth itself was very difficult, with a prolonged labor that eventually ended in a C-section. She decided going through that once was enough. And the thought of another miscarriage was ever present in the back of her mind. At least she had Becky. But now Becky's bed was unslept in, and here she was, sitting in the kitchen in an empty house, staring at the same ugly phone.

The phone rang. Catherine froze. It rang again. She snapped out of her reverie and snatched it up. "Becky?"

"Hi, Mom, it's me." Relief flooded through Catherine.

"Oh Becky, it's so good to hear your voice." Catherine was worried she might start to choke up.

"Mom, I'm fine. I'm sorry to leave like that. I know you probably freaked out. Did you get my note?"

"Yes, we saw your note. But oh sweetie, what's happening? What are you doing? We're so worried."

"Mom, I knew it would be impossible to explain it to you. I decided it would be easier to just go, and tell you after the fact. I knew you'd never agree and I didn't want to have a huge argument. Ricky and I have been planning this for weeks. He has a connection here who has a lead for a good job. You know, Silicon Valley. It's where all the action is. It would be a perfect job for him if he can get it."

"For weeks?" Catherine swallowed. "But you could have talked to me about it. I would have listened."

"Mom, the truth is, you would never have let me go, and you know it. You've never let me go. Would you seriously have been okay with me going to California with Ricky?"

Catherine was silent for a moment. "Where are you going to live? What are *you* going to do?" she said weakly.

"I'm thinking about graduate school. Maybe at Santa Clara, or San Jose State. We should be able to afford it if Ricky gets the job. We don't know where we're going to live yet—it depends on the job. Right now, we're staying with some friends of his in the city."

"Oh sweetie, why didn't you talk to us? We would have let you go." Catherine could feel tears welling up again.

"Mom, I don't think you're hearing me. I love you, and I know you love me. But you and Dad have been like this huge protective blanket swallowing up my life. I just needed to get away. You would never have let me go."

"But what about Ricky? We don't even know anything about him. What kind of a person is he? It seems like he has a really different . . . background than we do." Catherine bit her tongue as soon as the words were out.

Immediately, she could hear the defensiveness in Becky's voice. "Mom, are you saying that because he's black? That has nothing to do with anything. He's a great guy; I met him at Ithaca. You would like him too if you had taken the time to get to know him. I brought him by the house lots of times, but you never had any time for my friends. You never like my friends. We love each other. You have to let me live my own life."

Catherine wiped her eyes with the back of her hand. "Sweetie, I'm so sorry, I didn't mean that. And I have gotten to know lots of your friends. It's just that . . ."

Becky cut in. "Mom, I forgot to charge my phone, and I have to go soon. I'll call again later. Tell Dad I love him."

"Sweetie, don't hang up. Please. We need to talk about this."

"Goodbye, Mom. I'll talk to you again soon. I'm fine— please don't worry." The phone went dead.

Catherine felt drained. Was Becky right? Had they been a huge protective blanket? But why couldn't they have talked about it? Why did Becky see her as so unapproachable? She had always prided herself on her close relationship with her only daughter. How could she have been so blind? Her mind spun.

Suddenly she remembered Frank. Where was he? Oh yes, he went for a walk. And, as if prompted by her thoughts, at that moment she heard the click of the front door—another echo of that night twenty-five years ago.

"Hi, Catherine, I'm back. Did Becky call?" Frank appeared in the doorway.

"Yes, I just hung up with her. She said to tell you that she loves you."

"Well, what did she say? What's happening? Where is she?"

"She didn't say exactly, except that they're staying with friends. It wasn't a long conversation. She didn't want to tell us she was going because she thought we would just get into a big argument and never let her go."

"That's ridiculous," said Frank. "Is she coming back? What is she doing?"

"No, I don't think they're coming back. At least not right away. She said Ricky has a lead on a good job in Silicon Valley, although it still sounded kind of iffy to me. She said they love each other. She wants to go to graduate school out there."

"She *loves* him? I can't believe this. I knew this was all his fault." Catherine could tell Frank was starting to get angry again. "I remember him now. A creepy guy, always walking around with a smirk on his face, always talking about the great things he's going to do. I know his type."

"She said we have to let her live her own life."

"Well, not if she does crazy things like running off in the middle of the night with someone we don't even know. And I don't trust Ricky either. I'm going to go out there, find her, and bring her back." Frank's cheeks were flushed.

"Frank, we don't even know where she's staying. I don't think you can just go out there and bring her back. That's going to make things worse."

Frank slammed his fist against the door frame and Catherine could see the anger distorting his face. "Just you wait and see! I refuse to let some punk steal away my daughter!" He stalked out of the kitchen, opened the front door, and slammed it behind him.

Catherine put her head in her hands; she could feel the tears welling up again. Another memory came into her mind. This time Becky was ten or eleven and they were snuggled up together on the couch reading, the book illuminated by a warm pool of light from the antique floor lamp they had inherited from her parents—the same place she sat almost every evening now when she had work to do. At that age, and continuing through most of middle school, she had read to Becky every night before bed, starting with *The Chronicles of Narnia* and continuing with other classics like *Black Beauty, Watership Down*, the complete *Little House on the Prairie* series, and eventually *The Hobbit* and all three volumes of *The Lord of the Rings*. Often, if he didn't have to work late, Frank would join them too, sitting quietly in his big recliner on the opposite side of the room, listening with his eyes closed in the dim light, Fred sleeping on his lap. It had been Catherine's favorite time of the day. Even now, she could almost feel the warmth of Becky's little body nestled against her, the sense of peace and safety surrounding them, the house still and calm.

That particular night, something in the book they were reading, perhaps in one of the Narnia books when the children had to return back to the real world, had prompted Becky to say, "Mommy, I never want to go back to the real world." Catherine had laughed. "This *is* the real world, sweetie. And it's time for real little girls to go to bed." Now, remembering that night, Catherine wished with all her heart that she could be back on the couch again with Becky snuggled up next to her. "I don't like the real world either, sweetie," she whispered to herself.

FOUR

That same Saturday, Buddy stared out the window in his den and tapped his pencil against his front teeth. *This might be a little trickier than I thought*, he admitted to himself. *But do minor complications ever stop a master prankster? Not on your life.* He had to do this for his buddy.

The bar had been noisy on Friday, and they had only chatted for half an hour, but Buddy could tell that Frank was not in a good place. It had been several months since they had seen each other, and the long gap had made the changes in Frank more obvious. His face looked gray and pallid, and he seemed simultaneously more withdrawn—not even smiling at Buddy's terrible puns—and more on edge, like a balloon ready to pop. Buddy wasn't sure what the problem was, or even if there was a specific problem, but Frank did not seem like the easygoing, slightly sardonic, dryly funny friend he was used to hanging out with.

When inspiration had struck the previous evening, his idea had seemed brilliant and blindingly simple. This was typical of Buddy's inspirations. But complications inevitably crept in—"devilish details," he called them. The image that had suddenly flashed into his mind was a sign in the parking lot of Frank's suburban office building. He sometimes picked Frank up at work to go to a ballgame, and he was certain he could remember a prominent "Employee of the Year" sign above a parking spot right next to the front entrance. (*What a bunch of crock*, thought Buddy—*why not give them some real money instead of a pathetic parking spot?*) Might there be a parallel, it had occurred to him, between "employee of the year" and "research paper of the year?"

What I need, he thought, *is inside information*. And who better to help him than his old pal Cathy Simmons—she needed to be in on this anyway. He picked up his phone, and then put it down again. *Be smart*, he told himself. If he called now, Frank might answer. He had to get Cathy when she was by herself—which, now that he thought about it, couldn't be that hard: Frank had never in his life gotten home before six o'clock. *Patience, my friend, patience*, he counseled himself. Step one was getting Cathy on his team. *If only I had done that the first time around*, he thought, grinning to himself, and remembering the prank-within-a-prank.

THE FOLLOWING MONDAY, Buddy waited until four thirty, figuring that even dedicated school teachers like Cathy should be home by then. Just in case, he had an excuse up his sleeve if Frank answered ("Hey pal, we need to plan our first Phillies game"). Catherine picked up on the first ring. "Yes?" Her voice sounded tense.

"Hey Cathy, it's me, Buddy. Long time no see!"

"Buddy? Oh, hi, how are you. Frank isn't home yet— maybe try at seven."

"No, Cathy, that's why I'm calling now. I want to talk to *you*. I need your help with something."

"My help? With what?" Catherine said guardedly. Buddy began to worry that he had his work cut out for him.

"Cathy, Frank seemed kind of low when we got together on Friday. I want to cheer him up, and I had an idea. How about we try to organize a surprise party for his fiftieth? You know, do something special, get a bunch of his friends together." Buddy had figured Catherine would not be able to say no to a surprise birthday party.

"Well, I suppose that might be nice, but I don't know how you'll ever surprise him, especially not for his fiftieth. And we were thinking of going away that weekend. Besides, things are kind of stressful right now. I don't know if we can pull this off, Buddy. It's a great idea, but maybe this is not a good time."

Fearing she was about to hang up, Buddy quickly jumped in. "That's where I come in. I have a genius idea for surprising him. Remember that epic prank I pulled our junior year at U of O?"

"How could I forget that? Dementia hasn't set in yet! But what do you mean? You're going to prank him again?" Catherine's tone had shifted from discouraging to cautiously curious.

"Exactly. That's exactly what we're going to do, Cathy. Plus, we're not going to do it on his actual birthday." Buddy hoped the use of "we" would subtly move Catherine from "if" to "how."

"What do you mean? How is it a birthday party if it's not on his birthday? When are you going to do it?" Catherine sounded skeptical.

"Don't you remember how with our U of O gang we always tried to pull off surprise birthday parties? And how it got to be that everyone expected it, so it was impossible to surprise them anymore?"

"Yes, I do remember." Catherine smiled. "So we started having the parties when they wouldn't expect it, like two days before their birthday, or at six in the morning."

"Exactly. It started going to extremes after a while. Remember Garbo? He was pretty surprised to get a surprise party one week *after* he had already been surprised—which was really the surprise party for his *next* birthday, fifty-one weeks early."

Catherine was laughing now. "Maybe you're right: Frank really could use some cheering up. So, when are we going to do it? The weekend before?"

Buddy knew he had her now. "Not the weekend before, the *month* before. Frank's fiftieth birthday is on May fourth, if I'm not mistaken. So we are going to surprise him on April fifth, which just happens to be a Friday. Get it? Four slash five instead of five slash four? Like maybe we just got mixed up—it could happen with people like us who are getting close to dementia."

"Very clever. Yes, I think that just might surprise him. But how are you going to get him to the party? What's the prank?"

"Leave that to me. Let's just say I have a brilliant plan for getting him there. In fact, leave everything to me. It's going to be at a hotel, and Frank will go there directly from work that Friday. I'll take care of food and everything. I just need two things from you."

"Ok, sounds great." Buddy heard relief in her voice— she must have been worried he was going to dump a bunch of details on her plate. "I'm happy to leave every- thing to you; I have a lot going on right now . . . we're dealing with . . . with some family issues, so I don't think I would be able to pull something off on my own. What two things do you need from me?" Now Buddy could detect a note of tension returning to her voice. He wondered what she meant by "family issues." Frank hadn't mentioned anything like that at the bar on Friday.

"First, I need help with the guest list and inviting people. I'll invite the people I know, but you know his other friends better than I do, plus family. How many people do you think we should aim for? Obviously, me and Bunny, you and Becky, and maybe some of her friends—what about work friends or people in the neighborhood?"

There was a pause on the other end of the line. "I don't think Becky will be there. She's, uh . . . traveling with some friends these days. But sure, I can come up with a list. There's also a couple of church people, maybe an aunt and uncle and some cousins. Not a lot, though—maybe fifteen to twenty people total? Frank doesn't really like huge crowds anyway. What's the second thing?"

"I need an inside contact at his office. I know there's this guy Dave that Frank is always talking about. Do you think he would help? Can he keep his mouth shut? Do you know how to get hold of him?"

"Sure, that's Dave Murphy. He's probably Frank's best friend at work—only friend, really. We definitely need to invite him. Yeah, I think you can trust him. Depends what you want him to do, I suppose. Are you staying on the right side of the law with this prank of yours? I think I have Dave's email address. I can send it to you."

"That would be extremely awesome, Cathy." Buddy was starting to feel the excitement that always came when pulling off a scheme he had dreamed up. "This is going to be really great for Frank. I'm really worried about the guy. Thanks for humoring me—you're not going to regret it."

"Well, the original prank turned out pretty good for me," laughed Catherine. "So I guess I should trust you by now. Thanks for thinking about this, Buddy. Frank really could use something to brighten up his life a little. In fact, it's funny you should bring this up right now. I was just thinking this past weekend how Frank hasn't been his old self for quite a while, and for some reason I was even thinking back to the old U of O days. I don't know what put it in my mind—I guess great minds think alike. I'll look for Dave's email address right now, and put some thought into the guest list."

"And I'll let you know the details of time, place, etc. as soon as I have them nailed down. Bye for now, and thanks again!"

Buddy hung up the phone. Phew, he sighed in relief, that was touch and go at first, but so far so good. But he knew the next step would be even trickier: the logistics of the actual prank, not to mention persuading Dave Murphy to help. *Cathy sounds kind of stressed out*, he thought. *I wonder what's going on in that house. Maybe it's just living with Frank; that might stress out anyone.*

Remembering Garbo had made Buddy think about Mouse again. *What ever happened to him*, he wondered. Garbo and Mouse had been good friends. They had been roommates beginning their sophomore year, after Buddy had decided to room with Frank. They might have roomed together every year after that—Buddy wasn't sure. A wave of nostalgia swept over him. *Those really were the good old days*, he thought. *I wish I still had friends like that.* How come friendships after college were never the same?

Other faces and names flashed into his mind. He went through them one by one and tried to think who he was still in touch with, or at least how many of the old gang he had an idea where they were and what they were doing. He was shocked to realize that, other than Frank and Cathy, and Bunny of course, the answer was none of them.

What's wrong with me, he wondered. *What kind of a friend am I? I don't even know what happened to my best friends from college, not even my freshman roommate.* He suddenly vowed to himself: *I'm going to track down Mouse.*

THAT NIGHT HE HEARD Bunny in the kitchen at her usual hour, long after he had already microwaved his own dinner. He left the den where he had been waiting and went into the kitchen. "Hey, how was your day?" he asked.

"Same as usual, how about you?" she replied without looking up, continuing to chop vegetables for her nightly salad.

"Yeah, same old, same old . . . say, I wanted to ask you something: do you remember Mouse? My freshman roommate?" Buddy knew that Bunny kept track of people better than he did. She could reel off birthdates and phone numbers from memory and always seemed to know when someone was having a baby, going through a divorce, or having a midlife crisis. She also tended to read the alumni magazine. Buddy hadn't opened it in years.

"Sure, of course I remember Mouse. He's the only football player I've ever met who cared for anything besides football. Why do you ask?"

"Oh, I don't know. I've just been thinking about people from the U of O. Do you know what happened to him? Didn't he play for the Browns for a while?"

Bunny stopped chopping and thought for a minute. "Yes, I believe he did play for Cleveland for a few years, and did fairly well too. But then didn't the team fold? I can't remember what happened after that. Did he play with another team? Gosh, I don't really know. If you want to track him down, you might try contacting the alumni office. They might tell you."

"That's not a bad idea." Buddy hesitated, and then went on. "Do you ever feel like friendships after college are never as good as the friends we made during college?"

Bunny frowned. "I suppose there is something special about college. But no, I actually think some of my friends now are much more significant than my college friends. I still had a lot of growing up to do when I was in college."

"Not me," said Buddy. "I can't think of a single friend I've really cared about in all the years since we graduated, except for Frank, and he is a college friend."

"Do you want me to tell you what your problem is?" asked Bunny, pausing from her chopping and turning around to face Buddy.

"I'm not sure—how serious is it?" replied Buddy, only half jokingly. "But okay, go ahead and tell me."

"Your problem is that you wish you had all these great friends, but you don't actually do anything about it. Friendships don't just happen. You're like the little red squirrel who wanted to enjoy the cake but wasn't willing to do any of the work to make it."

"Hen," said Buddy.

"What?"

"It was the little red hen. And it was bread, not cake."

"Whatever. You know what I mean." There was an edge to Bunny's voice that Buddy wasn't expecting.

"Maybe you're right," he said, not feeling like arguing for once. "Anyway, I want to track Mouse down." He turned away to go back into the den and did not notice the look on Bunny's face. Not angry, but wistful: *What about me,* her eyes said.

Back in the den, he opened his laptop. The exchange with Bunny had made him all the more determined to find Mouse. He googled the Cleveland Browns and looked for old rosters, but he couldn't find anything online from the

1980s—before the digitization era, he thought glumly. Bunny was right, though: according to Wikipedia, the Browns were suspended by the NFL from 1996 to 1998. Mouse would have graduated in 1985 or 1986 . . . could he have played for Cleveland for ten years? That was a long time for an offensive linesman in the NFL, but certainly not unheard of. A search in the online archives of the main Cincinnati paper, *The Cleveland Plain Dealer*, turned up several references to him, mostly just on rosters in the sports pages. But Buddy found one article that highlighted Mouse as a "candidate for Rookie of the Year" in 1986, and noted that he had sung "The Star-Spangled Banner" at one of the home games—even mentioning his nickname, Mouse. *And I bet he didn't need a mic,* thought Buddy reverently. But the trail seemed to go cold after that, and Buddy could not even confirm whether he ended up winning the rookie award.

He switched gears and found the alumni page on the U of O website. On the *Contact Us* page he found an email address for general inquiries. *I need something that will get their attention*, he thought, tapping his teeth again. Suddenly inspired, he wrote:

```
Hi,

My name is Rudolph Kowalski and I was in the
class of 1985. I am a reporter doing
research for a retrospective on great
football players of the 1980s and was
wondering if you could give me any
information about Darnell Richards. He
graduated in 1986 and began his career
playing for the Cleveland Browns. Do you
have any information about his later career
and where he is now?

Many thanks,

Rudolph
```

That should work—alumni offices eat that kind of stuff up, Buddy said to himself as he closed his laptop. *They'll be begging me to share my story about Mouse. Might even be some good press for me in it.*

CATHERINE HAD BEEN AS good as her word and had sent Buddy Dave Murphy's email address shortly after their call. The next morning, from his office, he sent Dave a message. Dave replied later that afternoon that he would be happy to help, and suggested Buddy call him at work. Buddy dialed him right away. "Dave, it's Buddy. I think we met one time at a Phillies game."

"Hi, yes, I think we did. We were playing Atlanta, and Philly gave up seven runs in the last inning. Then we got dumped on by a thunderstorm."

"Ah yes, that was a memorable one. Listen, Dave, I'm hoping you can help me pull off a surprise birthday party for Frank. It's his fiftieth coming up."

"Sure, what do you want me to do? Isn't Frank's birthday sometime in the summer?"

"May fourth. But that's part of the surprise—we're doing the party a month early, on April fifth."

"Hmm, I guess that will definitely be a surprise. But why do you need me then?"

Buddy wondered how much of the backstory he should give. "It's kind of a long story, but I have a ruse in mind that I would like to connect to him getting an award at his job, if possible. Actually, I'm trying to recreate something similar to an epic prank I pulled on Frank back when we were in college—I can explain more later. The first thing I need to know is this: does your company have an award for employee of the year?"

"Employee of the year? We used to, but I'm not sure they still do that. It's been a while since I heard anything about it."

Buddy's heart sank. "But what about the sign out front, for the employee of the year parking spot by the front entrance? I'm sure I've seen that pretty recently."

"Oh, is that sign still there? I think the company president uses that spot for guests and VIPs—or he probably uses it himself." Dave sounded cynical.

"Do you think Frank pays attention to stuff like that? Would he know that the award is defunct?"

Dave thought for a minute. "You're probably right. There's a good chance something like that is not on his radar. Frank doesn't pay much attention to office events and doesn't hang out with other people in the office that much. He's kind of your typical bean counter in the back office that nobody ever sees."

"Ok, good. Here's the bottom line, Dave: I want to prank him that he's gotten an award for employee of the year. Do you think we can fool him?"

Dave laughed. "I don't know, that might be a tall order. It would certainly surprise him. It might be easier to pull off some kind of departmental award—you know, accountant of the year, or something like that. Frank might be suspicious about employee of the year, given he hasn't had a promotion in a really long time."

"Does stuff like that happen in your office? Would it seem really strange for the department to give out some kind of award?"

Dave thought again. "You know, there's one piece of good luck that's in your favor. We just got a new head of HR, and she's been talking about new ways to improve employee morale, and having more office events, picnics, and crap like that. You might be able to pin it on her, in which case it wouldn't matter if we've had awards in the past."

"Dave, that sounds perfect. Okay, the next thing is— and this could be tricky—how would an announcement like that normally be made, do you think?"

"Hmmm. I suppose HR would probably send out a department-wide email, but we can hardly do that, can we? That could be a big problem," replied Dave doubtfully.

Buddy groaned inwardly. *Looks like Dave does not quite have the prankster spirit. Guess I will have to be the creative guy here.* "No, Dave, I guess not. What about a phone call? What if someone called him to tell him about the award?" Buddy thought briefly about trying to hack into the company email system, and then remembered the part about not crossing any legal boundaries.

"I'm not too sure . . . company announcements always go out by email. No, I don't think that would work." Dave's skepticism was clearly on the upswing.

Buddy was not about to give up. "Ok, how about this. Suppose HR calls him to give him advance notice before the general announcement goes out. Would he buy that?"

There was a long pause. *Come on, Dave, work with me, we can make this work,* pleaded Buddy silently, his patience starting to wear thin. He could feel his jaw clenching and consciously tried to relax.

"Yeah, I suppose that might work. But how would that help?" Dave still sounded skeptical.

"This is what I'm thinking: Frank gets a call from HR to tell him he won an award, and that there's going to be a little reception at a nearby hotel to honor him and other awardees. They can even tell him it's on the down-low until after the event, at which point everyone would be informed." Buddy tried to sound upbeat.

"Okay, but why at a hotel?" objected Dave. "We have a departmental conference room where they usually do stuff like that. And is everyone in the department going to get invited? Won't he think it strange that no one else is going? Of course, it would be great if the whole department got to go, but that's a big crowd and most of them don't even know who he is. I'm not sure Frank is going to swallow this."

"Dave, these are all excellent questions, and I appreciate you helping me think this through. What if we tell him the reception is only for invited guests, and they are the only ones being informed at this point? If he asks, we can say the conference room is booked for another event, or, I know, even better, that the new HR director is trying to make it special and different, so that's why it's at a hotel. Also, we *can* invite the people who are his friends—those are the only ones he would ask about it. It should be fine as long as he thinks the company-wide announcement won't happen till after the reception. What do you think? Will it work?" *So many devilish details*, Buddy complained to himself.

The line went silent again; Buddy held his breath while he waited. "Yeah, I guess it might work," said Dave. "But who's going to give him the call? It can't be me or you, or any of his other friends, since he would recognize our voices. I don't really have any good connections in HR either."

Buddy breathed a sigh of relief. He had anticipated this problem. "That probably means Frank doesn't know everyone in HR either. I have a friend who can make the call, someone Frank doesn't know. But it does need to come from an internal office phone number. Can you sneak the two of us into your building and my friend can make a call from some other room? It should take less than ten minutes."

"Sure, that shouldn't be a problem. It's not unusual for people to have visitors . . . as long as Frank doesn't see you—which won't be a problem, since he rarely emerges from his office during the day. Like a groundhog in winter."

"Ok, Dave, this will be great. I think we have a plan. I'm going to figure out some of the details and email them to you. And then we can nail down the timing. Are you free after work on April fifth? Can you tell me who else from the office to put on the guest list? And don't forget—not a word to our buddy Frank."

"Sure, no problem, April fifth is good for me," said Dave. "And I'll send you an email about who to invite."

Buddy took a deep breath as he hung up the phone. *Accountant of the Year* was not as good as *Employee of the Year*, but he could live with it. This just might work. He smiled happily to himself.

FIVE

O kay, you've got the script, right? And you know what to say if he asks about the email?" It was the following Monday, and Buddy had picked up Lori—his *accomplice*, he kept calling her—on the way to Frank's office.

"Stop, you're making me tense. I can do this. I practically have it memorized. Didn't I tell you that in high school I played Miss Hannigan in *Annie*?" Lori was an attractive woman in her early forties. She wore a colorful blouse with a revealing neckline that was partially obscured by a necklace made of enormous brightly colored wooden beads. Her matching earrings were equally impressive. Buddy wished she had chosen something a little less memorable.

Buddy smiled as he pulled into the parking lot of Frank's office. "I know. You're going to be great—why do you think I asked you? Okay, if you're all set, let's do it. Remember, if he says something totally unexpected, just say you have another call and put him on hold for a minute. I'll be right next to you." Buddy paused and pulled out his phone. "Operation Prank Frank is officially underway," he announced dramatically. He dialed Dave

Murphy's cell phone. This was what he loved—the thrill of pulling off an "operation," the feeling of being in the thick of the action. Bunny said he had watched too many cheesy spy movies.

Dave was expecting his call and answered on the first ring. "Dave here; are we ready to roll?"

"Yes. Lori and I are in the parking lot."

"Okay, wait for me in the entrance lobby. The security guard has to give you visitor badges. What do we do if Murphy's Law strikes and Frank chooses this moment to emerge from his lair and wander the hallways?"

"Murphy's Law? Oh, you mean that other Murphy—I guess we improvise. How about we say I was in the area and stopped by to surprise him—and you just happened to be in the lobby?"

"Okay, sounds good—not likely to happen anyway. See you in exactly one minute." Dave hung up.

As they walked across the parking lot, Buddy said, "Hey, Lori, let's make ourselves a little more anonymous—you know, a little less memorable. Just in case. How about you call me Jack while we're in there? Who do you want to be?"

"Just in case what? We're not breaking the law, are we?" Lori stopped, looking slightly alarmed.

"Nah, this is just a prank. Totally harmless. But I just feel better not using my real name."

Lori gave him a quizzical look. "Okay, then I'll be Cleopatra. Or maybe Delilah."

"I don't think you're getting the concept. I said *less* memorable. How about Jill?"

"Jack and Jill? You don't think that's memorable? Okay, how about Lisa. But you already told Dave that my name was Lori. Isn't that a problem?"

"I did? When?"

"On the phone, just now, when you called him."

Buddy grimaced and mentally kicked himself. *Another stupid devilish detail,* he groaned inwardly. *Let's hope it doesn't get me in trouble.* "Damn, you're right, didn't mean to do that. Too late now—guess we'll have to improvise a way to let him know."

As he was speaking, they approached the main entrance. In the parking spot closest to the door, Buddy saw the slightly crooked "Employee of the Month" parking sign in front of a late-model BMW with a license plate reading QWIKLOT-1. *Hmm, I wonder whose car that is,* he thought wryly. The glass doors opened into a grand suburban office atrium where the marble-looking floor (was it real marble?) gleamed under lofty angled windows and several (fake?) trees and plants lined the walls. A tough-looking security guard sat behind the front desk.

At that moment Dave walked in from a side corridor. "Hey, Buddy and Lori, good to see you." Then, turning to the security guard, "Rich, these are my friends—here for a tour of the office."

"Same to you old buddy. This is Lisa," said Buddy, slightly emphasizing *Lisa,* and glancing meaningfully at Dave.

Dave looked confused and coughed into his hand, "Sorry, I mean Lisa."

The security guard pushed two nametags and a marker across the counter and said in a bored voice, "May I see some ID please."

Buddy sent a panicked look in Dave's direction, silently cursing him for not warning him they would be asked for IDs. He tried to stall by patting various pockets as if looking for his wallet. Dave stared back at him like the classic deer-frozen-in-headlights. Meanwhile, without batting an eyelid, Lori said smoothly, "Jack, honey, I seem to have left my purse in the car—would you go get it for me?" Then, bending over to write her name on the nametag, she made sure the security guard had a clear view of the front of her blouse, her dangling necklace almost touching the counter. "Dave, we didn't need IDs last time, did we?" she asked, turning her head toward Dave without shifting the angle of her body. Taking her time, and using large block letters, she carefully wrote *Lisa* on the first nametag and *Jack* on the second. She made sure Dave could see both nametags.

Dave cleared his throat again. "Uh . . . no . . . that's right, I'm sure we didn't." Then, rising to the occasion, he added, "Rich, Lisa and . . . uh . . . Jack are running late and will only be here for a quick tour. Can we skip the IDs this time?"

"No problem," replied Rich. "I just need a last name for the log." He kept his gaze fixed on Lori.

"Thank you so much, we really appreciate it," said Lori. "Sampson. Lisa and Jack Sampson." She smiled sweetly and straightened up, adjusting her necklace.

"Thanks, Rich. Why don't the two of you follow me." As they walked away, Dave raised his voice slightly to make sure Rich could hear him—*nothing to see here; just another ordinary tour of the accounting department.* "Let's start the tour with my department. It's actually one of the larger and more interesting parts of the company . . ." They followed him down the main hallway leading away from the lobby. As soon as they turned a corner, Dave said, "Quick, around the next corner, and we should be safe from Frank or anyone else." He took a sudden right and ducked into a small meeting room dominated by an over-sized oval table surrounded by several chairs. In the middle of the table was a phone.

"What's with the fake names? Is your name Lori or Lisa?" Dave asked as the door swung closed behind him.

"Her real name is Lori," answered Buddy quickly. "She's a good friend from way back, who is about to become our partner in crime. We just figured it was safer not to use our real names, that's all, but I guess it almost backfired on us. Thanks for saving the day, Lori—that was a close call. Dave, how do we work this phone? We need to know how to put Frank on hold if we have to. Also, can we do it on speakerphone so we can all hear what he says?"

Dave pulled the phone closer. "Here's the hold button. Just push it once, and it'll start flashing to show you're on hold. Then push it again when you want to start talking again. Sure, the speakerphone works great—just be sure to keep quiet because the microphone will pick up your voice anywhere in this room."

Lori took out her script and spread it out on the table in front of her. "Let's do this," Buddy said. "Dave, go ahead and dial Frank's extension."

"Wait," said Lori. "If I'm impersonating someone from HR, should I still use the name Lisa? Does Frank know people in HR? Lisa is a common name—there could be a real Lisa in HR."

"Good question. What do you think, Dave?" asked Buddy.

"That's a very good point. Actually, there *is* someone named Lisa in HR—quite a senior person too, someone Frank probably does know, and would maybe even recognize her voice. But I'm not too sure about just making up a random name either. What if he starts asking questions? Maybe this whole thing is not such a good idea after all. It could backfire somehow, just like it almost did at the front desk. I don't want to get in trouble." Dave suddenly sounded nervous.

Buddy knew he couldn't let this line of conversation continue. "Let's not overthink this," he jumped in.

"Everything is going to be fine. We'll just say Lori is a temp because someone's out sick, and she got assigned the job of calling people. Her name is Mary Smith."

"Mary Smith?" said Lori. "Can't you be more creative than that?"

"Ok, fine, Miss Magnolia Q. Waznooski, why not really be someone they'll never forget," Buddy said sarcastically, still thinking about her eye-catching necklace.

"Mary Smith is fine," Lori muttered. "Let's get this over with."

Buddy nodded. "Go ahead, Dave." They could hear the phone ringing over the speakerphone. Frank picked up on the second ring. "Hello, this is Frank O'Donnell."

"Mr. O'Donnell, I'm glad I caught you. This is Mary Smith from HR. I have some good news for you." Lori's voice was impressively professional sounding.

"Well, hopefully that's not HR-speak for some creative way to fire me," replied Frank. Buddy smiled—that sounded like Frank all right. "I didn't know we had a Mary Smith in HR—I used to know someone by that name. Are you new?"

"I'm a temp—just here for a day or two. They were short-staffed for some reason," replied Lori smoothly. "The reason I'm calling is to let you know that you're going to get a departmental award."

"An award?" said Frank. "I didn't know we had any awards. What have I done?"

"It's something new, I think. I don't know exactly what it is," said Lori. "I believe it's a new initiative from the director of Human Resources. Let me read the official wording on the memo I was given." She cleared her throat. "It says: 'We are delighted to inform you that you have won a departmental award. You are invited to attend an informal wine and cheese reception to honor you and the other award recipients. Your specific award will be announced at the reception. We regret that we cannot include spouses or significant others due to space limitations.'"

"Wow," interrupted Frank. "Wine and cheese. This *is* something new. I wonder what budget this is coming out of, but I guess I'll probably find out at the end of month. When will this glorious event take place?"

"The reception will take place on Friday, April fifth, at five p.m., in The Lincoln Room at the Gran Dorado Hotel," read Lori.

"Double wow! The reception is at a hotel? Are you sure? This does not sound like the company I know and love," said Frank. "Now I'm *really* wondering about the budget line item."

"All I can tell you is that's what it says on the memo," replied Lori. "It sounds very impressive to me. You must have done something amazing to win an award like this." *Uh-oh*, thought Buddy; *she's starting to ad-lib. Stick to the script Lori!* He tried to catch her eye and frown at her.

"Probably for the employee who's been here the longest without a raise," quipped Frank. "Can you send me an email with the details about the hotel and everything? I need something like this in writing."

"Of course, you will definitely be getting an email memo to confirm the details," said Lori without a pause. "May I mark you down as planning to attend?"

"April fifth, that's a Friday. Sure, why not. It's not like I go out dancing on Fridays. But I have a better idea, Mary. Why don't I stop by your office and you can give me a hard copy of the memo? I'm always afraid of losing things in my email inbox."

Lori could see Buddy jumping up and down and waving his arms. "Uh . . . I think I have another call coming in. Can I put you on hold for one minute?" She pushed the hold button and the light started flashing. "Yikes, what should I tell him?" she said with a panicky look.

Lori and Dave both stared at Buddy. He stared back. This was a wrinkle he hadn't anticipated. "What is he trying to do, hit on her? Dave, any ideas?"

"Um, she could say she doesn't have an office?" Dave stammered.

"How about she has to get permission from her boss?" offered Buddy. "Or, she's a temp and doesn't have a printer? Maybe her printer is out of toner?"

"This is taking too long," said Lori. She pushed the flashing hold button. "Hi, Mr. O'Donnell, sorry to make you wait. I'm afraid I'm already late for a meeting, and I'm pretty busy this afternoon, but I could print it out and leave it in an envelope at the front desk for you to pick up later, say after three p.m. Would that be okay?"

There was a pause. Buddy started to sweat. Then Frank's voice came over the speakerphone. "Sure, that would be great. Thanks a lot."

"You're welcome. And congratulations about the award." Lori kept her voice professionally upbeat in an HR kind of way.

"Thanks," said Frank. "I appreciate it."

"Goodbye," said Lori and hung up.

"Hook, line, and sinker!" exulted Buddy. "He fell for it! Lori, you just earned another drink on top of the dinner I already promised you."

Lori looked at Dave. "Do you think my idea will work? Can we leave an envelope at the front desk?"

Dave shrugged. "It's a little weird. But making you a temp was a good idea—it's something a temp might logically come up with, even if it's not that common. So sure, we can do that."

"It solves another problem too" added Buddy. "Now we don't have to worry about sending him an official email. Good thinking, Lori—we couldn't have done it without you. Dave, it would help if you reinforce it somehow in a day or two. Tell him you heard he won an award, or something like that."

"Okay, sure," said Dave. "What about the memo? Who's going to write that? We only have about two hours."

"No problem," said Buddy. "We can do it right now. If I write it out, can you type it up in an official-looking format on letterhead and drop it off at the front desk?"

WITH THE MEMO SAFELY in Dave's capable hands, Buddy dropped Lori off and went straight home without returning to his office in the city. They wouldn't miss him. Now he could follow up with Cathy before Frank got home to confirm the time and place of the party, as well as find out how many people she had invited. Then he could talk to the hotel about the food and order a cake. What about a present? Maybe something to remind Frank of the glory days at U of O? Cathy might have some ideas—or Bunny, for that matter. *This is going to be good*, thought Buddy happily, *as long as Frank remembers to show up at the right time. Dave can make sure of that. Accountant of the Year*, he smiled to himself again. *I'm a genius.*

He also wanted some time on his own to call the alumni office at the U of O. He had received a boiler-plate reply to his email thanking him for his interest, but informing him that they could not release any information about individual alumni due to privacy concerns. *He was in the NFL*, thought Buddy. *That's not incredibly private.*

He picked up the phone and dialed the number at the bottom of the email. "Hello, my name is Rudolph

Kowalski, class of '85. I'm trying to get some information about an old friend of mine and wondered if there was someone I could talk to."

"Certainly, sir. Let me forward you to one of our alumni care representatives," said a young-sounding voice. *Probably an intern being brainwashed into the alumni zone of hype and glory*, thought Buddy.

There was a short pause during which a stirring version of one of the classic U of O fight songs started to play. Buddy sang along, continuing a few bars after the song was interrupted midchorus by a voice that was so perfectly modulated Buddy thought it was part of the recording. "This is Megan, thank you for calling the Office for Alumni Relations at the U of O, forging the character of the next generation. What can I help you with today?"

Oops, did she hear me singing? thought Buddy, embarrassed. *I guess my character never got fully forged— maybe I should ask for a refund.* "Hi. My name is Rudolph Kowalski. I was in the class of 1985. I'm trying to track down an old friend of mine by the name of Darnell Richards. He was a football player, Class of '86. Everyone called him Mouse. Do you have any records about where he is now?"

Buddy heard keys tapping. "Mr. Kowalski, I see that you recently sent us an email about Mr. Richards. What newspaper did you say you worked for?"

Newspaper? thought Buddy, before remembering his fib about being a journalist. *These people are more efficient than I thought.* "Uh, I'm a freelancer, just doing a feature article—might be picked up by a few papers. Mouse was also a good friend of mine. I'm sure people would be interested in learning about his connection to the university. He had a great career in the NFL." *Which means he also must be rich*, he thought to himself, *which means you probably know every detail about his life.*

"Of course, we're always interested in hearing about the success stories of our alumni. But, as I'm sure you understand, we have to be careful about protecting their privacy."

"Well, even if you can't give me his address and blood type, can you tell me anything about what happened to him? Do you know how many years he played for the Cleveland Browns? I lost track of him after a few years." *This obsession with privacy is getting irritating*, thought Buddy.

"The information we report in the alumni magazine is publicly available," said Megan. "Have you had a chance to look through our archives?"

"No, I didn't know you had archives. That would be great. How can I get access to them?"

"I'm happy to inform you that we are currently offering the magazine archives as a special thank-you gift for donations of one hundred dollars or more. As I'm sure you know, the president recently launched the Sesquicentennial Campaign, which is aimed at building on the university's profound contributions to strengthening the foundations of excellence in . . ."

"Yeah, yeah, that sounds great," Buddy cut in, "I'd be happy to donate a hundred dollars. Sign me up."

"Thank you, sir. May I suggest that for a gift of another one hundred and fifty dollars you could also get high-quality digital reproductions of all yearbooks going back to 1887? Perhaps seeing the yearbooks would help jog your memory of other associates and friends of Mr. Richards who could help you locate him. If you're able to increase your donation to five hundred dollars, we can offer you a discounted price on season football tickets, and if you're feeling truly generous . . ."

Now that actually is a good idea, thought Buddy. *Those yearbooks could be helpful, although a hundred and fifty seems kind of steep.* "Sign me up," he interrupted.

"Why, thank you, sir! Your generous gift of one thousand dollars will make an enormous difference in the lives of deserving students who . . ." Buddy had not realized that Megan had continued talking while he was thinking.

"No, no, just two fifty for the archives and yearbooks. I like your idea of the yearbooks. Sign me up for that. Not a thousand." *Close call,* thought Buddy.

Well, that was not a total loss, he reflected after sharing his credit card information and confirming for the fifth time that he only wanted to donate $250, and no, he did not want a canvas bag with the university logo proudly stamped on both sides. The magazine archives and yearbooks would be coming on a DVD in the mail, along with free commemorative bumper stickers. And the suggestion of using the archives had given him another idea. Even if the Cleveland Browns had lousy records, the NFL was crazy about statistics. They must have all kinds of records, and would probably be happy to share them. *Still, finding Mouse is proving to be harder than I thought,* reflected Buddy. *Where are you, Mouse my friend, where are you?*

His mind drifted back to the fall of his freshman year. He could feel an uncomfortable memory lurking in the dark recesses of his mind. Buddy's normal strategy when memories bothered him was to crack open another beer and turn on the TV, but this time, for reasons he didn't fully understand, he cautiously let the memory emerge out of the shadows. Ever since he had conceived of reliving the old prank, something about Mouse had been getting under his skin. He touched the memory and winced, surprised that more than thirty years later a memory could still be so sensitive. That fall, Mouse had invited him to

Cleveland to spend Thanksgiving with his family. Buddy had hemmed and hawed and said he needed to check with his parents first. He had spent a sleepless night agonizing over what to say.

Buddy prodded the memory again. Why hadn't he wanted to go with Mouse? It wasn't that Thanksgiving with his own family was so great—in fact, he had grown to dread it. His mother always tried to pretend that it was such a precious family time, and when he was younger, Buddy had believed her. But by the time he was in high school, he had started to see through the charade. In reality, their extended family was riven with hidden stresses and fault lines—old grievances and slights simmering below the surface, suddenly laid bare by a caustic remark dropped into an awkward silence; issues never dealt with; textbook cases of passive-aggressive behavior. His father would retreat to the den and watch football as much as he could, slowly drinking himself into a stupor. The last couple years of high school, Buddy had joined him, secretly pouring beer into his frosted iced-tea glass.

So, no, it wasn't because he missed his own family so much, although his mother would undoubtedly have objected tearfully if he hadn't come home. Why hadn't he taken the chance of being away at college to escape from his family for once? Buddy gingerly poked deeper. Mouse had regaled him with stories about his huge, complicated, but, apparently, happy family, including hilarious incidents from previous Thanksgivings, like the time they didn't eat until after ten o'clock at night because his cousin had forgotten to defrost the turkey—a cousin known ever after as "Frozen Felicia." Was it possible that he was afraid of the comparison with his own dysfunctional family?

That might have been part of the reason, but there was something more. He dragged the memory more squarely into the light. Was it because Mouse was black? Was he uncomfortable being the only white person in a crowd of black people, or, worse, was he afraid of having to navigate a culture that seemed alien and different, and somehow beneath him: not his class, not his type of people? Did he think he was too good for Mouse? Was he afraid of what his family and friends would think? Buddy cringed at the memory and pushed it back into the shadows.

Whatever the reason, the next morning Buddy had come up with a lame excuse about how much his mother was looking forward to seeing him. Mouse had smiled, clapped him on the back—causing Buddy to stagger forward from the impact of his massive arm—and said softly in his deep, powerful voice, "Hey, no problem, I get it." *I wonder*, thought Buddy, *maybe he did get it, more than I ever did.* That spring, Mouse had hinted several times that he wanted to room with Buddy again the next year, but Buddy always studiously avoided the topic. Eventually, Mouse had connected with Garbo, and Buddy had ended up with Frank. It made sense, he always convinced himself—we were both in poli-sci; Mouse was on a different track. But, looking back, he knew two roads had diverged in a wood that Thanksgiving. Buddy stared unseeingly at the still-bare tree branches outside the window over his desk and sighed to himself: *Why didn't I take the road less travelled?*

SIX

The rest of March had finally crept past, one soggy day at a time. Frank was glad to see it go; March was his least favorite month of the year—not winter, not spring, sometimes one, sometimes the other—compounded by lots of pressure at work as tax deadlines approached. Now it was the day of the award reception, and Frank was tired at the end of another long week. He wished he could just go home and forget about the whole thing. Rupert had been on his case again all day. Giving them wine and cheese was just a gimmick anyway—did anyone really believe this was going to improve company morale? *Maybe if they would actually talk to their employees they might get some ideas about company morale*, he thought bitterly.

Dave poked his head in the door of Frank's office. "Hey, Frank, I guess today's the big day—getting excited? Whoa, that's impressive: you're wearing a tie—the last time I saw you with a tie was the Christmas party two years ago."

"No, I'm not excited. If you want to know the truth, I just want to forget about it and go home, and maybe I will. This tie is giving me a neck rash. There's a reason I hate wearing them." Frank stuck his finger underneath his collar and tugged at his tie. The tie was rather odd looking, with several colorful misshapen blobs apparently glued at random on a dark-blue background. Frank had thrown out most of his ties several years earlier, keeping only three: a black one for funerals, a garish Christmas one for office parties, and this one, which had been a Father's Day present from Becky when she was in kindergarten. Frank liked wearing it as a kind of protest against ties, daring anyone to comment on it.

"No, don't do that!" said Dave, sounding alarmed. "I mean, didn't you already commit to going—you can't back out now."

"Yeah, yeah, I know. But the whole thing is a bunch of baloney, and everyone knows it. Do you think Sandra Harris even knows who I am? She walked right past me in the hall this afternoon and didn't even glance at me. You'd think she might say something like, 'See you at the reception, Frank.' Also, it looked like she was headed to Vegas or something, dragging a carry-on suitcase behind her and heading out the door at three seventeen in the afternoon. That's definitely good for company morale."

"Who's Sandra Harris? Oh, the new HR director . . . um, I'm sure she'll be there, unless maybe some emergency came up? You just have to show up, stay for half an hour, and jet out. How bad can it be?"

"I wish you were coming," said Frank. "At least I'd have someone to talk to. Can you believe I've worked here for twenty years and hardly feel like I know anyone? Probably because no one else is dumb enough to stay here that long." He started loading up his briefcase. "Guess what? Rupert wants the reports by Monday again, so guess who's going to have a great weekend."

"Well, maybe the wine and cheese will cheer you up," said Dave, nervously twisting a mechanical pencil in his hands. "Do you have the address for the place?"

"Yeah, I should probably take that with me so I don't get lost." Frank ruffled through some papers on his desk and found the memo from HR. "Okay, here I go. Wish me luck. Maybe I'll at least get a raise out of this." He snapped his briefcase shut and headed down the hall, Dave trailing behind him as far as the door.

THE GRAN DORADO HOTEL was exactly what Frank had expected: predictable beige stucco with dark-green trim and incongruous gutter downspouts sprouting on the walls in unexpected places, fronted by an imposing covered entryway that looked like it had been built to welcome visiting sheiks from the Middle East. A few azalea bushes decorated the bases of the huge columns, which were surrounded by heaps of dark brown mulch spotted with bedraggled pansies, no doubt recently added in an attempt to add a touch of spring. Frank pulled through the grand entryway just for the fun of it and then found a parking space. There were not many cars in the lot.

He checked his tie in the rearview mirror, grimacing at his five-o'clock shadow and slightly balding head. After walking across tiles in the entryway that vaguely brought to mind fake Italian villas on the Jersey Shore, he entered through automatic sliding glass doors into a nearly deserted lobby. In one corner, a middle-aged man in a suit typed on his laptop. Frank paused to get his bearings, looking for signs for the conference rooms—probably down the hallway to the left of the reception desk. He strode confidently through the archway, passing the elevators and then several doors on the right before hitting a dead end with vending machines on both sides. *I guess I took a wrong turn,* he thought, and reversed course back to the lobby.

Frank did not like asking for help or directions. This was a frequent source of conflict with Catherine. "Just ask someone!" she would hiss in exasperation after the seventh circuit of the same three Home Depot aisles. He glanced around the hotel lobby, looking for any other likely doors. Could the conference rooms be on the second floor? The least they could have done was put up an event sign instead of making everyone ask the receptionist. Seeing no alternative, Frank reluctantly approached the front desk. "Excuse me," he said politely, "could you please direct me to The Lincoln Room."

The receptionist looked puzzled. "I'm sorry, what room was that?"

"The Lincoln Room," said Frank a little louder. "I'm here for a company event."

"I'm sorry, sir, we don't have a Lincoln Room. Perhaps you mean the Susquehanna Room?"

"No," said Frank irritably. "I do not mean the Susquehanna Room. I mean The Lincoln Room." Was she deaf? He fumbled in his pocket for the invitation memo, and then remembered he had left it in the car. "Damn, I'll be right back." He walked back through the sliding glass doors, crossed the parking lot to his car, retrieved the memo from the passenger seat, and returned to the front desk.

He pushed the sheet of paper across the counter in front of the bewildered receptionist. "Look at this; isn't this the Gran Dorado on Christhamom Drive?"

"Uh, we're on Chrysanthemum Avenue—perhaps you mean a different hotel?" she asked, looking even more confused.

"Yes, yes, Chrysanthemum, that's what I was trying to say," snapped Frank. "Look, isn't this where we are?" He jabbed his finger at the address of the hotel printed on the office memo.

She bent her head and looked closely where Frank was pointing. "Yes, that is the right address, and I see what you mean—it does say The Lincoln Room." She frowned. "Strange. Let me look up your name in our system."

"Well, it won't be under *my* name," snapped Frank, irrationally blaming the receptionist for the confusion. "It would be under my company name. I told you, I'm here for a company event. QuikLot—that's my company name." It was beginning to dawn on Frank that he hadn't seen a single person from his office, even though he was right on time—in fact, he hadn't seen anyone at all, other than that one tired-looking businessman typing on his laptop.

It was too late—the receptionist had already seen his name on the memo and typed it into her computer monitor. "Yes, I see your name—you do have a reservation, but it's for next weekend."

"What?" said Frank in surprise. "I'm telling you, the reservation is not for *me*. My *company* has a reservation. For the Susquehanna Room, no, dang it, I mean The Lincoln Room."

"I'm sorry, sir, we don't have a Lincoln Room." The receptionist eyed him warily, probably wondering if she should push the secret button to call the manager.

"How can I have a reservation? You must have me mixed up with someone else. There are lots of O'Donnells, probably lots of Frank O'Donnells. O apostrophe, double *n*, double *l*." Frank tried to lower his voice, glancing behind him to see if anyone was staring at him. The tired businessman seemed oblivious to the outside world.

"Are you the Frank O'Donnell of two sixteen Dogwood Drive?" said the receptionist, clicking through the reservation page on her monitor.

Frank was taken aback. "Wait a minute, that *is* my address. Are you sure? What's going on here?"

"It's right here, sir. You have a reservation for next Friday night, reserved under a Visa card ending in seven four three two."

It was Frank's turn to look bewildered. "That's not my Visa number, at least," he said. "But how did my name and address get in your system? I've never stayed here in my life."

"I don't know, sir. Would you like me to cancel your reservation?"

"For the last time, I don't *have* a reservation here," said Frank in exasperation. "Can you print that out for me—I want to look at it." A thought suddenly occurred to him. *I wonder if this is something Catherine did—that could be her Visa card. But why would she do it in my name?*

"Certainly, sir." The receptionist sounded relieved that Frank was calming down. A moment later she handed him a printout of the reservation confirmation.

Frank suddenly remembered the award reception. What could have happened? Could they have canceled it without telling him? *Wouldn't surprise me*, he thought. Maybe he should call someone. He felt in his pocket for his phone. *Shoot, I must have left that in the car too.* But who would he call? Most people would have left the office by this time. He could call Dave, but Dave was obviously as much in the dark as he was. There must be some huge screwup. Heads would roll in HR he hoped. His mood brightened. "If I can't *find* the reception, then I can't *attend* the reception," he said out loud. An image of a cold beer waiting for him in his fridge floated into his mind.

"Sorry, sir?"

"So, there's definitely no company events taking place here right now?" Frank asked, just to be sure.

"No, sir. But I can call our event manager if you would like to schedule one. You'll find the Susquehanna Room can be configured for a wide range of different events."

"No thank you! I'm afraid the wonders of the Susquehanna Room will have to wait for another day. Sorry for all the confusion, which is certainly not your fault. All's well that ends well. Thank you very much for all your help." Frank hoped he had not been too rude.

"You're welcome, sir. We look forward to seeing you next Friday."

Frank frowned. "Well, I'm not too sure about that. But thanks again." He walked out to his car, glancing one last time at the businessman in the corner, still engrossed in his laptop. As he slid into the driver's seat and loosened his tie, he noticed the message light flashing on his phone where he had left it on the passenger seat.

Uh-oh, I hope it's not a message from HR telling me that the reception is really at the Motel 6 down the road, he thought. It would be too awful to have to go through with it now, just when he was about to escape. He pushed the message button and held the phone up to his ear. "Hi, Honey, umm, I'm just wondering where you are . . . my plans have changed and I don't have to stay late at school after all. Can you give me a call as soon as possible?" Catherine sounded worried.

What a relief, the evil reception has not come back to life. But I'm sure I told her about it—why does she sound so anxious? Frank hit the call back button and Catherine answered immediately.

"Hi, Catherine, it's me. What's up? Good news, I'm on my way home . . . the reception is AWOL."

"What?" Catherine sounded surprised and confused. "What do you mean? Where are you? Aren't you supposed to be at the reception right now?" Frank thought he could hear voices in the background.

"Where are *you*?" he asked. "Sounds like a party. It's a mystery. I went to the hotel, and Lincoln seems to have drowned in the Susquehanna. There was no one there. Empty. Just a very sweet but confused receptionist."

"Frank, what on earth are you talking about? Do you mean the Delaware? What hotel did you go to?"

"The Gran Dorado on Chris-a-majig Avenue, you know, near the Walmart. Just like it said on the invitation. I assume there was some massive screwup at HR. Want to go out to dinner somewhere?" Frank started the car and pulled out of the parking lot. He was feeling better and better. "Hello, can you still hear me?" The phone had gone silent.

Suddenly the phone came back to life with a squawk. It sounded like Catherine had put it on speakerphone—Frank could hear voices and howls of laughter. He thought he could hear Buddy's distinctive booming laugh. What was Buddy doing there?

"Oh Frank, you'll never believe this. You were supposed to go to the Gran Dorado on Hyacinth Drive, near the train station!"

Now Frank was bewildered, for the second time that night. "There are *two* Gran Dorados? But I went to the address on the memo! I checked! There was no one there! And how did *you* get involved in this?"

"Frank, it's a surprise birthday party for you, but you went to the wrong place! Buddy was trying to prank you again and he screwed up! Or actually it worked better than he ever imagined—the first time it was the wrong day, this time it was the wrong place!" It sounded like Catherine was having trouble talking through gasps of laughter.

Now Frank could hear Buddy's voice. "Get your butt over here, Frank! The crowd is getting hungry!"

"But it's not even my birthday!" protested Frank, starting to laugh despite his confusion. "Okay, okay, I'm on my way!"

THIS GRAN DORADO LOOKED the same as the last one, but this time the parking lot was much fuller and there was a prominent sign in the entryway: *QuikLot Reception in The Lincoln Room.* In the lobby, another clearly labeled sign pointed down the hallway to the left, where the sign over the door said: *The Lincoln Room.* Frank pulled open the door and a cheer went up. Buddy shouted, "Here he is! Let's sing for the birthday boy!" A massive cake on the table proclaimed, "Accountant of the Year—may the next fifty years be even better than the last!" Frank saw Dave standing against the wall, smiling and looking pleased. Buddy came over and clapped him on the shoulder. "Once again, the prank's on me. Glad you made it, old pal—happy birthday to my best friend!"

Catherine had been hovering near the door, phone in hand. Frank could see the relief on her face as she gave him a quick hug. "Happy pre-birthday, honey—this is just the first installment. Sorry for the mix-up about the place—when Buddy organizes something, anything can happen."

Frank laughed. "No kidding—but it's still a great surprise!" Buddy and Dave were busy lighting fifty candles on the cake. The crowd started singing and Frank did his best to blow out all fifty candles with one huge breath, causing much hilarity from the bystanders.

A small group of well-wishers gathered around Frank and Catherine. "Hi, Bunny," said Frank. "Great to see you—it's been a while."

"Happy birthday, Frank," said Bunny with a smile. "I know—I don't know where the time goes. The four of us should get together for dinner sometime."

A large, lumpy-looking woman whom Frank did not recognize, carrying the hugest bag he had ever seen, suddenly let out a squeal. "Bunny Valentino! I thought it was you! It's Wendy Fletcher, although now of course it's Wendy Lewis, ever since my darling husband Gregory came into my life. What an *amazing* coincidence to see you here! Gregory was *just* saying as we were driving over that seeing Frank again was almost like a high school reunion, and now here *you* are! And Buddy too—I had no idea! You look absolutely marvelous!"

A light went on for Frank. He had heard that his best friend from high school, Greg Lewis, had recently re-married, but he had never met his new wife. How interesting that she had gone to the same high school as Bunny (and Buddy, of course, since that's where Buddy and Bunny had first started dating). "Nice to meet you, Wendy—I didn't even realize Greg was here." Frank looked around and saw Greg standing behind the drinks table.

"Wendy! What a surprise," said Bunny. Frank couldn't help but notice that her enthusiasm didn't quite match Wendy's. Just then, Buddy and Dave walked up and started handing out giant pieces of cake precariously balanced on flimsy paper plates.

"So, Dave," said Frank, "I guess you were in on this all along! You sure had me going! But who was it who called me on the phone? Was HR in on it too? And why did you send me to the wrong Gran Dorado?" Frank started laughing again, thinking about the confused receptionist.

"I just did what Buddy told me to do," said Dave, joining in the laughter. "Buddy's friend Lori was the one who called you. Is she here?" Dave looked around. "She was great. Although maybe Lori wasn't even her real name—Buddy was being very mysterious about it!"

Buddy coughed and said, "Uh, no, she couldn't make it unfortunately. Excuse, me, gotta get some more cake." He moved off in the direction of the food table.

There was a brief lull in the conversation. Everyone seemed to have a fork in their mouths. Wendy and Bunny had been having an animated discussion on the side—at least Wendy had been animated—but now Frank saw Bunny looking at Dave with a thoughtful expression on her face, her fork stopped halfway to her mouth and her brow slightly furrowed. Then the noise of the conversation swelled again as more people came over to greet Frank and wish him a happy birthday.

His cake eaten, Frank looked around the room to see who else was there. It was not a big crowd, but he was surprised to see several people like Greg that he hadn't seen in years. Another high school friend was talking to Greg at that moment. And, on the far side of the room, he saw a former member of their church who had moved to North Jersey chatting with one of their neighbors. *Catherine must have had a hand in this*, he thought. *Must not have been easy coming up with a guest list for an introvert like me.* Standing by herself against one wall, he saw Denise, his former assistant who had recently been promoted to work for Rupert. *I bet that's been a blast*, Frank thought. *Dave must have invited her. I guess I'd better say hi.*

He moved in her direction. "Hi, Denise, glad you could make it tonight."

"Hi, Frank—happy birthday! And congratulations on the 'accountant of the year award!'" Denise waggled her fingers to make air quotes. "Maybe this will inspire HR to actually do something like this—you would definitely win if they did."

"Thanks, Denise. Don't hold your breath about HR doing something reasonable." There was an awkward silence. Now that she wasn't working for him anymore, Frank couldn't think of anything to say. "So, how do you like working with Rupert?" he finally asked.

"Well . . . it's definitely had more variety than what I was doing before." Denise's voice was flat.

Yeah, I'll bet, thought Frank. *Very diplomatic—I hope it's worth the extra pay*. Another awkward silence.

"It's been encouraging to see the upward trend in sales since I left," Denise said brightly. "I always pay special attention to those reports, because I remember working on them with you."

"Upward trend? Really? Not what I would have said, but I guess things could be worse . . ." Just then, Frank caught Greg's eye. "Say, Denise, I need to talk to an old buddy before he leaves. Stop by my office and say hi sometime." Frank forced himself to smile as he edged away in the direction of Greg.

The party slowly wound down. Frank forced himself to make the rounds and talk to all the guests before they left, and by the end he felt like his smile was pasted on his face. He and Catherine were the last to leave, except for Buddy who was still wrapping up the leftover cake and packing up the stereo he had brought. Bunny had apparently already left in her own car. They walked over to say goodbye. Frank punched Buddy in the arm.

"Thanks, Buddy. It was really great. I had a good time. And great classic tunes, too." Frank broke out in a snatch of song, accompanied by the strum of an air guitar: "Baby, we were born to run . . ."

Buddy grinned happily. "Well, it didn't quite go as planned, just like the original prank, but I think we can still call it a success. What do you think, Cathy?"

Catherine laughed. "Your pranks always scare me, Buddy—you never know what will happen! But, yes, it was great, and thanks so much for organizing everything. I never would have done this without you."

As they walked away, Frank called back, "Hey, don't forget our first Phillies game—the Tuesday after next, right? Got that in your calendar?"

"You bet, wouldn't miss it," said Buddy with a wave.

LATER THAT NIGHT, when they were at home lying in bed, Frank asked Catherine, "So who got the hotels mixed up? Was it really Buddy's fault?"

"Who knows? Unless Dave wrote it down wrong when he typed up that invitation? But Dave came to the right place, so Buddy must have given him the wrong address, and Dave never noticed it. They said they had to write that memo in a hurry—apparently it was a last-minute change in the plan, from what Buddy said."

"Well, I really swallowed it. Just like the first time. And look how that turned out." He squeezed her hand and they were both quiet for a moment. "Thank you for the thoughtful gift—that was your idea, wasn't it?"

"The initial idea was mine, but Buddy did most of the work pulling it together. Somehow, he had copies of all these great pictures from our last year at U of O. I contributed a few pictures too." Frank had been presented with a memory book full of pictures of their college days. All the guests at the party had signed it, and most had written personal notes.

"Well, it brought back a lot of good memories." Frank was quiet again. "I had a good time. That might be the first time I've ever enjoyed a surprise party—although, I guess it wasn't really a surprise. Definitely better than wine and cheese with Rupert!"

Catherine smiled at him. Then she leaned over and kissed him as she turned out the light. "You're lucky to have Buddy for a friend."

SEVEN

Bunny pulled into the driveway in front of the dark house. *I'm glad we went to the party in separate cars,* she thought. Sharing a ride home with Buddy would have been unbearable. She walked briskly up the sidewalk to the front door, expertly navigating the curb and steps with feet trained by years of coming home after dark. Finding her way to the kitchen with the help of the street light filtering through the windows, she turned on the light over the kitchen range and looked in the cabinet for a wine glass. The shelf was empty. She groaned out loud, but then remembered she had turned on the dishwasher before leaving the house that morning. Opening the dishwasher, she saw a row of clean wine glasses gleaming in the dim light. In the fridge, she found a previously-opened bottle of chardonnay and carried it to the counter that divided the kitchen from the dining area. She slid onto a bar stool and filled the glass almost to the rim.

The off-hand comment from Dave about Lori had been a shock. She swallowed a big gulp and leaned her elbows on the cool granite countertop. *So that's how it ends,* she thought bitterly.

One day the previous summer, Buddy had gone to work and forgotten his phone on the kitchen counter. The buzzing of the phone was driving her crazy, and she had finally picked it up to silence it. Without meaning to, she had seen the text from Lori on the screen. *It was this same counter*, she remembered, sipping her wine and staring dully at the swirling patterns in the granite, picturing the phone vibrating in a bright patch of sunlight on that hot August morning. The soothing buzz of the wine began to do its job, calming her, and relaxing the tense, coiled muscles in her back.

On that hot summer night, when Buddy had finally come home after midnight, she had screamed at him, *"How could you see her again?"* She had held the phone inches from his face, demanding that he call her and end it once and for all, threatening to walk out, her eyes dry but her voice boiling with fury, spilling out the rage that had been building up all day. He hadn't denied it—how could he, with the evidence literally in her hand. But he had sworn it was the last time, he had been drinking and made a mistake, that he was under a lot of stress at work, that he was sorry, that it would never happen again, that he loved her. She had given him an ultimatum: one more time and the marriage would be over.

The ultimatum must have had some effect, because things appeared to get better. Buddy was more attentive and made an effort to be home more on weekends, although he still traveled frequently for his job. It was so hard to know what was going on below the happy-go-lucky persona he loved to present to the outside world. Still, Bunny began to believe the affair with Lori had been a passing stage, a midlife crisis that was now past. And then, that evening: the party for Frank, Dave's passing reference to Lori, the damning revelation. She had no illusions. *I guess he's getting better at lying*, she thought caustically. *I suppose that has always been one of his strong points—pranking and deceiving his friends. Well, that's the last time. I'm done.*

Bunny sloshed more wine into her glass and felt the oppressive weight of the dark house bearing down on her. She didn't want to keep the house after the divorce: too big, too empty, too many crushed dreams. *Would it have been different if we'd had kids?* she wondered for the hundredth time. But after they'd gotten married, her real estate career blossomed; she had loved it—still loved it—and it had taken over her life. Buddy had occasionally talked about starting a family, at least in the early years, but never with much enthusiasm. He seemed to feel it was the expected thing to do—and he had insisted on buying the ridiculously huge house with room for a family of five, plus a yard big enough for a pool that was never built. But Bunny had a hard time imagining him actually being a dad. It didn't really fit his lifestyle. *Appearances, that's all he cares about—as long as he looks like a happy suburban guy with lots of money, a fancy car, a big house in a nice neighborhood, and, oh yes, an attractive, successful wife—in that order—it doesn't matter what the reality is.*

She became dimly aware that a phone was ringing somewhere. She jumped up, almost knocking over the empty wine glass. *Is that my business phone? Where is my purse? Tomorrow is Saturday, probably a client.* She had learned to expect calls at any hour of the day or night, no longer surprised at the random, trivial questions that people thought were important enough to call her about at three in the morning. She scanned the shadows for her purse, and then saw it on the counter by the fridge, the bright screen of her phone faintly visible through the fabric. Hoping it might stop ringing before she could get to it, she took her time walking across the kitchen, opened her purse, and retrieved her phone. The number on the screen was not in her contact list, and she paused, staring down at the screen. Then, impulsively, she touched the answer button. *Even a junk call might distract me,* she thought with a sigh.

"Hello, this is Bunny. What can I do for you?" She hoped her voice didn't sound slurred.

"Oh, thank goodness you picked up, I wasn't sure you would, I know it's awfully late." The high-pitched voice sounded vaguely familiar. "I know that I *never* answer my phone after ten p.m., especially not on a weekend. It's just *never-ending* if you don't set limits—the way people are these days, with all these horrible devices that everyone is glued to, never a moment of rest or privacy, I really do *not* like certain aspects of this modern world . . ."

The speaker seemed to be pausing for her first breath and Bunny jumped at her chance. "I'm sorry," she cut in. "Could you remind me who you are?"

The voice squeaked in what might have been a laugh. "Oh dear, I keep forgetting we hadn't talked for *such* a long time before an hour ago, how could you possibly recognize my voice? Even though, honestly, *your* voice has not changed even the slightest bit. I would have recognized it anywhere, not to mention that you are still just as attractive as ever—how on earth do you do it? It's me, Wendy, we just spoke at the party for Frank—was he really accountant of the year?—and you gave me your card, and I know it's *dreadfully* impertinent of me to call so soon, and at such a late hour, but I simply did not know who else to turn to, and I said to myself, perhaps it wasn't just coincidence that we were so wonderfully reunited tonight. I don't know about you, but I really do *not* believe in coincidences, not anymore, not after . . ."

Bunny could feel the conversation spinning out of control. She quickly cut in. "Wendy! Of course! I'm so sorry I didn't recognize your voice. Is there something I can help you with?" Instantly, she regretted the wording of her question.

Without missing a beat, Wendy swerved into a new topic. "Oh, that's so sweet of you to offer. It's my granddaughter. Or, I should say, my daughter. Her ex-husband—such a horrible man—I warned her, you don't know how many times I warned her—had promised to help, because my daughter is working tomorrow and the daycare is closed on weekends. But he was in Detroit and his flight got canceled, so he doesn't even get to the airport until ten—just like him to mess up his flight—and then he claims he doesn't have anyone to pick him up. Of course, my daughter asked her neighbor, but her mother is in the hospital and she has to go get her. So that means it's up to me." Wendy paused for another breath.

Bunny was getting lost. "You want me to pick up your daughter's ex-husband at the airport?" she asked dubiously, wondering where this was headed.

Wendy squeaked again. "Oh, no, I don't care about *him*; he can rot in baggage claim for the rest of his life for all I care. I can watch the baby, but I promised to show a house tomorrow morning, and it's right in your neighborhood . . . would there be any possible way you could fill in for me? I've already rescheduled them twice, and I do so hate to disappoint such a lovely young couple looking for their first home—it's really very sweet."

There was a sudden silence. "Oh," said Bunny. Another amazing coincidence Wendy had discovered that evening was that both of them were in real estate. And, as it happened, one of Bunny's clients had canceled on her just that afternoon and her morning was open, a rarity on a Saturday. *I might regret this*, she thought. She hesitated, stalling, and then thought about being alone with Buddy in the morning. *Okay, Wendy, maybe you're right about coincidences.* "I guess I could do that. What time? Where is it?"

As if breaking through a temporary log jam, a new flood of words came gushing down the line. "Oh, I *knew* I did the right thing calling you. I told you, coincidences do *not* just happen; there's always a reason. Thank you *so* much—it's extremely kind of you and I absolutely *insist* on returning the favor anytime you need something. That's what old friends are for, isn't that right? It's at ten a.m., just off Route 41 . . . it can't be more than fifteen minutes from your place. Was it Stream Hollow? Let me see, where is that scrap of paper . . ." Her voice faded and Bunny could picture Wendy rummaging through her giant bag. Bunny knew the area well and had never heard of a Stream Hollow. "Oh dear, it must be on my desk. I'll have to text it to you in the morning. Or would you rather I call?"

"No, no, that's quite all right, texting is fine," said Bunny quickly. "Uh, I'm afraid I can't stay on the phone much longer . . ."

"I understand, I understand, it's very late," said Wendy. "I'll let you go. We simply *must* get together for lunch sometime and get properly caught up now that we've rediscovered each other—and to think that we both went into real estate! Again, thank you *so* much! I really was at a loss and didn't know what I was going to do, and then I reached into my bag for my phone and your card just *fell* into my hand, and I just *knew* it was a sign, like that time last year when . . ."

"Yes, that would be nice . . . so sorry, I have to go, good night, Wendy," interrupted Bunny, afraid of being regaled with an endless stream of amazing coincidences. Even before she put her phone down, she was starting to regret her decision. *I could easily have come up with an excuse,* she thought. *What am I getting myself into?*

Headlights flashed through the window and she heard Buddy's car pulling into the driveway. She quickly put the wine in the fridge and slipped up the back stairs, thankful she hadn't turned on any overhead lights. She knew Buddy would go into the den and watch the eleven o'clock news, and she wanted to be in bed long before he came upstairs. Her thoughts were too unsettled to talk to him yet. She knew sleep would elude her, but she had long ago perfected the art of faking it. Buddy never seemed to notice.

At quarter of ten the next morning, Bunny was ready to leave, dressed in her usual realtor version of business casual. But Wendy still hadn't texted her the address. She sat on the deck enjoying the morning sun and a second cup of coffee while she waited. Buddy was still in bed. In spite of the emotions churning inside her, the moment was surprisingly peaceful. A pair of sparrows chased each other around the forsythia bushes bordering the deck, their blossoms starting to explode in brilliant yellow. Half hoping Wendy wouldn't respond, she sent her a text, adding a reminder to include the lockbox code so she could get into the house. *Wendy hasn't changed at all since high school*, she thought, but then had the uncomfortable thought: *What about me? Have I changed?* She and Buddy had started dating in high school, and she had followed him to the U of O. Getting married had seemed a foregone conclusion, to her and all of their friends. *What if I hadn't gone to the U of O? Would we still have gotten married?*

Another five minutes went by. Bunny was just getting her hopes up that Wendy had forgotten all about the appointment when her phone buzzed: "its 38 brook haven dr, code 3838, asking 195k, their names are ted and jane, very sweet young couple just married, thanks a million, yr the best, cant wait to have lunch, lots of love, W."

Even her texts are long-winded, thought Bunny as she sent back a thumbs-up. *Doesn't she know never to use the house number for the lockbox? Brook Haven, not Stream Hollow—just like Wendy to mess that up.*

She stood up to leave and suddenly stopped as if jolted by an electric shock: *Thirty-eight Brook Haven—that's our old house!* In a daze, she went inside, walked through the garage, and got into her car. She and Buddy had bought thirty-eight Brook Haven Drive the week before they were married. What was happening? Ever since running into Wendy, the coincidences did seem to be piling up uncontrollably. A vivid image leaped into her mind: a tiny white ranch with sky blue shutters and a gray shingled roof, a large bay window overlooking a modest front yard bordered by a crumbling driveway, a huge maple in the back shading an overgrown back yard where she had always longed to build a deck.

Buddy had soon grown to hate the house—too cramped, too close to the neighbors, too many leaks in the roof. But she had always had a soft spot in her heart for their time together there. Was it really almost twenty-eight years ago? They had lived in the house for three years. By a stroke of good fortune, they had timed their purchase perfectly, right before a boom in the local housing market had allowed them to quickly trade up to their current monstrosity. In fact, the experience of buying and selling that house was what had first interested Bunny in real estate.

Bunny signaled left and turned onto their old street, lined on both sides with rows of identical houses. By now, most of the old asbestos wall shingles had been replaced with vinyl siding, resulting in a hodgepodge of pale pastels and mismatched creams and off-whites. The street soon curved to the left, and she held her breath waiting for number thirty-eight to appear on the right. *There it is*, she exhaled. *It looks just the same.* Amazingly, it had never been enwrapped in the dull vinyl sameness of the other houses and was still painted a fresh-looking white, but the shutters were now a dark green instead of sky blue. The maple was still there too, even larger now, the newly unfurled leaves looming over the house. She could see a small black hatchback in the driveway. Thanks to Wendy, she was a few minutes late.

As she pulled up to the curb, the doors of the black car opened and a man and woman emerged. Bunny walked up the driveway and extended her hand. "You must be Ted and Jane," she said. "My name is Bunny."

The man and woman exchanged confused glances. "Wendy's not coming?" asked the woman.

"I'm her colleague," fibbed Bunny smoothly. "I'm afraid Wendy had an unexpected family crisis this morning."

"Again?" said the man.

Bunny winced. *I guess that excuse has been used a few times.* "I'm sure I can answer your questions," she said with a forced smile. "Let's go inside and take a look." She extracted the key from the lockbox and opened the door, trying to ignore an overwhelming sense of déjà vu. She was pleased to see that the house had been well cared for. Someone had even added the deck and sliding glass door she had always dreamed of, and the kitchen had new cabinets and appliances. The young couple wandered around the rooms, seemingly unimpressed. Bunny followed them, barely paying attention, a flood of memories coursing through her mind.

"I thought it had three bedrooms," said Ted. "And where's the dining room?"

"The room at the end of the hall *is* a bedroom," answered Bunny. "It's perfect for a nursery or a study." She stood in front of the sliding doors that opened onto the deck and spread her arms. "This charming eat-in kitchen catches the light beautifully in the morning. And you can extend your table into the living room when you have guests. We used to sit a dozen people without a problem." *Oops,* she caught herself. *Shouldn't have said that.* She was biting her tongue, knowing they would never believe her if she told them this had been her house when she was a newlywed. But they didn't seem to notice her slipup.

"Let me show you the basement," she said, leading them downstairs. "There's tons of room for storage, and you could easily add another bedroom or family room down here. It's dry—I can guarantee it doesn't leak."

"Really?" said Jane, looking around doubtfully at the clean but unfinished space. "How do you know? Anyway, it just seems kind of cramped. And only one bathroom," she added dismissively.

As Bunny followed them back upstairs, she wanted to scream at their backs. *Can't you see how perfect it is? It's not all about the number of bathrooms—you can be happy here!* But instead, she smiled politely. "Well, just give Wendy a call if you want more information. This house probably won't stay on the market for long at this price. Especially in such a quiet neighborhood, and with woods behind the backyard."

But they didn't seem interested in the backyard or the woods, and before long Bunny was watching them back their car out of the driveway. *Oh well,* she thought with a touch of spite. *They're the wrong type anyway.* She walked back through the rooms to make sure all the lights were off and was about to leave when she saw a glimmer of light under the basement door. She went back down the stairs and discovered that the light over the washer and dryer had been left on. She switched it off and was turning back to the stairs when she noticed the cover of the circuit-breaker box underneath the staircase was open. She rolled her eyes. *It was probably Ted . . . what is it about men and circuit breakers? They always want to look at the circuit breakers. What do they expect to find?*

She was about to slam the cover shut when something caught her eye and she froze. Something was scratched into the paint on the inside of the small gray metal door. The weight of the memories that had been building in her mind all morning suddenly made her legs feel like they were going to buckle. "Oh," she said, "Oh my goodness." She leaned her back against the rough basement wall and then, not caring if she snagged her expensive jacket, slowly slid to the floor until she was sitting hunched on the cold cement, clenching her arms tightly around her knees.

Years ago, back at the U of O, Buddy had come up with a clever way to combine their two names by merging the *n's* and *d's*. He had spent hours perfecting it until, looked at from one direction it looked like *Buddy*, and from another like *Bunny*. It had become their secret signature, something they had never shared with anyone else. That first year in the house there had been a mysterious electrical problem, leaving them with no working outlets in the kitchen, and Buddy had been trying to fix it by staring into the circuit-breaker box. Not known for his handyman abilities, he had eventually given up and called Frank.

While they were waiting, he had carefully etched their secret signature into the paint with the tip of his screwdriver and outlined it with a heart, like a teenager carving their initials into the bark of a tree. *The heart of the house*, he had called it. Bunny could remember laughing and saying, *If it's the heart, we'll have to live here forever.* Buddy had enfolded her in her arms and given her a big sloppy kiss.

Forever. How could I have forgotten this was here? What happened to us? Bunny felt tears pricking the backs of her eyelids. *Where did we go wrong?* In those early years, Friday nights had been special. They had always gone out somewhere together, to a favorite restaurant, to a movie, or just for a drive on winding country roads. Then, at some point, Buddy had begged for a Friday off to play poker with some golf buddies. Just this once, he had said. And then somehow, without any conscious decision, the poker game had taken over their Friday nights together. *Is that when it started? Something as simple as that? Would we still be together if Buddy hadn't started playing poker?*

Bunny leaned her head against the wall and stared at a beam of sunlight feebly slanting through one of the dirty basement windows. The window looked like it hadn't been cleaned since they had lived there. *That's how it happens. One speck of dust at a time, layer by layer, until the grime is thick and impenetrable. What can clean twenty-eight years of grime?*

She remembered another Friday night. It was later, after they had moved, not long after she had started her real estate career. She had had a terrible day and was on the verge of giving up. Buddy had taken one look at her and bundled her into his brand-new Mazda MX-5, retracted the convertible top, and before she knew it, they were speeding down the Atlantic City Expressway toward the Jersey Shore, the warm summer wind whipping back her hair. They had ended up in Cape May, at an amazing Italian restaurant that Buddy somehow knew about. Afterward, they had walked on the beach under a huge golden moon, and she had poured out her heart to Buddy. He had listened, really listened, and told her that he believed in her. Looking back, that had been a turning point in her career.

Bunny sighed and pulled herself up off the floor. *Was it really too late?* She went back up the stairs, locked the door behind her, and climbed into her car. As she drove away, she caught one last glimpse of the house in her rearview mirror, and for a moment a trick of the light made the shutters gleam sky blue.

THE REST OF THE DAY passed in a blur. Bunny had several appointments during the afternoon and she didn't get home till nearly seven o'clock, her legs and feet aching.

Buddy's car was in the driveway, and she guessed he would be in the den. Bunny paused in the kitchen, and then, before she could lose her courage, strode into the den. The TV was on and Buddy was staring fixedly at the screen, a glazed look on his face.

"Hello, Buddy. That was a great party last night."

He started at the sound of her voice and turned his head toward her. "Oh, hi, Bunny. Yeah, in the end it turned out good, I guess." He picked up the TV remote from the arm of his recliner and clicked the mute button.

"You seem to be on a real memory-lane kick these days. Any luck tracking down Mouse?"

Buddy frowned. "Actually, I keep hitting dead ends. But I haven't given up yet."

Bunny tried to make her voice sound bright and carefree. "Speaking of memory lane, do you remember that time you took me to Cape May, when I almost gave up on real estate, and we walked on the beach? Do you remember the name of that restaurant?"

Bunny thought she saw his eyes light up for a moment. "410 Bank Street. Man, I haven't thought about that place in years. I wonder if it's still there."

"Buddy, let's go back there again. Let's look for it. It's been years since we've done anything like that."

Buddy looked surprised. "Go back to 410 Bank Street? When? Right now? I'm not sure that's such a good idea . . . I'm kind of tired . . ."

"No, not right now. How about Friday? I'll cancel all my appointments. Buddy, let's walk on the beach again. We can talk, really talk. We can remember the old times at the U of O."

Bunny saw his eyes shift. "Umm, Friday might not be good for me." He fumbled for his phone and clicked on something. "Nope, can't do it on Friday. Out of town on business."

Suddenly, Bunny could tell he was lying. Her heart ached. "Please, Buddy. Can't you cancel it?"

"Nope, can't do that." He avoided her eyes and looked back at the TV. "How about a different Friday?"

Bunny sighed. "Okay, maybe another time. But you know what? I'm going to keep Friday open just in case you change your mind. Please, just think about it, okay? It's not too late to change your mind."

"Sure thing, but you know I can't cancel business trips just like that."

"Right." Bunny sighed again. Then she turned around and walked back into the kitchen. Behind her she could hear Buddy unmuting the TV. Opening the fridge, she took out the bottle of chardonnay.

EIGHT

The morning after the surprise party, Frank was awakened, as usual, by Fred jumping on his feet at precisely six o'clock, purring furiously and demanding breakfast. *No such thing as sleeping in around here*, he groaned to himself. Slipping quietly out of bed, he dragged himself downstairs, dumped a scoop of tuna-flavored Purina Cat Chow in Fred's bowl, and opened the sliding glass door to the deck. The fresh spring air washed over his face. For a moment, the dreariness of his life lifted and he turned his face to the east where wisps of pink-tinted clouds painted a delicate filigree across the sky. The dawn chorus of birds welcoming the new day filled the air, and a rich earthy smell rose up from the onion grass in the back yard, full of the promise of renewed life.

Then his eye caught the corner of the deck railing where the water-proofing sealant he had laboriously applied in the fall was already peeling off. Beyond that, at the back of the yard, he could see the wire fence sagging from a large tree limb that had dropped in the last snowstorm. The fallen limb reminded him that the same snowstorm had ripped the gutter downspout off the corner of the house. *The joys of homeownership*, he thought sourly, and turned back into the kitchen, sliding the door closed behind him.

Catherine was just walking into the kitchen, yawning and stretching. "Sorry to wake you up," said Frank. "Blame it on the beast." He bent down and scratched Fred, who was rubbing against his ankles and purring joyfully. "What's the latest news from Becky?"

Catherine frowned. "I haven't talked to her since last weekend. She seems willing to talk to me about once a week, on the weekend, so I've given up trying to call during the week. Hopefully, I'll talk to her today. I don't get the impression much has changed. She's barely posted anything on Facebook. It's hard to believe it's been over a month since she left. I really missed her last night."

"Me too," said Frank. "So she's still sleeping on a couch on the twenty-seventh floor of some high-rise in San Francisco? What about the job for mister computer genius?"

"Yeah, still staying with their friends. The job is still up in the air, as far as I know. She seems strangely unconcerned about that. To be honest, she sounds pretty happy." Catherine pulled out a chair and sat down at the kitchen table as Frank scooped coffee into a fresh filter.

"The good times won't last," said Frank, watching the coffee trickling into the pot. "Just wait, she'll hit bottom and come running back home with her tail between her legs. Or her lover-boy will dump her."

"Maybe. But I can't get out of my head what she said that first time she called—that we've been a huge blanket smothering her for her whole life. Is that really true? She *is* an only child, and sometimes parents are the blindest of all when it comes to their own children. I wonder." Catherine took a turn scratching Fred behind his ears.

"No, it's not true," said Frank. "She had a normal childhood, no different from anyone else. Better than most, in fact. We were the ones encouraging her to discover herself, to be all that she can be, to live up to her potential, and all those other stupid clichés. When did we ever smother her? Kids these days don't know how good they have it, and then they moan and groan when things don't go their way." He jerked the coffee pot out before the machine had finished dripping, and filled his mug. Several drops of coffee sizzled and steamed on the hot plate.

"Well, I've been thinking a lot about it the last week or two. Besides, if that's how *she* feels, how can you argue with that? We did have a lot of rules, you have to admit. Like how much TV she could watch, and what shows, and what friends she could hang out with. We were really strict about curfews. And we didn't let her get a cell phone until she was sixteen. Remember that time I got in a fight with her teacher about watching an R-rated movie in school when she was only fifteen? I have to admit that seems kind of ridiculous now." Catherine stood up and opened the sliding glass door to the deck to let in some fresh air. She stood with her back to Frank, watching the sunlight hit the new spring leaves at the top of the trees behind the house. Fred meowed to be let out, and she slid open the screen door just wide enough to let him squeeze through.

"Those are normal rules. You were just doing your job as a mother. All families have rules about stuff like that. And you were a great mother—she has nothing to complain about. If she wants to complain about something, she should say it to our faces, not run off somewhere and hide without even talking to us." Frank opened the cabinet where they kept breakfast cereal and stared at the choices. *Same old boring stuff*, he thought.

Catherine returned to her seat at the kitchen table and picked up a lavender scrunchie Becky had left behind on the table, twirling it mindlessly in her fingers. Once, Frank had tried to put the scrunchie away in Becky's room, but Catherine had stopped him. "I know it's silly," she had said, "but leaving it there helps me pretend she's just out with her friends, and might come bursting through the door any minute. Lavender was her favorite color, you know." Frank did not think this was wise, but he had kept his mouth shut. He had not known lavender was Becky's favorite color.

Catherine tilted her head to one side and stared at the scrunchie, her brow furrowed. "Okay, maybe, maybe you're right, but maybe we never gave her a chance. She might have tried to talk to us and we never noticed. It's not always easy for kids to push back against their own parents, especially a quiet kid like Becky. Here's another example I thought of: summer camps. We sent her to a lot of summer camps, but did she ever get to choose which one? How did we decide? Did we even ask her what she wanted? It's strange, I can't remember really involving her, although I always thought she had fun doing the things I chose. And I spent a lot of time figuring out what would be the perfect camp for someone with her personality and gifts. Like that writers' camp . . . was that the summer after eighth grade? I thought she loved it, but maybe I just assumed that and never asked her."

"How many kids even get a chance to go to summer camp? You can hardly call sending your kid to expensive camps smothering her. Besides, that was in middle school. Was she smothered in high school? She seemed to have plenty of friends. We let her choose her college, and then paid for it. I don't call that smothering." He let the door of the cereal cabinet snap shut and moved on to the freezer, looking for a bagel or waffle.

"Frank, you're forgetting the two hundred-mile rule! That was *your* idea, by the way. We told her she could go to any school within two hundred miles—and why? Because we wanted her to be within a three or four-hour drive, so she could come home on weekends, and so we could go to school events. It was all about what we wanted."

"Yeah, but two hundred miles goes from Washington all the way up to Boston! Do you know how many universities and colleges that covers? Besides, what's wrong with staying close to your family?" Frank had found a frozen bagel and jammed it into the toaster.

"There's nothing wrong with it. But two hundred miles does not include Ohio, say, or Michigan, not to mention Texas or California. You even said Pittsburgh was too far. Be honest, Frank. We wanted her close by and we wouldn't budge. That was the biggest argument I ever remember having with her, and she was not the type to argue. And don't you think it might be significant that the school she finally chose was two hundred fifty miles away? Don't you remember how hard she had to fight to get you to budge an extra fifty miles?"

"I still think Ithaca was too far; it sometimes took five hours when traffic was bad," Frank said grudgingly. "And it wasn't just me who wouldn't budge—it was you too. I thought she loved Ithaca. Where did she *want* to go?"

"That's the whole point," said Catherine. "I don't even know where she would have chosen if it was completely up to her. That's what I'm saying—maybe we really *were* smothering her. And don't you remember the huge discussions about her major? We were all very polite and reasonable, but we did strongly encourage her in certain directions. We kept reminding her how much Ithaca was costing us, and how she needed to be sure she could get a good-paying job. So she ends up doing education. But that's what *I* love—is that what *she* loves? And then we're all excited about her living at home as soon as she graduates, and so she does it. She comes home, back to her old bedroom, and we think everything is just great. I don't know, maybe we weren't listening." Catherine's voice trailed off, and she looked out on the deck again, where Fred was crouched in a hunting pose, staring at something just off the edge of the deck.

"Well, she sure didn't choose accounting," said Frank, stabbing a knife into a tub of cream cheese. "Okay, maybe you're right. Maybe she thinks we did try to control her life to some extent, but that's what all parents do. And does that justify her running off to California with Ricky Raccoon without telling us?"

"Ricky Raccoon? Where did that come from? Frank, that's offensive—you can't call him that!" Catherine turned and stared at him, shocked.

"I don't care. It's those huge glasses he wears. It makes him look like a raccoon. And he sneaks around like a raccoon too. This never would have happened if he hadn't been in the picture." Frank realized his voice was rising and his fingers were so tightly clenched around his coffee mug that he wondered if it might crack. He was suddenly afraid of the anger he could feel boiling up inside him. Once, when Becky was a toddler, something had infuriated him—he couldn't remember what—and he had flung one of her toys against the wall, hitting a picture frame and causing it to shatter on the floor. No one had been hurt, but that moment had terrified him, revealing something uncontrollable inside him that he hadn't known existed. He consciously took a deep breath and tried to calm himself.

"Anyway, I can't sit here and talk about this all day— Rupert is bugging me again about another stupid report that he wants on his desk first thing Monday morning. What a jerk. Let me know if Becky calls." Frank left the kitchen, mug in one hand, his thumb hooked through the center of the bagel, and with his other hand grabbed his briefcase where he had left it by the front door. Behind him, he heard Catherine sigh as she opened the fridge to get her breakfast. He went into the office and pulled out his laptop.

Frank clicked open the spreadsheet for Rupert and stared at it, finding it impossible to focus. Gradually, his heart rate subsided. He had a nagging feeling he was forgetting to do something. What was it? Something related to Becky? To the party? That was it. He stood up and walked back into the kitchen. "Hey Catherine, I almost forgot to ask you—a strange thing happened when I was at the wrong Gran Dorado yesterday. The receptionist insisted there was a reservation in my name for next Friday. That's partly what confused me. Are you cooking up some other surprise you haven't told me about?"

Catherine looked up from her bowl of yogurt, fruit, and granola. "No—are you crazy? Do you really think I would pick the Gran Dorado by Walmart for a surprise night out? It must be a mix-up with someone else with the same name."

"That's what I thought. But she knew our address— that's why I thought it might be you. That reminds me, she printed out the confirmation page. Now where did I put that?" Frank headed upstairs to check the pocket of his sports jacket and was soon back in the kitchen. "Are these the last four digits of your Visa card: seven four three two?"

"No idea. You know I can never remember numbers like that. My card is upstairs in my purse, or you can check the file in the office." Catherine was extremely organized about filing, unlike Frank who tended to leave papers stacked in giant piles on his desk. "I know exactly where everything is," he always claimed. And, even though Frank was the professional accountant, Catherine was the one who always made sure the monthly bills were paid on time. "I don't trust your filing system," she had told him early in their marriage after several bills went missing in one of the piles.

"Ugh, I was just upstairs." Frank went back into the office, opened the filing cabinet, and pulled out the file labeled "Visa–Catherine," neatly filed before "Visa–Frank." He took out the latest statement. The last four digits of her card were 6383, not 7432. He put the file back in the drawer and, on an impulse, pulled out his Visa file. After working with accounting records his entire working life, he knew strange things could happen with numbers, either from computer glitches or human error. Was it possible the whole thing was some kind of bizarre mix-up that had somehow linked his name to a different card in the hotel database?

He pulled out the last few months of bills and scanned down the entries looking for anything that seemed odd, not even quite sure what he was looking for, but trusting his accountant's intuition. There were no references to the Gran Dorado or any other hotels—just the usual predictable charges for gas, insurance, car repairs, his *New York Times* subscription, the occasional restaurant, and other random purchases. *This is ridiculous*, he decided. *Catherine pays the bills—she definitely would have noticed anything strange. The only thing this proves is that I have a boring life—not that I needed any proof of that.*

He was stuffing the bills back in the file when he was surprised to see a second January statement tucked in the back of the folder. *Aha!* he thought. *Maybe Catherine is not so efficient after all—it looks like she filed her statement in the wrong file.* He pulled out the page, found the "Visa–Catherine" folder again, opened it and was about to slip the January statement in its place behind February when he suddenly froze. Catherine's January statement was already there. He looked more closely at the statement in his hand and realized it was not a statement after all—it was a memo, addressed to him, with the subject line:

"Thank you for joining the Visa Family!" An account number was shown at the top of the page. The last four digits were 7432.

"Catherine," he shouted. "Are you still in the kitchen? Can you come in here for a sec?"

"What's the matter?" Catherine asked as she walked into the office. "Can't you find the Visa folder?"

"I found it alright. Look at this. Do you remember filing that?" Frank handed her the Visa welcome memo.

Catherine looked at it. "What is it? I think I vaguely remember it. It was something to do with Visa and it had your name on it. So I stuck it in your file. Is it a problem?"

"It's thanking me for ordering a new card. And the last four digits are the same as the ones from the wrong Gran Dorado."

"I don't understand. What does it mean?" Catherine looked confused.

"I think it might mean identify theft," said Frank. "Someone could have created a Visa account in my name and is using it to pay for hotel rooms at the Gran Dorado and who knows what else. This could be bad."

"Are you sure?" asked Catherine. "Maybe you ordered it accidentally. You know, those scam calls where they trick you into saying 'yes' and you end up ordering something you don't want."

"First of all," said Frank with exaggerated patience, "I would never do that. Second, even if I had, I definitely did not accidentally reserve a room at the Gran Dorado. No, someone else is using a card that's in my name. That's identity theft."

"But why did we get the welcome memo but no other statements? It doesn't add up. Anyway, if that's what happened, call Visa and report it. Will we be responsible for all the charges? How much has been charged so far?"

"Good question. Let me see ... according to the welcome memo, the credit limit is twenty-five thousand dollars, so it could be quite a lot. I'm not sure if we're responsible. Probably not, but it could be a huge headache to straighten out. I've heard some horror stories. Shoot, just what I needed—a new problem." Frank grimaced.

"I've seen some headlines lately about credit card data breaches at big companies—could this be the result of something like that?"

"I suppose so—yes, that's very possible—although our current Visa cards were not hacked. This seems a bit different because a new card was created. But it could be that hackers would be able to get personal information they need from that kind of data breach in order to set up a new card, like social security numbers and addresses, for example." Frank paused, wheels turning in his head. "I'm very curious about what's been charged on that card. It seems like such a strange coincidence that a card created in my name by some random hacker would end up being used so close to home."

Frank turned his attention back to the welcome memo. "It says here that we can set up an online account by calling this eight hundred number. Do you suppose it would be possible for me to do that? Or would the hackers have already set one up?"

"Frank, just call Visa and report the problem. Don't start messing around and trying to figure this out yourself." Catherine knew that Frank had a tendency not to let go of an idea once it had lodged in his mind.

Frank had already picked up his phone and was dialing the 800 number. "Let's just see what happens. Don't worry, I'm going to report it. I'm just curious if I can get access to the statements."

"Hello, I'm calling to set up an online account for my new credit card—I just got it in January but haven't set up an online account yet. Frank O'Donnell: O apostrophe d-o-double-n-e-double-l. The card number is 9462-8661-5129-7432. The last four digits of my social security number? Sure." The Visa rep also asked Frank to confirm his home address and his mother's maiden name, and to provide an email address. "Sure, I can hold . . . yes, that's correct. Wait, let me write that down. Okay, got it, great. Thank you very much. Goodbye."

"Wow, that was really easy. Looks like the hackers never bothered to set up the online access. Now, there should be an email in my inbox with a link, and he gave me a temporary password . . . yes, there it is . . . let's see if this works . . ." Catherine peered over his shoulder as he clicked on the link. The website prompted him to create a new password. Frank thought for a moment and carefully keyed in "d!ehackersD!E," cackling fiendishly under his breath.

And then he was in. A welcome message asked if he wanted to review the award-winning, convenient, user-friendly features of their new interface, designed for professionals like him. Frank clicked *No thanks* and stared at the screen. "First, let's see what the current balance is . . ." He clicked on a link labeled *Account Dashboard*.

"Oh no," said Catherine. "Over eighteen thousand dollars. Yikes, that's bad. That's a lot in only three months . . . what are they spending it on?"

Frank clicked on *Statements*, and then randomly chose February. "Look," he said, pointing with his mouse. "A Gran Dorado charge, on February fifteenth. So this week's reservation is not the first time they've stayed there—sure wouldn't be my first choice for a hot Valentine's date. Wow, look, I guess that wasn't a joke: a hundred and eighty-nine dollars for flowers on Valentine's Day from that florist next to Walmart!" Frank scanned down the rest of the entries. "In general, it looks like a lot of hotel and travel charges. Let's see if I can download

PDFs of all the statements right away. I don't know if the hackers will somehow find out that I've accessed the account." He studied the screen and finally located a download icon in the corner. Then he carefully opened all the monthly statements and downloaded them onto his laptop. "Okay, now let me go through these a little more carefully. I guess I can logout of the site for now."

Catherine had been craning her neck over Frank's shoulder. "This is giving me a headache. I'm going back to the kitchen—let me know if you find out anything interesting. Aren't you going to call Visa to report this? Eighteen thousand dollars is a lot of money."

"Yes, I'm going to call, but I just want to take a quick look at this first." He decided to start with the January statement and work his way forward.

Thirty minutes later he burst into the kitchen, where Catherine was working on a shopping list for the week ahead, carrying his laptop. "There's something very disturbing about this, Catherine."

Catherine looked up. "What do you mean?"

"First of all, the hackers have been paying the minimum balance on time every month. Why would they do that? Why not blow the entire twenty-five thousand dollar credit limit in the first month, before anyone notices? Or on the first day, for that matter? A lot of the purchases look like the kinds of things you do on vacation—there's some hotels, car rentals, fancy-sounding restaurants, high-end stores like clothing and jewelry. To me it smells like a guy traveling with a girlfriend with expensive tastes. But then, weirdly, there's also some more budget hotels, like Gran Dorado—in fact, Gran Dorado shows up a few times. But here's the kicker—airline tickets. There are a few of them—some of them business class to exotic foreign places. But the one that hit me over the head with a hammer is this one. Take a look at this." He sat down next to Catherine at the kitchen table and pointed to the laptop screen.

"American Airlines, $467.58," Catherine read out loud. "What's so strange about that?"

"No, read the whole thing, including the numbers."

This time Catherine read: "'American Airlines, CONF-5GX47K-03-01-13, $467.58.' So what?"

"Can't you see? The confirmation number includes the date of travel—March first."

"I don't get it," said Catherine.

Frank looked Catherine in the eyes. "That's the day Becky flew to San Francisco."

"Frank! What are you saying? That Becky is somehow involved in this? That she's connected to the credit card hackers?"

"Not Becky necessarily—but maybe Ricky. It fits everything. He was in and out of our house who knows how many times, probably lots of times when we weren't here. It would have been easy for him to have access to our confidential information to open a credit card in my name. Plus, he's mister expert on identity theft—he told me all about it that one time we talked."

"Frank, I don't believe this! If it's true, Becky must not have known."

"Maybe not. The one thing that's a little strange is that the amount of money doesn't look enough for two airfares—but there's not enough info on the statement to know for sure. Also, it doesn't say the destination, but four seventy sounds about right for the West Coast."

Now it was Catherine's turn to stare at Frank. "They didn't fly together that night. She told me that he had gone out a week earlier. I must have forgotten to mention that to you."

Frank scrolled up on the page, then clicked over to the February statement. "Look, right here. Another American Airlines ticket, a similar amount of money, confirmation number 7QP83L-02-22-13. That's exactly one week earlier—probably the same flight."

This time they both stared at each other. After a moment Frank broke the silence. "This could also explain why we never saw any of the other statements. Ricky could have been intercepting our mail—maybe we got lucky and he just missed the first letter because you're so efficient at filing things right away. Or maybe Becky was helping him."

"Frank, don't say that. I can't believe Becky would be involved in something like this." Catherine was still looking at Frank's laptop and Frank heard a sudden intake of her breath. "Frank, look, Victoria's Secret—that's the one at the Moorestown Mall. I saw a Victoria's Secret shopping bag in Becky's closet . . . could that be something he bought her? Oh Frank, this is awful!"

"Honestly, I'm not as surprised as you are. But one way or another, I'm going to get to the bottom of this. Ricky Racc . . . okay, you don't like raccoon? Then rat, that rat is not going to get away with this."

Catherine looked at him helplessly. "Oh Frank, what is happening to our little girl? How did we end up here?"

Frank reached out his arm and gave her an awkward hug across the gap between the chairs. "Don't worry, my love. We'll get through this somehow. I know we will."

NINE

This whole prank thing has been a real trip down memory lane, thought Buddy the day after the party. His laptop was balanced on his knees, a cup of coffee in one hand, and a huge slice of leftover cake perched precariously next to him on the arm of his leather recliner. He had slept late, and, as usual on a Saturday, Bunny was already out of the house by the time he came downstairs. Thanks to his call to the alumni office about Mouse, the promised yearbooks and alumni magazines were now safely stored on his laptop. The yearbooks had been a godsend in putting together the memory book for Frank's party. He was surprised how many memories the pictures stirred up. Just seeing the faces of people he hadn't thought about in decades brought back a rush of vivid memories and emotions.

And it wasn't just pictures of people that had triggered memories. Clicking through the yearbooks, he had glimpsed the fountain outside the library in the background of one photo. That was the fountain where he and three dormmates had stripped off their clothes and cavorted in the knee-deep water at four in the morning after an epic frat party. The outing ended with one of the frolickers slicing his head open on a sharp corner of a bronze mermaid, staining the water an ominous pink as blood poured from the gash on his head. He hadn't thought about that episode in at least twenty-five years, but now he could remember the exact shirt he had been wearing, the taste of the metallic, chlorinated water on his tongue, and the flashing red lights of the ambulance throwing huge, distorted mermaid shadows against the side of the library. Strange, how the brain worked.

At first, he had thought the digitized alumni magazines would provide the fastest answers to his questions about Mouse. Surely, a famous alum like Mouse would get frequent mention in the class notes, maybe even a feature article or two. Everyone in the class of '86 had known Mouse. But Buddy had been disappointed. The first problem was that the text of the magazines was not searchable (*maybe I had to donate another five hundred to get that feature,* grumbled Buddy). As a result, he had to painstakingly open each issue separately and browse through the pages one by one, scanning for any references to Mouse, Darnell Richards, or football in general. The first three issues had raised his hopes with several notes in the class pages about Mouse's promising early years with the Browns. But then the references disappeared, and Buddy's labors were fruitless. *I guess the glory days were over,* thought Buddy in frustration.

The problem wasn't that the alumni didn't care about football. They cared plenty, but the only team that mattered to them was the university team: the glorious Fighting Eagles. The endless hype and absurd, jingoistic chest-beating about the team began to turn Buddy's stomach by the time he had skimmed through thirty or forty issues of the magazine (typical headline: "Inspiring Fourth-Quarter Stand Brings Eagles Within an Inch of Victory—Coach Optimistic for Next Season"). The irony was that the team had had a terrible record during those years, and, in fact, that particular coach had been fired, prompting endless soap-operatic speculation and rumors in the pages of the magazines. *Maybe because eagles don't actually fight that much*, thought Buddy. *Don't they just soar majestically by themselves and pity the pathetic humans scurrying below like ants?*

The NFL avenue of inquiry had been more fruitful, at least regarding the facts of Mouse's football career. Buddy had phoned the public relations number on the NFL website, using the same guise of being a free-lance reporter, and got an enthusiastic response. He had been connected to a research analyst who had been happy to tell him that Darnell Richards had been an offensive tackle with the Cleveland Browns from 1986 to 1995, when the Browns suspended operations for three seasons. He had signed with the Detroit Lions the following year, but had apparently left the team after one year without completing his contract. The analyst didn't know the reason why; his database only had numbers, not the reasons behind the numbers. Nor did he have detailed year-by-year player statistics at his fingertips. However, for a small fee Buddy could order a custom report on an individual player. He could also order copies of gamebooks for any NFL game back to the 1950s. The gamebooks included detailed statistics for every player, as well as play-by-play summaries of every game. Buddy had sighed—more money out of his pocket, but at least this time without the propaganda about *character building*—and ordered the custom report for Mouse, as well as the gamebooks for every game in his last year as a player at Detroit.

He had been pleasantly surprised when the materials had arrived in his inbox a few days later. The player report revealed that Mouse had had a stellar career with the Browns. For ten years, he had started almost every game and rarely missed an offensive snap. He had received the team Player of the Week award several times, and had been selected for the Pro Bowl in 1991. As far as Buddy could tell, he had had significant injuries only twice—in 1992 and 1994—but in both cases had only missed three or four games. As a host of other linesmen had come and gone, Mouse had been a steady presence anchoring the offensive line. This sounded like the Mouse Buddy remembered: not a flashy player, not seeking the spotlight, just quietly doing his job. *It's easy for players like that not to be noticed*, thought Buddy. They're the kind of people everyone takes for granted until they don't show up one day and everything falls apart.

Sadly, the reason for his brief career at Detroit was quickly evident. The player profile showed that Mouse had only played in the first two games of the 1996 season. Buddy pulled up the gamebook for the second game, a home game against the Tampa Bay Buccaneers on September 8, 1996. Detroit had won decisively, twenty-one to six, thanks to four turnovers by the Bucs. He carefully scanned the play-by-play summaries. There it was, early in the second quarter: "B. Sanders middle for no gain; tackle by M. Jones; D. Richards injured (out of game)."

That was it—the last play of Mouse's NFL career. No details, no honoring the end of an impressive career. Just the terse note: "injured (out of game)." A few minutes later, Barry Sanders had scampered fifty-four yards up the left side, scoring Detroit's first touchdown of the day. No doubt that had quickly erased any memory of an aging offensive tackle being carried off the field on a stretcher. *People only care about stars like Barry Sanders*, thought Buddy. *Nobody notices linemen like Mouse, unless they cause a stupid penalty, or get injured and delay the game.*

Buddy took another big bite of cake and washed it down with a gulp of coffee. He could see his reflection in the black rectangle of the TV directly in front of him. For once it was dark, but he wondered what percentage of his life he had spent staring at it, mesmerized by tiny, brightly-colored figures chasing after one kind of ball or another. Sometimes he hated sports, especially football—the hype, the money, the glorification of violence, the lure of fame and riches often ending in lives shattered by injuries after a few years. He had read somewhere, when searching for information about Mouse, that the average NFL career for an offensive lineman was only three-and-a-half years. *What a waste of a human being*, thought Buddy. *Even though I watch the damn games every weekend.*

Unfortunately, knowing the facts of Mouse's NFL career was not helping Buddy find him. In fact, they only raised more questions. Why would he sign with another team after such a long successful career at Cleveland? Wouldn't it have made more sense to retire when the team had folded in 1995? He must have had plenty of money by then. Buddy knew that, despite his skill as a player, Mouse had not really been that passionate about football. How serious was the injury that had ended his career? And, more importantly, what had he done after his NFL career, and where was he now? Buddy felt like he kept hitting dead ends.

Buddy stood up and went into the kitchen for a refill of coffee. *Might as well have some more cake too,* he decided. *Who needs breakfast or lunch when you can have cake?* Back in his chair, he pondered what to do next. Maybe the alumni office rep was right—the key was tracking down someone else who knew him. Buddy turned his attention back to the DVD and clicked on the yearbook for 1996. He found a picture of the football team. There was Mouse, standing in the back row, looking straight at the camera. The camera had caught him with a pensive look, maybe even a touch of melancholy (*probably be-cause of the team's 1-12 record that year*, joked Buddy to himself); everyone else had the requisite tough-guy look. Even surrounded by other football players, Mouse looked huge.

Who would have known Mouse the best? Some of his teammates, most likely. A football team at a major state university lived in a bubble all its own, with specially arranged classes and meals that would fit into practice and travel schedules; nothing could be allowed to get in the way of winning games for the glorious Fighting Eagles. But, Buddy knew, the U of O was unusual in that it did not require athletes to live in special dorms. And Mouse had liked getting out of the football bubble. Buddy remembered him saying once what a relief it was to talk about something besides sports. After their freshman year, Mouse had ended up rooming with Garbo. Had they continued rooming together? Buddy wasn't sure, but Garbo would be a good place to start.

It was kind of strange how many of their circle of friends had nicknames, mused Buddy: Garbo, Mouse, Buddy, Bunny—and there were others too: Prettyboy, Mitch, Grover (or was that his real name?), Roach (that actually *was* his last name, a no-brainer for a nickname). Except Frank. Frank had refused to be called anything but Frank. Maybe it was because he hated the first nickname Buddy came up with: Wiener. *Understandable*, thought Buddy, smiling—although he had meant it as a joke. *I guess a nickname means you belong. Everyone wants to belong. Maybe that's why I never dumped my nickname.*

Most of the nicknames had stories behind them. Take Garbo, for example. Buddy would never forget that night in the cafeteria their freshman year. Garbo—whose real name Buddy was currently blanking on—was sitting at the table with the rest of the gang as usual. Out of nowhere, his girlfriend had walked in, grabbed a container of garbanzo beans from the salad bar, and dumped it over his head. Why she did this was never exactly clear. Knowing Garbo, Buddy wasn't too surprised; he seemed to have a different girlfriend every month. Garbo was tall and skinny with a crewcut (thanks to a ROTC scholarship), an impressive nose, prominent ears, and an infectious laugh. The avalanche of garbanzo beans had rolled off his head, slid down his face, and bounced off his shoulders onto the table and floor. A handful of beans got caught in his glasses, and a good number found their way down the open neck of his polo shirt. A moment of shocked silence was followed by howls of laughter. Garbo ate it up, climbing up on his chair and taking a dramatic bow.

At first, they called him Garbanzo, remembered Buddy, but that was too many syllables to stick. On a subsequent night, the cafeteria table had taken a vote and settled on Garbo. *The Great Gonzo* of Muppet fame was a close second—a vocal minority pressing their case based on the shape of Garbo's nose—but was ultimately voted down because it had even more syllables.

Oh, for a picture of that, Buddy thought. He set his empty cake plate down and scrolled through the pages of the yearbook on his computer screen, picturing the garbanzo bean scraps still stuck in the bristles of Garbo's crewcut. He still couldn't remember Garbo's real name; it would be hard to find him without knowing his name—too many pages of faces to scroll through. He clicked on a few more random pages of miniature faces in the year-book. Noticing a stern face with a perfectly flat crewcut staring rigidly out of the page gave him an idea: maybe there would be a page for ROTC graduates.

Buddy clicked on the 1985 yearbook (they had been in the same class) and scanned through the table of contents. Sure enough, there was a ROTC page, and a couple of clicks later, there was Garbo, grinning at the camera out of a sea of dress uniforms. What was he holding? Buddy squinted at a slightly-blurred blob in Garbo's hands. An oddly-shaped cake? A stuffed animal? Buddy smiled. Typical Garbo—amazing they let him get away with that in a ROTC picture; every other figure was perfectly aligned with military precision, down to the exact angle of their faces. Buddy zoomed in on the caption below the photo. Yes, that was him: Bob Branson. *No wonder I couldn't remember his name*, thought Buddy. *Garbo is much better.*

Buddy clicked back to Garbo's picture in the main section of the yearbook. In that picture, he was wearing a novelty hat that made it look like an arrow was piercing his head, directly through his large ears. Buddy started to smile again, but then his eye caught another name on the line immediately below Garbo: Reginald Brantley, III. The face stirred something in the pit of Buddy's stomach; not every memory from the college days was a good one. Reginald Brantley had been known simply as Brantley. *Did a last name count as a nickname?* wondered Buddy. *It was more because his first name was so preppy*, he thought with a touch of spite.

Why had Buddy disliked him? Obviously, not just because he was preppy and rich, or even that he had attended a private school outside of Boston, which Buddy considered the height of preppiness. There were plenty of other people like that at the U of O whom he had gotten along with just fine. Was it something about the way he talked, or the way he looked at you, like you were somehow beneath him? A way of sizing you up, calculating how you fit into his life plan? There was no question that he was highly ambitious. *But so was I,* thought Buddy.

In truth, he didn't have that many specific memories of Brantley, except for one late-night debate—argument?—about trickle-down economics. It was the prototypical late-night college discussion that is supposed to shape your life in profound ways; *maybe even build your character*, thought Buddy sardonically. Brantley was smarter than he was, Buddy had to admit. More articulate too. Buddy could remember a helpless feeling that even though he *knew* Brantley was wrong, Brantley kept twisting his words and throwing them back at him to mean something different.

But Buddy knew the real reason for his reaction to the yearbook photo was a painful episode that had happened much later, long after the U of O days. Staring at

Brantley's yearbook photo, Buddy at first tried to block out the memories. But then, uncharacteristically (was it because of the prank, the yearbooks, his quest for Mouse?), he let them surface. His mind went back. He was thirty years old, married for seven years, and about to lose his job for the fourth time. He couldn't bring himself to tell Bunny that he was being let go again. He hated the job anyway, but his career seemed to keep hitting brick walls. He kept getting trapped in useless, two-bit companies that weren't going anywhere. He needed a break, a way into the kind of company that actually had a career ladder to climb, that would get him out of always starting over and spinning his wheels at some place that didn't understand him.

One night after dinner, when Bunny was scanning through the alumni magazine, she had asked him if he remembered Brantley; he had just gotten a job in Philly and moved into the area. "He might be our neighbor," she said.

"What kind of job?" asked Buddy.

"Looks like one of the top jobs at a company called Bryn Aston Holdings—have you heard of it? Sounds like a big company," replied Bunny. "I wonder if he remembers us."

"I doubt it," said Buddy. "We don't move in those circles."

But later, after Bunny had gone to bed, he looked at the alumni magazine. In the class news section, he found the page Bunny had been looking at. Most updates were one or two lines of text, but occasionally someone would be profiled in a longer article. That was what must have caught Bunny's eye. The article briefly described Brantley's new job, including a short profile of Bryn Aston Holdings.

That's more like it, Buddy thought. *That's the kind of company I need to get into. A big company, with lots of different divisions, lots of products and services, lots of places for marketing geniuses like me.* He needed to get his foot in *that* door. But how? *Would* Brantley remember him? Could this be his big break? He was not surprised to see Brantley getting such a plum job. *That's exactly what he was angling for way back when we knew him. I guess his life plan is right on track. Unlike yours truly.*

The article included a nice photo of Brantley with his wife. Buddy didn't recognize her, but she had apparently also graduated in their class. The article quoted her as saying how much she had been enjoying exploring the local area, and that Reginald had even joined the neighborhood gym already. Buddy studied the picture carefully. The front of Brantley's new house was visible in the background. Buddy recognized it as one of the new McMansions that had sprung up on the west side of town.

An idea was beginning to form in Buddy's mind. What he needed was a way to meet Brantley and renew their old "friendship." There was only one gym on the west side of town, at least only one that someone like Brantley would be likely to go to. The next day Buddy went to the gym and paid for an annual membership. That Friday was his last day of work, and without telling Bunny he had lost his job, he continued leaving the house at the usual time every morning and went to the gym multiple times a day, trying to guess when Brantley might show up. Buddy did not even know for sure if Brantley had a membership there, but it seemed plausible based on where he lived, and Buddy was getting desperate. Bunny didn't yet realize how precarious their financial situation was. When he wasn't at the gym, he spent hours in the public library or at one of the various coffee shops in the area.

Buddy spent as much time as he could in the locker room and entry area of the gym where he would be sure to encounter Brantley if he came, stalling as he changed and showered, pretending to work on his laptop in the small waiting area, as if he were waiting to meet someone for a squash game. The gym attendants soon knew him by name. His hopes went through the roof when one day, one of them confirmed that someone fitting Brantley's description was a regular, although the attendant couldn't say for sure when he usually came to the gym.

Buddy redoubled his efforts, spending even more time at the gym at a variety of random times. It was an expensive gym, and the membership included a subscription to a fitness magazine. Bunny noticed it in the mail one day and asked Buddy, "Are you a member at this gym? We can't afford that." Buddy had quickly lied—claiming the magazine was some kind of freebie through his office. He just couldn't bring himself to tell Bunny that he had been fired again.

And then one day, there Brantley was. Buddy was just coming out of the locker room around lunchtime when he saw Brantley striding into the gym, an expensive-looking duffel bag slung over his shoulder. Buddy had imagined this scene for so long that he couldn't believe his eyes at first. He froze. Then the adrenaline started pumping through his veins. *This is it*, he thought. His throat felt dry, and the sweat drying on his body from his recent workout turned cold and clammy.

Buddy had memorized and practiced a variety of opening lines. He went with option C. "Brantley, is that you? It's me, Buddy, from the old U of O days." The hardest part was making sure the surprise sounded genuine. Buddy hoped the adrenaline would take care of that. In his own ears, his voice sounded strained and too high-pitched.

Brantley stopped, a puzzled look on his face. He looked around, and then saw Buddy across the room. "Buddy? Buddy Kowalski? No one's called me Brantley in years.

Buddy! Is that really you? I didn't know you lived around here. Small world! Are you a regular here?"

"No," lied Buddy. "Just joined—the sedentary life of a desk job was starting to show." He patted his stomach. "I heard a rumor you had moved into the area." That part was true at least.

"Yeah, I'm working in Philly now. Just moved here a month ago. You live around here?"

"Just across the way, as a matter of fact," replied Buddy vaguely. "Hey, it's great to bump into you—we should have a drink sometime and catch up. Talk about the good old days." Buddy held his breath. He could feel his heart pounding.

Brantley paused and pulled out a small black appointment book. He studied it for what seemed like hours. "Sure," he said. Buddy breathed again. "How about next Friday at, say, six p.m.? I'm working from home again that day. Know any good places around here?"

Buddy was ready for this question. "How about Del Monte's, over on Laurel Avenue?" Buddy had picked a popular up-scale bar that he figured Brantley might have heard of.

"Perfect," said Brantley. "I've been wanting to try that place. Great—see you then; sorry, I can't chat now—got to stick to my schedule!"

"Sure, no problem. See you next Friday at six." Buddy smiled as authentically as he could as Brantley headed past him into the locker room. Success. Step one. Brantley had remembered him. So far so good.

That was the last time he went to that gym, Buddy remembered. In reality, he hated exercising, especially working out at gyms. Bunny would have been amazed to know how many hours he had spent there. *I guess I got my money's worth*, he thought.

The drinks at Del Monte's had gone even better than expected. The only awkward moment came in the first few minutes when Brantley made it clear that Buddy should call him Reginald. "College nicknames, Buddy—so juvenile," he said, with a forced chuckle, apparently forgetting that *Buddy* was a college nickname. After reminiscing about the U of O—Buddy did his best to exaggerate how many memories they shared without sounding like he was exaggerating, playing up how much the late-night discussion about macro-economics had deeply affected him—Buddy carefully turned the conversation to the real reason for the get-together. "So, tell me about your new job, Brant—I mean Reginald."

"Oh, it's a wonderful company," said Brantley. "Bryn Aston Holdings—you must have heard of it. Very much an up-and-coming place. Lots of growth. I'm looking forward to making my mark there. I've got the sales portfolio right now. Where are you these days?"

Sales—perfect, Buddy breathed to himself. And now for the big lie—a *calculated risk*, he kept reminding himself. "Oh, I'm in marketing—assistant VP at Johnson and Johnson. Great company. But honestly, I feel like I've gone about as far as I can there. You know, a place like that can get a bit stuck in the traditional ways of doing things." Buddy was gambling that Brantley would never see his resume. He crossed his fingers, offered a quick prayer to any god that might be listening, and squeezed the lucky keychain in his pocket that he always took to Phillies games.

"Very true, very true." Brantley looked at Buddy with a thoughtful expression. "You know, I've got a bit of a leash to bring in my own people. There might be a place for someone like you. What do you think—any interest in a move? Might be a step down from your current position—but, like I said, we're on an upward trajectory."

Buddy had practiced this moment in front of a mirror for hours. He needed to project the perfect blend of surprise, reluctance, interest, skepticism, and openness—all without seeming too eager. "Hmm. Interesting. I certainly know of Bryn Aston's reputation. Let me think about that," he said, nodding and stroking his chin. "Not sure how J and J would take it. But definitely an intriguing thought."

And it had worked. Amazingly, it had worked. Buddy had gone through an interview, but it seemed a formality; apparently a green light from someone like Brantley was good enough for HR. He was careful not to lie on his resume, but he wasn't sure they even looked at it. Within three weeks he was sitting in an office on the eleventh floor of a building in Center City Philadelphia. When he told Bunny that he had run into Brantley—Reginald—who had offered him the position, and that he had resigned from his previous job, she was thrilled and never questioned any of the details. And, fortunately, Buddy did not report directly to Brantley, so they rarely crossed paths in the office. Buddy began to relax and let his guard down. It really was a good company and a good job. He was beginning to feel the satisfaction of knowing he was good at what he was doing.

But six months later, somehow, Buddy never figured out how, Brantley had found out the truth. He had called Buddy into his office on a Monday morning and hadn't beat around the bush. "You lied to me about Johnson and Johnson," he said without preamble.

Buddy's heart stopped. His face burned. He could feel Brantley's eyes boring into him. Finally, in a low, agonized voice, his eyes staring at the intricate pattern of the richly colored Persian carpet in front of Brantley's desk, he pleaded, "I was desperate. I was almost out of cash. My credit cards were maxed out. Please, I'm sorry, don't fire me. I can do this job. Let me prove myself. I'm not that kind of person."

Brantley had looked at him in disgust. "I'm not going to fire you. But please, never lie to me again. You could have told me the truth. I still would have given you the job."

Buddy sighed, still gazing at Brantley's face in the yearbook photo, the dark eyes staring at him accusingly out of the screen. He could still visualize the pattern of that carpet in Brantley's office. *Literally called on the carpet*, he thought, wincing at the memory. He clicked his mouse, and the picture disappeared from the screen. If only he could click the memory and make that disappear too.

A few years later, Brantley had moved on to CEO of an even bigger company. Buddy didn't know where he was now. Once, he and Bunny had seen him with his wife in the local supermarket. Bunny could not understand why Buddy ducked his head and refused to go say hello. "He helped launch your career!" she hissed. "Bryn Aston has been a great place for you." But Buddy had just shaken his head and slipped out to the car, leaving Bunny to finish shopping on her own.

The next step was to find Garbo. *Let's try Facebook*, said Buddy to himself, savagely jabbing the mouse with his finger and clicking the familiar blue and white logo much harder than he needed to.

TEN

Having concluded Ricky might be involved in stealing his identity, Frank needed to convince Catherine they should not call Visa right away. "I know you don't believe Becky could be mixed up in this, but what if she was? We don't want to get her in any trouble." He and Catherine returned to the kitchen so Frank could refill his coffee cup.

"I guess you're right," Catherine conceded. "But in the meantime, the hackers are racking up bills on our account."

"True, but they're already almost at the credit limit. Besides, they seem to spend in fits and starts. That's one of the weird things about this. A few more days is not going to make any difference. When Becky calls, don't say anything. I need some time to think what to do."

Although it was a lovely spring day, Frank spent the rest of Saturday inside pacing around the house. Catherine was catching up on grading and banned him from the den, where she liked to sit curled up on the couch, a cup of tea at her elbow and papers piled in stacks on the coffee table. Fred napped in the opposite corner of the couch. Becky didn't call.

By dinner time, Frank was ready with his plan. "I'm going to stake out the hotel," he announced, taking a bottle of Yuengling beer from the fridge and twisting off the top.

Catherine raised her eyebrows. "Stake out the hotel? Seriously? Do you have one of those white, unmarked vans with computer thingies in the back? Or are you going to creep around in the bushes?"

"Whoa, since when did you get so sarcastic?" he countered with a wounded look. "Yes, I am serious. We know, thanks to the amazing coincidence of my going to the wrong hotel, that there's a room booked under my name this coming Friday. I'm going to see who checks in. I'm putting my money on Ricky the Rat."

"Sorry, honey. I just don't see how you can possibly stake out the hotel. Are you going to sit in the lobby for ten hours wearing dark glasses? Oops, sorry, I'm getting sarcastic again, aren't I?" She spooned out leftover pasta salad onto their plates. "Also, Ricky is in San Francisco. Why would he come back to New Jersey?"

"Who knows? He used to live here. There could be any number of reasons to come back. Maybe he just wants to hang out with his old partners in crime. The credit card shows that the hacker has stayed at the hotel several times. It doesn't cost him anything," he added bitterly.

"Okay. Tell me how you're going to do it then."

"My first idea was to just check into the room myself, as soon as the hotel will let me. After all, it's in my name. Then I could be sitting there when Ricky walks in."

"Stop saying Ricky," Catherine demanded.

"Okay, the hackers. Is that better? But then I realized there's a major flaw with that plan. When Ricky—I mean the hackers—try to check in, they'll be tipped off that someone's already there."

Catherine looked suddenly alarmed. "Also, if it's not Ricky, don't you think it might be dangerous? We don't know what kind of people we're dealing with."

"Hmm. I hadn't thought of that. And, even if it is Ricky, I'm not sure I want to confront him right away. I might, I suppose. I'm not sure."

"Okay, so you're not going to check in. What *are* you going to do? Sit in the lobby?"

"Yes, that's exactly what I'm going to do. If it's Ricky, it's no problem—I'll recognize him walking in. But if it's not Ricky, I still want to know who it is. That means I have to be close enough to the reception desk to hear what they're saying. I know the layout, because I was there last week. I think it will work."

Catherine frowned. "Won't they think it's strange? Some guy sitting in the lobby for hours? What will you do all that time?"

"If anyone asks, I'll say I'm meeting a business colleague whose flight was delayed by a few hours. That hotel is close enough to the airport that it has a free shuttle. I'll pretend to work on my laptop. When I was there last week, there was a guy doing that and no one seemed to care."

"There was a guy pretending to work on his laptop?"

"Very funny. How would you like to help? You could take a turn watching."

"Are you serious?" Catherine was incredulous. "No way. I'm not getting involved in this. I still think you should just call Visa. How long are you going to sit there? From three p.m. till midnight?"

"Well, maybe not till midnight. Yeah, I know it is a really long time, but I don't know what else to do. If this doesn't work, I'll call Visa and report it," promised Frank. "But I predict I'll see Ricky walking into that hotel."

"You know what you should do? You should ask Buddy for help—this kind of thing is right up his alley. Just like another prank."

"That's not a bad idea," said Frank. "He does have good ideas—although not always so good at implementing them." Frank smiled, thinking about Buddy's latest prank. "Maybe I'll give him a call. He might even help me pull it off. Are you going to call Becky today?" he asked, changing the subject and draining the last dregs of his beer.

"No, I don't think so. I feel like I'm always the one initiating the calls. This weekend I decided to just wait and see if she calls me. I'm trying to take seriously what she said about the blanket thing. It's hard though. I'm trying to keep my mind off of it."

Frank nodded sympathetically. Poor Catherine—Becky's absence was really taking a toll on her. His attention drifted back to the stakeout . . . something was bothering him, but he couldn't put his finger on it. Something about the hotel . . . yes, that was it. "Uh-oh, I just thought of a potential flaw in my plan: the receptionist. What if it's the same person as last week? It might be, because it's the same shift, and it might have been a memorable incident for her. She might recognize me and say, 'Hello, Mr. O'Donnell, are you ready to check into your room?'"

Catherine thought for a moment, tilting her head to the side like she always did when she was concentrating. Frank loved the way it made her look like the sparrows that lived in the bush in front of their house, cocking their heads as they peered out between the leaves. "Can you make yourself look different?" she asked. "Wear different clothes? A hat? How about wearing your contacts instead of your glasses? I know—grow a beard!" Catherine laughed. "I can just picture it: this bearded guy lurking in the lobby wearing sunglasses and a baseball cap. The receptionist is definitely going to call the cops after you've been sitting there for eleven hours."

"Ha ha, very funny. I can't grow a beard in one week, although I could get fashionably scruffy. But maybe you're right. If I look different enough, she won't make the connection; she must see hundreds of guests every week. The contacts are a good idea. See, I don't need Buddy—I have Catherine as my fellow plotter." Frank poked her playfully in the ribs with his finger.

WHEN FRANK GOT INTO the office on Monday morning, there was an email in his inbox from Sandra Harris, the HR director, requesting him to come to her office at ten o'clock. She didn't say why. *Probably to pick up my Accountant of the Year award*, thought Frank. *Too bad she missed the party.*

While he was waiting, he dialed Buddy's cell phone. The call went straight to voicemail. Frank hung up without leaving a message and tried Buddy's office number instead. His assistant answered the phone. "You've reached the office of Rudolph Kowalski. How may I help you?"

"Hi, this is Frank O'Donnell. Is Buddy in today?"

"Hello, Mr. O'Donnell. No, I'm afraid not. He's traveling most of this week."

"Oh, that's too bad. Do you know if he'll be around Friday afternoon?"

Frank could hear computer keys clicking in the background. "No, unfortunately not. It looks like he gets back in town on Saturday sometime—he won't be back in the office until the following Monday. Would you like to leave a message for him?"

"No, there's no point if he's not in town. I was hoping he could help me with something on Friday afternoon. I'll catch up with him some other time. Thanks for your help." *Oh well*, thought Frank, after he had hung up. *I guess Buddy won't be any help after all.*

He carefully timed his walk to Sandra Harris's office to ensure he arrived at her door at precisely 10:03. Frank's motto for what he called the paper pushers of the world was "always keep them guessing." Depending on his mood, this might lead him to provide the minimal amount of information as late as possible, or alternatively, vast quantities of redundant information—however, he was always careful to stay out of trouble.

Once, he had come close to crossing the line by carefully checking the "other" box on every question of an online HR survey and then filling in on the explanation line "See response to Question 2"; but in the response to question two he wrote "See response to Question 3," and so on, eventually ending up at the last question of the survey, which asked (as he knew it would) "Do you have anything else you would like to add?", where he wrote that he preferred to opt out of completing the survey (the survey had been optional to begin with). He had hoped this would brighten the day of a paper pusher somewhere in the maze of cubicles in the HR department. Instead, he got a terse email that his survey response was "not helpful" (proving, Frank had pointed out to Catherine later, that the survey was not as anonymous as they claimed it was).

He tapped on the director's door and heard her reply, "Come in, Frank." Sandra Harris was an imposing woman, both in size and manner. She looked impassively at Frank from behind her desk, which had a single open folder perfectly centered in front of her. The rest of the desk was completely barren except for an empty inbox in one corner. The vast mahogany surface reflected the fluorescent lights above it. "Please take a seat."

Frank's earlier bravado evaporated as he perched on the edge of a simple wooden chair placed in front of the gleaming desk, which seemed to loom larger and more ominously moment by moment. "What did you want to see me about?" he asked, thinking, *All we need to complete the scene is a naked light bulb hanging over the chair.*

"I won't beat around the bush, Frank." Her voice was surprisingly deep and powerful. "Your supervisor has submitted a complaint about your performance."

"Um, I'm sorry to hear that . . . he hasn't mentioned anything to me. I've always had the impression he was satisfied with my work." Frank racked his brain. *What was Rupert up to?*

Sandra picked up the top sheet from the folder in front of her. "Specifically, he says there has been a pattern in recent months of missing important deadlines. This has reflected poorly on the department and has resulted in extra work on his part, according to his statement. Is it true that you have missed important deadlines?" Sandra's face remained impassive.

Frank considered the best way to respond. Better play it cool, he decided. "He must be referring to the monthly reports, which he usually asks to have on his desk first thing Monday mornings. Yes, I have been late a couple of times, but I believe I completed them by the end of the day in all cases. I've been dealing with some personal stress at home." He could feel a wave of anger boiling up inside him, but he gritted his teeth and kept his voice level. "It won't happen again."

"I'm sure it won't, Frank. I took a look at your annual performance reviews, and you have an impressive record over many years. I'm not going to put a formal note in your file. But please take this little conversation seriously." She symbolically closed the folder on her desk and placed the sheet of paper to the side. "Thank you for your time."

Frank stood up. "Thank you," he said through clenched jaws. Seething with anger, he strode down the hall. *What a load of crap,* he raged to himself. Rupert didn't even have the guts to talk to him directly. The least he could have done was show up at the meeting with Sandra. *What a coward—sitting at his desk and emailing a nastygram that he's too chicken to say to my face. How can he submit a complaint to HR because of two reports that were a few hours late? And as always, HR always assumes the boss is right—what about the fact that Rupert doesn't even need those stupid reports until Wednesday? Why does he always make me submit them by nine a.m. on a Monday? Why not the end of the day? Does it ever occur to the Sandras of the world that the boss might be a jerk?*

Frank was so absorbed in his internal raging that he didn't hear Rupert's voice until it was almost too late. He had forgotten that Rupert had somehow managed to have his office moved to this section of the building, presumably, Frank assumed, so he could suck up to the senior managers. He could hear Rupert in the hallway around the corner, saying to someone in his high-pitched nasal voice, "That's exactly what I was thinking when I realized she hadn't even looked at the actual results. It's just incredible how people think they can get away with that kind of thing . . ." He heard the other person guffaw and say something unintelligible.

The voices were getting closer. Frank looked around frantically. He did *not* want to run into Rupert right now. He didn't trust himself to keep his anger in check—or Rupert's next complaint might be a little more credible, especially if there were stitches involved.

Frank knew there was an executive conference room around there somewhere—yes, there was the door about ten yards ahead of him. He took three gigantic leaping steps, praying the door would be unlocked and the room empty. There was no light under the door. He grabbed the handle and pulled. Thankfully, the door swung open, and he lunged inside, pulling the door closed behind him as quietly as he could. Trying not to make a sound, he stood in the dark, his heart pounding. He must have made it in the nick of time. He heard Rupert's voice right outside the door and suddenly had a terrible thought: what if they were coming to a meeting in this room? He quickly flipped the lights on—it would be even worse to be caught in the dark. Quick, he needed an excuse to be in here; could he claim to be lost? Rupert was saying, "Yeah, let's see how she deals with that. I bet she won't like it." The other voice replied, "Serves her right." And then he heard Rupert's voice fading as they kept moving down the hall, "I remember the last time she tried something like this . . ."

Frank breathed a sigh of relief. He looked around the room curiously. He had rarely been in this conference room; these days it was used exclusively by senior management. It looked like it had been recently upgraded: the floor was covered with a plush carpet, and several modern-looking works of abstract art hung on the walls, the colors carefully selected to match the carpet. Expensive executive chairs covered in leather surrounded a large oval conference table made from what looked like solid oak.

The polished sheen of the table was marred by finger prints, and several empty coffee cups and paper napkins were scattered around the table. *Looks like the cleaning service hasn't been in here yet*, thought Frank. That's right, he remembered: the monthly senior management meeting would have been the prior Friday afternoon in this room. It was always held the first Friday of the month, unless the first day of the month was a Friday. That's why Rupert always wanted the monthly sales figures at the beginning of the month. *What do they actually talk about in those meetings?* he wondered. *Probably a huge waste of time. I'm glad I don't have to go to them—although they might serve some tasty snacks.* He looked hopefully at several serving platters on the sideboard on the opposite wall, but there were only a few crumbs left. *Brownies and fresh strawberries, I bet*, he thought based on the crumbs and a few stray leaves.

He was about to turn out the lights and leave when he noticed some papers piled on one of the chairs near the sideboard. Out of curiosity, he walked over to see what they were. Maybe the meeting agenda, he thought. It looked like a handout from one of the managers' reports; the first page was a colorful graph. He looked more closely. Wait a minute—those were the sales figures. This was Rupert's report. The graph displayed a trend line showing the growth in sales over the past year. He suddenly remembered what Denise had said at the party: something about a positive trend? Frank hadn't really been paying attention to her. If he had, he would have been quick to point out that the trend so far this year had hardly been positive—at best, flat, and definitely worse than the previous year. Denise was a good numbers person. Why would she have said that?

That's strange, he thought, looking at the graph again. *This line* does *show a positive trend—what numbers is Rupert reporting?* On the second page was a chart comparing the quarterly goals with the actual results: in every case, the goal had been met or exceeded. *No way*, thought Frank. *We have definitely not met every goal—maybe we came close a couple of times, but there's something wrong with this.* He stared at the report. "I'll be damned," he said out loud. "Is Rupert fudging the numbers?"

He quickly folded the handout and stuffed it into his pocket. Then he turned out the lights and carefully opened the door a crack. The coast was clear—no sign of Rupert. As soon as he was safely back in his office, he examined the first page of the handout more carefully. The graph was formatted in such a way that the exact figures were hard to decipher, but the trend definitely showed an upward slope for the past six quarters. There was an asterisk at the end of the title at the top of the page. On the bottom of the sheet, in small print, Frank read: "Preliminary figures; subject to revision."

"Also known as *cover my ass*," snorted Frank.

He thought for a moment, tapping his mechanical pencil on the desk. He knew that Denise would be able to shed light on what was going on with the numbers, but he didn't want to get her in trouble. She had been a faithful helper for many years before getting the promotion into Rupert's office. He opened his email and clicked *New Message*.

```
Hi Denise,

It was great seeing you at the party on
Friday. Thanks for coming! We hardly see
each other anymore. The party was a lot of
fun. Hard to believe I'm turning 50. :-)

You might be able to do me a favor that
would save a lot of time. I've been asked
to do some follow-up on Rupert's latest
sales report. Would you happen to have the
numbers behind the charts he presented last
week? I have a feeling you'll be able to
pull them up faster than Rupert. :-)

Thanks a lot!

Frank
```

Frank knew Denise would love the emoticons—he had had to overcome deeply-held principles to include them. He had also thought long and hard about the wording of "I've been asked to do some follow-up . . ." It wasn't exactly a lie, he told himself. *I have been asked to do some follow-up—it's just that the person doing the asking is me.* He clicked *Send*.

Frank leaned back in his chair and gazed out the tiny window above his computer monitor. Getting an office with a window had been one of his "promotions" a few years before. The window had an inspiring view of a rusted fence at the back of the parking lot; still, it was better than the cubicles he'd occupied for years, and at least he could see the sky. Typical for April, the weekend's sparkling sun had been replaced by a cold drizzle, and heavy gray clouds were obscuring the horizon, making it hard to see the boundary between parking lot and sky. Frank sighed heavily. As the adrenaline from meeting with Sandra and evading Rupert subsided, the sense of dreary hopelessness that was always under the surface bubbled back to the top. And now he had a new problem to deal with. What was Rupert up to? Frank sighed a second time and turned back to his computer.

ELEVEN

Finding Garbo had been ridiculously easy. Once Buddy had remembered Garbo's full name with the help of the yearbook, his Facebook search had gotten an almost instant hit. Bob Branson was a fairly common name, but not when paired with his alma mater and year of graduation. Buddy had tried the same thing with Mouse, but had come up empty, concluding that Mouse must never have joined the social media giant. Buddy generally avoided social media, but had to admit it had its uses.

Garbo had accepted his friend request within the hour and happily shared his phone number via private message, suggesting that Buddy call him the next day, Sunday, early in the evening. Buddy scrolled through some of the pictures on Garbo's Facebook feed. *Not as skinny anymore*, he thought, *but I would recognize that nose and ears combo anywhere.* It must be over twenty years since they'd seen each other. He was surprised to see an African American woman in many of the pictures, and then sheepishly realized she was Garbo's wife. There were lots of pictures of kids of different ages. He wondered if Garbo had stayed in touch with other members of their circle of friends.

What is it about me? he asked himself. *Why do I lose touch with all my friends?*

ON SUNDAY AFTERNOON, Buddy had a hard time not watching the clock. *This is ridiculous—I'm acting like a kid waiting for school to let out*, he told himself, trying to lower his expectations. *Why is this such a big deal for me? Garbo might not even know anything about Mouse.* But even watching golf on ESPN with a cold beer at his elbow couldn't distract him. Finally, at six o'clock, he decided it was early evening and dialed Garbo's number.

"Buddy Kowalski. I knew it had to really be you," said Garbo. "No one has called me Garbo for at least twenty-five years."

"What do people call you now?" asked Buddy.

"Bob," said Garbo. "You know . . . my name . . . they call me Bob."

"Not as great a name as Garbo," cracked Buddy. "I'll do my best, but I'm not sure I can call you Bob."

"Be careful, there are a few stories I could release to the public that you might not want released," retorted Garbo, with the same infectious laugh Buddy remembered so well. "What are you up to these days?"

The next few minutes passed sharing updates about family, jobs, and the like. After doing his required stint in the military, Garbo had moved to Cleveland and started working as an assistant manager at a warehouse. Eventually, he had bought out the business and expanded it to other cities. "Why Cleveland?" asked Buddy. "I thought you were from Virginia."

"To be near Grace," answered Garbo without hesitation. "Her family has been here forever—actually, that's how I got into the warehouse business, through her uncle."

Garbo and Grace had raised five kids; two of them were still at home. "Nope, no kids," Buddy replied when asked. "I guess the time just never seemed right for us. Bunny's done really well with her real estate career, but it was tough getting it off the ground. I'm not sure I'm the dad kind of guy, anyway. But I'm sure you're great at it." Buddy meant it—Garbo had the kind of exuberant, fun-loving personality that kids would love. He wondered what Grace was like, and how Garbo had ended up in an interracial marriage. They seemed satisfied with their lot in life. Buddy felt a pang of regret, wishing for a moment that he was more like Garbo and less like himself. The whole family thing had kind of passed him by somehow.

"So, what prompted you to get in touch with me?" Garbo finally asked after the updates petered out. "Are you planning something? Being Buddy, you must have something up your sleeve."

"No, not this time," replied Buddy. "I do need your help, though. It's a long story, but somehow, I got to thinking about our college days, and I started thinking about Mouse. I completely lost touch with him. I figured you might have stayed in touch. Didn't you room with him for a few years?"

"Mouse," repeated Garbo thoughtfully. "I haven't heard that nickname for a long time either. Did you know he stopped using it a couple of years into his NFL career? Most people just called him Richards. He hated people making comments about his size, so maybe that's why he didn't like being called Mouse."

"No, I didn't know that," replied Buddy. "Like I said, I lost touch with him. I've been trying to track him down, and keep hitting dead ends. Did you stay in touch with him? Do you know where he is now?"

"Yeah, we stayed in touch alright. Actually, it's funny you should mention Mouse, because he's the real reason I'm in Cleveland. That first year we were roommates, my sophomore year, he invited me to his home for Thanksgiving, and that's how I met Grace—at his church. In fact, we ended up going to that church for a long time, although Grace and I didn't attend nearly as regularly as Richards did. He lived right in Cleveland all the years he was playing for the Browns, and after the injury at Detroit he moved back. He grew up around here; he has a huge family—tons of cousins and second cousins, scattered all over the country, but a lot of them are still in the area."

"I heard about the injury, but not any details. What actually happened?"

"It was his knee, the right one, I think. It just bent back the wrong way underneath him; another lineman was lying on top of him. Think about it, a combined weight of over six hundred pounds bending your knee backward. People on the sidelines said they heard it pop, like the sound of a champagne bottle. He'd had surgery on that knee once before, back when he was with Cleveland. Maybe it was never as strong after that. Of course, he was out for the season, and the Lions dropped him like a hot potato. He had multiple operations, but always had a limp after that."

"Ugh," winced Buddy, imagining the scene. "Why did he keep playing so long? More than ten years, wasn't it?"

"Let's see . . . the Browns folded after the 1995 season so, yeah, Detroit was his eleventh year in the NFL. It wasn't because he loved football, that's for sure. It was all about the money. Everyone thinks you get rich playing in the NFL, and maybe most players do, but not Richards. The problem was his huge family. He has such a soft heart, and most of his family lived—still lives—below the poverty line. I don't know how many people he was paying rent for, making car payments, bailing out of jail, paying medical bills, you name it. He also made some bad financial decisions, although I think some of his cousins flat-out cheated him. Do you remember the dot-com bubble in the late 1990s? That was after Richards quit the NFL, but one of his cousins suckered him into investing a ton of money in some stupid online start-up—cyber something, cyber jewelry, something like that—and he lost a butt-load of money. On top of that, I wouldn't be surprised if the CTE wasn't already affecting his decision-making."

"CTE? Oh, is that the problem with concussions that the NFL has been getting so much bad press about lately?" Buddy was only vaguely aware of the issue.

"Yeah. I forget what it stands for, but it's what happens after you get hit in the head fifty times a day for twenty years. You figure, someone like Richards probably started playing Pop Warner Football when he was five years old. Anyway, yeah, Richards was a poster child for CTE— memory loss, confusion, dizziness, trouble walking—he had every symptom, and in my opinion, it was already starting before he quit the NFL. Or rather, when the NFL booted him out; the Lions treated him really badly. In those days, the coach didn't pull you out of the game unless you couldn't stand up. Linemen were supposed to be tough, and they were—Richards was as tough as they get—and that meant you didn't moan about a little bang to the head. You went back out and played, no questions asked. Things are different now—although not that different. Did you know that Richards had the Browns' record for the longest streak of consecutive snaps at one point? I think it was something like five thousand plays."

"Wow, I had no idea Mouse was dealing with all that. That's terrible." *What a waste of a human being*, Buddy thought to himself for at least the third time. "So, what did he do after he left the NFL?"

"Well, it was tough for him to get a job—I'm not sure he even wanted a job. And he did have some money, at least at first. The surgery, rehab, all of that took close to a year. After that he basically helped his family and did charity stuff. He loved working with kids, although he refused to have anything to do with youth sports—partly because of his knee injury, but I think he also hated the way sports had put him in a trap he felt he couldn't get out of. He had the misfortune of being born big, and that was seen as a ticket out of the ghetto. He didn't like it when kids saw him as a model for success." Garbo paused reflectively. "Yeah, it was like a trap. Maybe that was another reason he didn't like being called Mouse."

Buddy could hear something in the background. "Hold on a sec, Grace is saying something," said Garbo. "What was that, Grace? Yeah, yeah, I was just getting to that." Garbo's voice got louder again. "She wants me to tell you about his singing. That was one thing he kept doing right up till he left. I think that's why he loved church so much. We have a great gospel choir, old style; those big choirs are not so common anymore in Black churches. He sang almost every week. That's mostly how we stayed in touch. We would see him at church, and sometimes he'd come home with us for Sunday dinner." Garbo paused. "Man, those were good years."

"Did he just sing in the church?" Buddy asked, wishing he could have heard Mouse sing one of the Gospel classics.

"Mostly, but every once in a while, he'd get asked to sing for some kind of community event. People in the area got to know about him. In fact, when there were special Sundays at church, not just Christmas or Easter, you know, Mother's Day, things like that, when people knew Richards would be singing, the church would be packed. The minister told me once that more people came to hear Richards sing than to hear him preach—and he was a good preacher too."

"Yeah, I've never forgotten his incredible voice. I always thought his talents were wasted on football. I bet *he* would have been a good preacher." Another memory flashed into Buddy's mind: once, in their freshman dorm, a class outing had been descending into chaos. Mouse had stood up and with a single powerful word brought instant order. Then, without another word, he had simply sat down again.

"That's true, he probably would have been an amazing preacher. Nobody could ignore that voice." Garbo paused again. "Talking to you is bringing back a lot of memories. My favorite memory of Richards singing was on one of the September eleven anniversaries. No, wait a minute, Grace is holding up one finger, it was the very first anniversary—yeah, she's right, that's why the crowd was so huge. We live outside of Cleveland, in the Eastlake area, and our town was one of the first to get a piece of steel from the World Trade Center and put up a memorial. It was already put up by the first anniversary. It's out by the City Hall, and there's a big grassy area there. I don't think they were expecting the size of crowd that turned up. The memory of nine eleven was still pretty raw. Anyway, they asked Richards to sing, and he got up there and sang 'Amazing Grace' like it's never been sung before, Buddy. If you were sitting here, you would see Grace nodding her head and agreeing with me. I will never forget that moment. When he was done, no one could talk for maybe five minutes. Nobody clapped or cheered—it was like a holy moment. There were a lot of tears, too. When he was done singing, he just quietly walked off into the crowd, and the spotlight stayed on the flags around the memorial."

Buddy could tell Garbo was starting to choke up just remembering it. Not knowing what to say, he said awkwardly into the silence on the line, "Gosh, I wish I could've been there . . . I never heard Mouse sing except in the shower. Even that was amazing."

Garbo regained his composure. "Yeah, Richards could really sing. We really miss that."

Buddy asked, "So, where is he now? It sounds like he's not around Cleveland anymore. I guess he never got married?"

"Nope, he never married. He saw what other NFL wives had to put up with, and he told me once that he didn't think it was fair to put a wife or kids through that. At one point, when he was done with football, we thought he was sweet on someone in the choir, but nothing ever came of it. I guess he had his hands full with all the family he already had. And the CTE kept getting worse and worse. His memory was shot, and he would get confused about where he was. For a while, a nephew was living with him, but something happened with that, I don't know . . . maybe the nephew got a job somewhere else. The family was trying to take care of him—that was the least they could do after all the money they had sucked out of him. He had nurses' aides coming every day for a while. But the dementia started getting bad. And then I think the money ran out. So, apparently, he had another cousin out in New Jersey, who was able to get him a spot in a nursing home out there. One day he was gone. We haven't seen him since. Can you believe it? A nursing home when he was still in his forties."

"Did you say New Jersey? I live in New Jersey." Buddy couldn't believe his ears.

"I thought you said you were in Philadelphia."

"I work in Philly . . . but I live in New Jersey, right across the Delaware River."

"Oh," said Garbo. "I guess my East Coast geography is a little weak."

"You mean Mouse has been right here in New Jersey this whole time I've been looking for him? When did they move him out here?"

"Grace, do you remember what year Richards left? It's been a while." Buddy could hear Garbo calling out to Grace. "She thinks 2006 or 2007, sometime around then."

"More than five years ago . . . I can't believe it," said Buddy. "Do you know where the nursing home is? Is he still in the same place?"

"I suppose so," replied Garbo. "As far as we know. To be honest, we tried calling the first couple of years, but without the visual cues, I think he was having a hard time remembering exactly who we were. So we haven't been in touch for quite a while. We've been sending Christmas cards every year, and I don't think they've been returned. Let me find the address. Grace! Where can I find Richards's address?"

Grace was efficient, and a moment later Buddy had written down the address on a scrap of paper: Golden Manor in Cherry Hill, New Jersey. Cherry Hill! That was twenty minutes from Buddy's home.

"Garbo—Bob—I can't thank you enough. I've been beating my head against the wall for the last few weeks trying to track Mouse down—I should've called you first. I still can't believe he's practically my neighbor."

"Well, it was fun getting caught up. Brought back some good memories. When you see him, say 'hi' from us and tell him we miss him. I hope he remembers you—I think he will; the older memories are stronger, and he'll be able to see you face-to-face. He's a good man. We've always felt terrible how football screwed up his life."

"Sure thing—I'll give him your love. Say thanks to Grace, too. I hope I can meet your whole family sometime. Goodbye." Buddy hung up the phone. He thought again how his life might have been different if he had accepted that Thanksgiving invitation from Mouse all those years ago. *Would I be living in Cleveland with someone like Grace and a houseful of happy memories?* he wondered a little wistfully.

But he was elated about finding Mouse. After so many dead ends, it looked like his quest was finally coming to an end. He immediately opened his laptop and Googled "Golden Manor Cherry Hill." The website had a professional look to it, full of pictures of smiling senior citizens surrounded by their families or being expertly cared for by attractive, well-proportioned medical staff. *Maybe he hasn't run out of money after all,* thought Buddy hopefully. *I might even be able talk to him right away.*

He found the phone number on the website and dialed it. The phone rang and rang without an answer. Eventually, after about ten rings, it went dead with a click. *Hmm, that's strange,* thought Buddy. He checked the number and tried again with the same result. He looked at his watch; Sunday evening—maybe they're short-staffed on Sundays, or they're between shifts. Impatiently, he put down his phone. Over the course of the evening, he tried several more times, always with the same result. Finally, he gave up and went to bed.

MONDAY MORNING, HE WAS out of the house before Bunny woke up. He liked getting to work early to beat the traffic over the Ben Franklin Bridge, and he had a busy week ahead of him. Midmorning, he had a break in his meetings and tried the nursing home number again. This time someone picked up on about the eighth ring. "Golden Manor, howmayIdrectyrcall," said a tired-sounding voice.

Buddy's face brightened. He didn't have much time, but maybe he could at least say hi to Mouse. "Hello, I was hoping to speak with Mr. Richards," he said, trying to sound as professional as possible.

"Richard? Richard who? You're gonna have to give me a last name," said the voice on the other end.

"Richards *is* his last name. Mr. Darnell Richards, with an *s* at the end," Buddy repeated patiently.

"Okay, okay, Richards, Richards. Nope, no one here with that name. Want me to check for a last name Darnell?"

"No, his last name is Richards. Darnell Richards. Are you sure? Can you check again? I'm sure you would know him if you saw him—a huge, tall guy, used to play in the NFL." Buddy's patience was quickly wearing thin.

"Sorry, I'm new here. I already checked the system again—there's no one here with that name. Maybe you've got the wrong place. Excuse me, I got some other calls coming in." The line went dead.

Buddy took a deep breath, counted to ten, and dialed the number again. This time it went to ten rings and he heard the familiar click, followed by silence. "Damn," he said out loud, looking at his watch. "I'll have to try again after lunch." He was already late for his next meeting. He cursed again.

The same voice answered when he tried after lunch, this time on the ninth ring. Buddy decided to lead with his calm, professional voice again. "Hello, I called earlier about Mr. Darnell Richards, and was told there was no one there with that name. If that's the case, would you be able to tell me if he was previously a resident at Golden Manor?"

"Nope. Unless they left in the last week. Anything else I can help with?"

What help? thought Buddy. He could sense the voice starting to hang up. "Please, don't hang up yet. Why can't you tell me if he was there previously?"

"Company policy. Personal and confidential."

"I'm not asking for anything confidential. I just want to know if he *used* to be there. I'm not asking for his address or medical history, for God's sake." Buddy tried to keep his voice level.

"Definitely can't release medical history. Personal and confidential."

"I'm not asking for his medical history. That was meant to be a contrast to show you that what I'm asking is *not* confidential." Buddy's irritation level was rising dramatically. *Why am I explaining myself to this fool?* "Look, is there anyone else I can talk to? Someone who can explain the policy to me?"

"Nope. I can take a message for my supervisor. She'll call you back. Everything about our residents is personal and confidential. Company policy. I got some other calls coming in."

"No, no, don't hang up!" Buddy's voice was no longer calm and professional. "Do you know how hard it is to get anyone to answer your goddamned phone?"

"Well, we got a lot of technical problems with the phones. I got another call coming in right now."

That sounds like a lie, thought Buddy angrily. *I bet the technical problem is you.* "Okay, please take a message for your supervisor. My name is Kowalski, that's K-O-W-A . . ." Buddy realized the phone was dead again. *Damn these people!* He slammed down the receiver. That was one thing he liked about land line phones—you could slam down the receiver; with smartphones, all you ended up with was a cracked screen.

He was so close and now another road block. He could feel the frustration boiling up inside him, but nothing would make him give up now. He was traveling the rest of the week, so whatever his next step was, it would have to wait till after the weekend. Obviously, phone calls to

Golden Manor were not going to get him anywhere. But he could be patient when he needed to. Wherever Mouse was, a few more days were not going to matter.

TWELVE

Catherine, you have to help me! I'm serious. I need you." It was Thursday evening, the day before the stakeout at the Gran Dorado, and Frank had just gotten back from work. Fred was winding himself around his ankles, politely requesting dinner. Catherine was cutting vegetables in the kitchen. "Rupert just sprung a meeting on me at four o'clock tomorrow, right when the stakeout is supposed to start. I can't not show up to his meeting. He just submitted a formal complaint about me on Monday!"

"Frank, you know how I feel about this. I don't like sneaking around spying on people. Also, I don't think Ricky will show up. There's some other explanation. This is all a waste of time—or else you're going to get mixed up in something serious. I don't like it." Catherine kept her eyes focused on the carrot slices tumbling off the edge of her knife in perfect ovals.

"But I can't get out of this stupid meeting! Rupert is being a pain in the butt—who else would schedule a meeting at four o'clock on a Friday afternoon? All you have to do is sit in the lobby until I get there, probably five thirty at the latest. It'll be a piece of cake. You can even get some work done. Check-in at the hotel is three p.m. I guarantee, if no one's watching between three and five thirty, that's for sure when they'll show up; Murphy's Law would never pass up a chance like that." Frank's voice seethed with frustration as he paced back and forth behind Catherine, almost stepping on Fred.

"No, Frank. I don't want to do it. Do you know how tense I would be sitting there? The receptionist would probably think I was having a heart attack and call 9-1-1. It just won't work. Find someone else to help you." Catherine had switched to cucumbers.

"Who? I already tried calling Buddy—he's out of town, not coming back till Saturday. Do you really want me to ask our church friends to help with a stakeout of our daughter's boyfriend who we think is some kind of criminal robbing us blind? I don't think so. Fred, can you cut it out?" Fred was getting more insistent about the dinner problem, meowing and getting tangled up Frank's feet.

"Why don't you just feed him? That's the problem, Frank. You're asking me to do something crazy and maybe even illegal for all I know. If a church friend wouldn't do it, why would I do it?"

"Okay, okay, let me think." Frank dumped a scoop of food in Fred's bowl, buying a reprieve for his ankles, and scratched the five days of stubble on his chin. "How about a compromise. You don't have to go into the lobby—you can sit in your car somewhere where you can see the entrance. If anyone asks, you're waiting for a friend. People do that kind of thing all the time. You *are* waiting for a friend—me."

"How will that help? Are the bad guys in this drama wearing dark trench coats and sunglasses? How will I know if someone is checking in under your name?"

"You won't—I agree, it's not ideal. I'm trying to compromise. But at least you'll know if Ricky shows up.

That's one bad guy you *will* recognize. It's better than nothing. Catherine, please, I really need your help. I know you don't like my Ricky theory, but it really fits the facts. I've been studying those credit card statements. I can't prove it, but there are a number of air tickets that could easily be him flying back and forth to SF. For all we know, Becky's been with him. She might even be there tomorrow."

Catherine stopped chopping and frowned. "No, I don't believe it."

"Okay, if you don't believe it, then all you're losing is a couple of hours sitting in your car in a parking lot. Nothing will happen, I'll show up, and you can go home."

Catherine sighed. "Okay, you win. I guess I can do that. I can't get there exactly at three, but I'll try to leave a few minutes early from school and get there as soon as I can. What do I do if I do see Ricky?"

"Nothing. In fact, if that happens, you can call me and leave a message, and go home right away. I'll make sure my phone is on in silent mode so you can leave a message without interrupting my meeting."

Frank started to calm down. He grabbed a Yuengling from the fridge and went out on the deck to wait for Catherine to finish getting dinner ready. He was determined not to lose this opportunity. Catherine might be blinded by motherly love, but he was convinced Ricky would show up at the Gran Dorado. What would happen then was another question.

* * *

IT WAS FRIDAY AFTERNOON, and Catherine was running late. Frank had texted her to remind her to leave, but it had been hard to get out the door. She liked to leave her desk neat and organized before the weekend. At 3:07

p.m., she pulled into the parking lot of the Gran Dorado and circled around looking for a spot that would offer an unobstructed view of the entrance. There were not many cars in the lot, and she was about to back into a spot opposite the two giant pillars supporting the covered drive-through in front of the hotel entrance when she suddenly slammed on her brakes.

A taxi had just pulled up and two people were climbing out, a man and a woman. From her angle, she could only see their backs as they exited the car on the side opposite her position. The man was short and scrawny, a backwards-facing baseball cap on his head. The woman was slender and almost as tall as the man, with light brown hair pulled back in a ponytail that was tucked into a brightly-colored scrunchie. Worse, she only caught a brief glimpse, but the patch of skin on the back of the man's neck was clearly African American; she couldn't see his companion's skin color. As she watched, the couple walked through the automatic sliding doors into the lobby, pulling a wheeled carry-on bag behind them. Panic-stricken, Catherine thought, *Oh no, could that be Ricky and Becky? That's how she wears her hair, and I think Ricky used to wear his hats like that.*

Instead of taking the time to finish backing into her spot, Catherine yanked the transmission into drive and lurched forward into a handicapped spot right next to the entrance. She jammed on the brakes and jumped out, slamming the door behind without bothering to lock it. *I hope no one is watching this handicapped person sprint into the hotel,* she thought. As she walked through the doors, she slowed down and scanned the lobby. The couple was already standing in front of the reception desk, still with their backs to her. She paused uncertainly in the middle of the floor. *Now what? Somehow, I need to see their faces.* She could just make out the words on the baseball cap: San Francisco 49ers. Her heart sank.

Where would they go next? Looking around desperately, she could see two options: a hallway to the right leading to the first-floor rooms and another entryway to the left where she could see the elevator doors and a couple of vending machines. Instinctively, she gambled and headed for the vending machines, like a drowning swimmer seeing a lifeboat. A moment later, she pretended to scan the choices in the displays while straining her ears to hear the voices behind her at the reception counter. She couldn't make out any words; why were they taking so long? How long could she stand there pretending to agonize over choosing Coke or Dr. Pepper? Finally, the voices fell silent and she heard the sound of the carry-on wheels getting louder. Her gamble had paid off—the couple must be headed her way. Taking a deep breath, she turned and looked directly in their faces as they approached the elevator doors. The man had a salt-and-pepper goatee and the woman was wearing heavy, cakey makeup. They appeared to be in their forties or fifties. Not Ricky. Not Becky. They paid no attention to her and pushed the up button, staring at the blinking numbers above the doors.

Catherine fed two dollar bills into the vending machine and randomly pushed one of the buttons. A Diet Coke clunked into the drawer. Ugh, she hated Diet Coke. Taking the can and scooping up her change, her hand shaking, she walked back through the lobby and climbed into her car. "Thank God it wasn't them," she breathed. She backed out and pulled into an adjacent non-handicapped space. From there she would have a better chance of seeing the faces of anyone walking in the entrance—her first spot directly opposite the door had been a bad choice.

Slowly her heart stopped pounding and she started to relax. *What would I have done if it* had *been them?* she wondered. *Frank, why did I let you talk me into this?* A car pulled into the parking lot and a balding middle-aged man in a business suit went into the hotel. Definitely not Ricky. Catherine still doubted that Ricky would show up. Frank wanted to believe that Ricky had stolen his identity and stolen their daughter; he wanted a fairy-tale ending, the bad guy in jail, and Becky safely back home again. But Catherine knew the true narrative was not that simple. Was Ricky a bad guy? Had he stolen their daughter? Is that why he was a bad guy? Or had Becky chosen him? Could she live with Becky choosing him? With Becky choosing anyone? Grief bubbled up inside of her. Was she losing her daughter? Had she already lost her?

Her mind went back to another day of loss that was etched into her memory: the day they had dropped Becky at Ithaca College her freshman year. It had only taken a few minutes to unload the car. They had already had a tour of the campus and met her roommate. The college admissions staff had scheduled an orientation meeting for new students at four o'clock and gently let it be known that parents were not invited. They had stood awkwardly on the sidewalk outside the dorm; no one could think of anything else to say. Finally, Catherine had thrown her arms around Becky and held her. Becky had hugged her back, but Catherine could feel that she was eager to go. A new door was opening in her life, a door she had been waiting for, a door she was ready to walk through.

For Catherine, it felt like a door slamming shut. "Goodbye, sweetie," she whispered and got into the car. She heard Frank say, "We'll call you when we get home." Catherine turned her head and looked back as they drove away. The small figure of Becky waving dwindled into the distance and then disappeared as they turned a corner. "Goodbye, sweetie," Catherine had whispered again as her eyes blurred with tears.

She could feel tears pricking the back of her eyes now as she stared unseeingly at the hotel entrance. A van pulled up and several passengers got out, all of them with suitcases or carry-on bags. Must be an airport shuttle. Suddenly remembering why she was there, she shook her head and quickly scanned their faces. There were only two men, and she got a good look at both of them. Nope, and nope again; not Ricky. She hoped she hadn't missed any cars while she had been lost in thought. For the next hour and a half, she tried to block out the thoughts swirling in her mind and focus on her task. A steady trickle of people came and went, but surprisingly few for a Friday afternoon. Only two were remotely similar to Ricky, and Catherine saw both of their faces clearly.

Finally, her phone rang. It was Frank. "I'm on my way—be there in ten minutes. Anything to report?"

"I had one close call just when I got here, but it wasn't them. So far, so good: no Rickys to report."

"Good," replied Frank. "See you soon."

Catherine did a double take when someone tapped on her window a few minutes later. A man with a scruffy beard wearing a baseball cap, T-shirt, and sunglasses was staring at her. "Oh, Frank, it's you!" laughed Catherine, rolling down her window. "I didn't recognize you at first!"

"Eef a man's vife doesn't recognize him, you know zat ze disguise is verking," said Frank in a fake-sounding accent. "I have my contacts in too, in case I need to take off my sunglasses inside."

"Except you can't carry a huge expensive leather briefcase like that. That doesn't fit with the T-shirt and jeans. You need a backpack. Why do you need your briefcase?"

"I need my laptop," said Frank. "And I have a newspaper to hide behind."

"Take out your laptop and newspaper and give me your briefcase. You can't take that in with you. Hmm, your shoes aren't ideal, but I guess it's too late to worry about that."

"Yeah, I forgot about my shoes. No one will notice. You're right—here, take the briefcase. Okay, no time to lose—wish me luck."

"To be honest, I hope your mission is a failure!" replied Catherine. "But I also don't want you to get killed—so good luck not getting killed! Let me know if you're going to be really late." She started the engine, waved, and drove off.

* * *

HOLDING HIS LAPTOP AND newspaper, Frank walked into the hotel lobby. It was almost deserted. A middle-aged couple, the man wearing a backwards 49ers baseball cap, was seated on a couch watching a CNN news update on a large flatscreen TV. He glanced quickly at the receptionist; just as he had feared, it was the same woman as last week. *Yikes, I need to stay away from her. Let's hope my disguise works*, he thought. There were several small round tables scattered around the lobby, the tall kind with glass tops often found in coffee bars. Frank chose the one nearest the reception desk and pulled a chair around so his back was to the desk. From this angle, he could also see anyone who walked in the entrance. He sat down and opened his laptop. *My first stakeout*, he said to himself, feeling a nervous tingle of anticipation in the pit of his stomach.

He connected to the hotel's free Wi-Fi service and opened the *New York Times* website. No, he decided, his alter ego would not read the *New York Times*. He opened YouTube instead and tried to look as interested as possible as he scrolled down the page. Belatedly, he remembered that he had left his headphones in his briefcase. *Oops,* he thought, *guess I'd better switch to Facebook.*

Behind him, he heard the receptionist say, "How may I help you?" as a guest walked up to the desk.

"I'd like to check in—Walker, Samuel Walker." Good. He could hear clearly from this distance. Now he just had to wait. He hoped it wouldn't take too long.

An hour passed. The excitement of his first stakeout began to fade. The chair was remarkably uncomfortable; when he used the footrest, his knees bumped into the bottom of the table, but the seat was too high for his feet to reach the floor. The edge of the chair was starting to cut off the circulation in his legs. A soft-looking lounge chair tempted him across the room, but he was afraid it would be out of hearing range, and moving the chair would attract too much attention. He shifted uncomfortably. He had gotten bleary-eyed scrolling through Facebook's endless feed and was now pretending to read a travel blog. He had thought about analyzing the spreadsheet with Rupert's sales figures that Denise had sent him a couple of days previously, but decided he wouldn't be able to focus. So far, nothing suspicious had happened. Not that many guests had even checked in. He wondered if this Gran Dorado, which was relatively new, was going to make it with this level of business.

He thought about Catherine. It had been sweet of her to agree to help out. For her sake, he hoped he was wrong about Ricky, but he had a bad feeling he wasn't wrong. This whole situation was really hard on Catherine. Was Becky right? Had they been too protective? What had it been like for her to grow up as an only child? *I was kind of an only child too*, remembered Frank, but his mind instantly recoiled from the thought. That was different. *Please, I don't want to go there*, he pleaded, not sure who he was pleading with. His memory, that's who. If only memories could be boxed up and sealed away in an archive—or better yet, permanently deleted. Memories were like social media posts and email: once you clicked *Send*, they could never be completely expunged. He had tried to banish this particular memory many times, but he knew it was part of his DNA. It was this memory that had driven him away from Catherine that awful night of her miscarriage. That was another memory he wished he could expunge.

He heard the automatic sliding door whoosh open and glanced over at the entrance. Another airport shuttle had dropped off a load of passengers. None of them fit Ricky's profile, but he tried to listen closely as they checked in, straining to hear the magic words: *Frank O'Donnell.* Another receptionist joined the first one to handle the mini-rush, making it hard to distinguish individual conversations and names. As he strained to listen to the voices behind him, Frank's eyes stayed focused on the glass entrance doors. Beyond the columns of the drive-through, he could see dark thunderclouds looming on the horizon. It looked like the first big thunderstorm of the year might be unleashed on them any minute.

The dark clouds immediately prompted the forbidden memory back to his consciousness. He pushed it away again. *Please, no, I don't want to go there*, he begged again. Dark clouds on the Jersey Shore, the sunlight still shining incongruously on the sand and crashing surf. The sound of kids' voices laughing and shouting as they ran through the shallow surf chasing seagulls. The black clouds were behind him, towering over the boardwalk. *Just don't look that way, the wind will blow them away, we just got here, please don't let it rain.* He was eleven years old. He had been looking forward to this day for weeks. The Jersey Shore! Finally, burning hot sand shifting under his feet, ocean air blowing in his face, sun warming his bare back, after all the months of dreary rain and homework. No more school for three months! The summer beckoned to him with all its promise of freedom and fun. He turned his head back to the boardwalk and felt a cool, rain-scented breeze on his face. The angry clouds were inching closer but the sun was still bright on the beach. *It's going to be fine*, he thought hopefully, turning back to the waves.

He could see his little sister, Julie, holding her beach pail and standing near their mother, who was struggling to set up a beach umbrella in the strengthening breeze. Julie was only six, quiet and reserved, always cautious about trying new things. *Where was their father?* Frank wondered. He could hear his mother calling him to come and help her with the umbrella. Frank sprinted down the beach, his arms outspread like a World War II fighter plane, and made a dramatic crash landing, leaping into the air and skidding feetfirst toward the umbrella. His mother had finally got the umbrella stabilized. "Frank, honey, you just kicked sand over everything. You'll get it in Julie's eyes. Can you just sit here with Julie for two minutes? I want to catch your father—he's going back to the car to get the lunch bag we forgot, and I need to remind him to grab the new bottle of sunscreen."

"Okay, Mom. That wasn't sand; those were machine-gun bullets." His mom started jogging in the direction of the boardwalk. Frank grabbed the pail from Julie and began scooping sand into it. "Want to make a sand castle, Julie?" The sand was hot, and he stuck his feet into the hole he had just dug to cool them off. Behind him, he heard the lifeguard's whistle, but he ignored it. He packed the sand down in the pail and dumped it in front of Julie . . .

"Excuse me, sir, is there anything I can help you with?" Frank started out of his reverie with a jump to see the receptionist—the same one he had spoken with a week earlier—looking down at him. The lobby had suddenly emptied. "I noticed you've been sitting here for a while," she added.

"Uh, no, I'm fine . . ." stuttered Frank. "A friend . . . I'm waiting for a friend. His flight out of Chicago was delayed for a few hours. Is it okay if I sit here?"

"Sure," she replied, "no problem. Would you like a more comfortable chair? There's plenty of options over there." She pointed across the room. "Also, we have vending machines by the elevators if you need a snack."

"Uh, I really like these little tables . . . they're uh . . . good for my laptop . . . and uh . . . better for my back." He hadn't planned a response to that question. *Ugh, that sounded lame*, he thought, *don't attract attention, gotta try to act normal.*

"Suit yourself!" She smiled and returned to the reception counter. Apparently, she hadn't recognized him.

Frank focused on his laptop again, grateful that the interruption had cleared his mind and brought him back into the present. He heard a rumble of thunder and decided to check the weather on his laptop. Just then, a woman came through the sliding doors and walked up to the reception counter. He heard her say, "Hello, I'm meeting a Mr. Frank O'Donnell—has he checked in yet?" Frank froze, one finger suspended above the keyboard, feeling the adrenaline surging through his veins. This was it! Was she the hacker? Damn, he had been distracted and hadn't gotten a good look at her. He carefully turned his head, trying to get a glimpse out of the corner of his eye. He could hear the receptionist answering, "O'Donnell? With an oh apostrophe? That sounds familiar . . . let me check . . . no, he hasn't checked in yet. What time were you expecting him?"

"He should be here any minute. I'll just have a seat and wait for him." The woman's heels clicked on the tile floor as she walked by Frank's table and took a seat in one of the lounge chairs across the room. He caught a whiff of perfume as she passed by. It felt strange to hear people talking about him when he was sitting ten feet away. He cautiously raised his eyes above his laptop screen to see what she looked like: shoulder-length dark hair, slightly heavy, attractive, lots of jewelry . . . early forties maybe?

She didn't look like a hacker to him, but maybe he had the wrong stereotype of hackers. Or, the guy she was meeting was the real bad guy—Ricky? But would Ricky be meeting someone like her? Something at the back of his brain was trying to get his attention. He didn't think he had ever seen her before, but there was something familiar about her. What was it? Maybe it was just his adrenaline-fueled imagination playing tricks on him . . . lots of people looked similar to each other. Frank lowered his eyes and racked his brain.

Ten minutes passed. Frank took several deep breaths, trying to slow his pulse. This was the critical moment— *please, don't let me screw this up now*. If he was right, he would see Ricky walking in the door any moment. If it wasn't Ricky, then he would get a glimpse of the real hacker. He placed his phone on the table next to his laptop. He had already made sure the camera app was open and ready to go. If it wasn't Ricky, he wanted to try and snap a surreptitious photo of the hacker—and the woman too—if he could pull it off without being noticed. What would he do if it *was* Ricky? Should he confront him? He had gone back and forth in his mind. Now that the woman was here, he suddenly decided not to. He didn't want to create a scene—better to confront him later.

He had brought the newspaper to help hide his face if the need arose. Maybe he should open it now, so he didn't have to fumble with it at the last minute. Yawning casually, he unfolded the newspaper and, opening it to a random page, held it in front of his face.

Another five minutes passed. Frank's tensed arm muscles were starting to cramp when he heard the sliding doors swoosh open, followed by heavy-sounding footsteps crossing the floor. He could feel the muscles in his jaws tightening. A voice said, "Hello, I'm Frank O'Donnell— I'd like to check in." At almost the same time, the woman called out, "Hi, Frank, I'm over here!"

For a moment, the world shifted into slow motion. Frank's brain dutifully recorded the headline inches from his face: *Stocks Rise Sharply After Upbeat Jobs Report.* He heard the glass doors whooshing as they closed and the clicks of the keys on the receptionist's keyboard. He stopped breathing. He would know that voice anywhere. It was Buddy. Something else clicked in his brain. The woman's voice: it was Mary Smith from HR, except Mary Smith was really Lori, according to Dave, and who was Lori?

At the same instant he heard Buddy reply, "Oh, hi Lori, sorry I'm late." Frank heard her heels clicking, caught the whiff of perfume, heard the sound of a kiss. Frank held the newspaper frozen in front of his face, not daring to move. Buddy finished checking in and Frank heard them walking toward the elevator. He heard Buddy asking Lori about restaurants, then the ding of the elevator bell, and then he counted to one hundred. When he was sure they were gone, he folded the newspaper, grabbed his phone and laptop, and walked out into the pouring rain.

THIRTEEN

Buddy didn't get home until late Sunday night, and he was up early Monday morning. He had planned to return home on Saturday, but the thought of spending the weekend at home had filled him with dread. Instead, he had called multiple friends and acquaintances until he found someone who was willing to play a round of golf with him, after which he had drunk too much at the clubhouse bar and ended up crashing on his golf buddy's couch. On Sunday, he had gone back into the office to catch up on some work, coming back late, after Bunny was already in bed. She was still sleeping on Monday morning when he slipped out of the house and headed to his favorite place for coffee and a fresh bagel.

To be honest, he hadn't enjoyed spending weekends at home for a long time. Weekends were the busiest days of the week for real estate agents, so Bunny was rarely around, especially at this time of the year. The big empty house was too quiet for Buddy. But even when Bunny was home, he often felt uneasy. They always seemed to be walking on eggshells around each other, especially after that big blowup last year—although fortunately that seemed to have more or less blown over.

Over the years, their lives had gradually drifted apart. Buddy figured most marriages were probably the same. No one could sustain the intensity of "first love" over the long haul; it was normal to develop other interests—new friends, hobbies, that kind of thing. He supposed their separate careers didn't help. His job required him to travel regularly to the company's regional offices, with the result that sometimes days would go by without them seeing each other. In the early years, they would always let each other know where they were—even if it was just a hastily scribbled note by the phone—but they had gradually stopped bothering. It didn't seem worth the effort.

The previous week was a case in point: Buddy couldn't remember if he had even seen Bunny since the party. *Wait,* he recalled as he washed down the first bite of cinnamon-raisin bagel with a slurp of hot coffee, *I must have seen her at least once, because she asked me about that restaurant in Cape May.* The bagel was delicious, still warm, with a perfect chewy texture. There was something about New Jersey bagels; even in Philly, he hadn't been able to find anything to match them. *What had made her suddenly remember that night in Cape May?* he wondered. It wasn't like her to dredge up the past like that. Could the surprise party and his quest to find Mouse have triggered memories for her too? But why had she suddenly been so insistent about it? Even trying to talk him into going right away on Friday. *Oops, that would have been this past Friday,* he remembered guiltily, an image of the Gran Dorado flashing across his mind. *I probably should have bought her flowers or something. Oh well, I can always take her out to dinner another time—but no way am I driving all the way to Cape May.* Maybe Bunny was right, though: they needed to do something to liven up their marriage. *Let me find Mouse first, and then I can focus on Bunny,* he promised himself. *It'll be fine.*

Finding Mouse was why Buddy was sitting in the coffee shop and not in traffic on the Ben Franklin Bridge. He was taking a day off work to try to finish his quest; well, technically, it wasn't a day off—his boss thought he was working from home because of a doctor's appointment. Buddy hated wasting vacation days, and even though it was only April, he had already used up his quota of personal days for the year. He had concluded that phone calls to the nursing home were a waste of time; instead, he was going to drive to the nursing home and somehow persuade them to tell him what they knew about Mouse. He knew that it was much harder to say no to someone standing in front of you, especially when that someone was Buddy Kowalski. At a minimum, if Mouse really wasn't there— Buddy didn't completely trust the receptionist, who seemingly had trouble with basic office skills like answering the phone—he was determined to find out when he had left and where he had gone. If that failed, his only other idea was to go back to Garbo and see if he could help him track down Mouse's New Jersey relatives.

Buddy finished his bagel, briefly considered buying another one for the road, and then got back into his car, taking his half-finished coffee with him. According to Google maps, it should have taken twenty-three minutes from the coffee shop to the nursing home in Cherry Hill, but the algorithm didn't seem to have predicted the traffic accurately. He soon found himself inching along State Route 41, passing one identical strip mall after another. Each red light seemed to last an eternity. As he crept along, he pondered how to persuade the nursing home staff to release information about Mouse. Obviously, he would have to go over the head of the receptionist, who had apparently been trained to repeat the mantra "company policy, personal and confidential" no matter what the question. (*Why not hire a parrot*, thought Buddy, *it would be a lot cheaper and more entertaining.*) But he didn't think the journalist cover story he had used on other occasions would work. First, he didn't have any credentials or ID if he was asked. Second, they might be afraid of the publicity a journalist could bring.

He swallowed the last dregs of his coffee, staring at the back of the truck he had been stuck behind for the last three miles and wishing he could pass it to get away from the black smoke belching out of its exhaust pipe. What other excuse could he use? He could hardly claim to be a family member. What about a lawyer representing the family? But why would they need to send a lawyer? He would need a convincing cover story, and nothing was coming to mind; plus, a lawyer would definitely scare them about confidentiality and publicity. The speedometer briefly hit twenty-five mph before the next light turned red. Buddy banged the back of his head against the headrest. How about something connected to the NFL? That might work—a retrospective on great linemen of the past? Or, on a darker note, a profile of CTE sufferers? But how could he convince them that he worked for the NFL?

Buddy was finally able to worm his way into a right turn lane and get off of Route 41; he knew the traffic wouldn't be as bad the rest of the way. Google led him through several pleasant-looking neighborhoods with neatly manicured lawns. *The American Dream*, thought Buddy sourly. *Just don't ask what goes on behind the white picket fences*. Then the route took a sharp turn to the right, dipped under a railroad track, and wound behind what looked like abandoned warehouses. After two more turns, Google announced brightly, "Your destination is on the left."

"How about an apology for taking thirty-eight minutes instead of twenty-three," Buddy complained out loud to his phone as he pulled into the parking lot.

There were only a handful of cars parked near the entrance, which Buddy assumed must be the staff's cars. The parking lot asphalt was lined with cracks, from which a fresh new crop of spring weeds was beginning to emerge. Brownish-gray deposits of leaves from the previous fall were clumped along the curbs and it looked like the landscaping contractor hadn't shown up for a few years. The outside of the building had a dreary, run-down look to it, completely unlike the photos Buddy had seen on the web page. In fact, he wasn't even sure it was the same building—hadn't the pictures shown a much grander entrance, with flower beds lining the sidewalk and smiling seniors sitting near a fishpond? Were the pictures of cheery, professional-looking staff also faked? Maybe it was hard to get through on the phones because there was literally no one there to answer them. It was beginning to look like Garbo was right after all: Mouse's NFL wealth really had run dry.

Buddy pulled open the door and stepped into the lobby. The familiar nursing home smell hit him like a furnace blast. A long-buried memory instantly popped into his mind: he was eight years old, holding his mother's hand, as she dragged him on weekly visits to his dying grandmother, his mother insisting that he kiss her cool, leathery cheek, fear and dread gripping his heart. The sickly smell of those over-heated corridors and rooms was indelibly etched in his memory.

Buddy paused to gather his courage and looked around the room. On the right, several residents in wheelchairs were lined up in a row along one side of the lobby. Their shapeless bodies were slumped against the armrests of their chairs, dull eyes staring straight ahead and seeming not to notice Buddy's entrance. The receptionist's counter was directly in front of him. The chair behind it was empty and he could hear a phone ringing. He was tempted to reach over and answer it. "Sorry, we can't help you, personal and confidential, company policy," he would say and hang up.

A staff member wearing a washed-out green nurse's uniform came through a door on the left pushing another resident in a wheelchair, expertly maneuvering it into position next to the others. "Excuse me," said Buddy, trying to catch his attention.

"The receptionist will be with you in a minute, sir," he said politely in a practiced monotone and returned the way he had come, not breaking his stride or turning his head.

Buddy leaned over the counter and tried calling out in a loud voice, "Hello, could someone help me please?" There was no response. He took a deep breath and tried to quell his rising impatience, almost gagging on the stale smell of disinfectant and age. There were several faded plastic chairs along the wall across the room from the row of wheelchairs. Not knowing what else to do, Buddy took a seat and tried not to look at the wheelchairs. Before he lowered his gaze, he couldn't help notice a line of drool trickling from the corner of one resident's mouth. He shifted his body in the chair and angled his face toward the deserted counter. Somewhere in the distance he could hear a TV turned up too loud, and a murmur of voices and clinking dishes. He still hadn't decided what cover story to use. Buddy pulled out his smartphone and checked for messages from his office. The phone at the front desk was ringing again.

Much to his surprise, the ringing suddenly stopped and Buddy heard a familiar voice: "Golden Manor, how-mayIdrectyrcall." He looked up and saw a petite young woman with heavily-framed glasses, neatly and professionally dressed, her hair pulled back in a perfectly round bun, holding a clipboard in one hand, a container of some kind in the other, and the phone receiver wedged precariously between her shoulder and ear. "Yes, ma'am, I'll make sure she gets the message. Thank you."

Buddy leaped up and practically sprinted to the counter. "Excuse me, can you . . ." but before he could finish his sentence, she had disappeared again, a frantic look in her eyes. Buddy groaned in frustration and returned to his plastic chair. This time he stayed perched on the edge, eyes glued to the counter, muscles tensed to spring into action. He did not have long to wait before the phone started ringing again. This time Buddy made it to the counter before the receptionist did and he was waiting for her when she emerged from the back room like a bird darting from its nest. "Excuse me, I really need to talk to you," he said in what he hoped was a loud, commanding voice, firm but polite.

"Golden Manor, howmayIdrectyrcall. Extension two twenty-seven. Yes sir, got it." She expertly punched several keys on the console and finally turned and looked at Buddy. "I'm sorry, sir, everything is going haywire this morning and Jill called in sick again." She took a quick breath and looked up at him with worried eyes magnified by her huge glasses, making her look even more bird-like. "How can I help you? Visiting hours are normally after lunch."

Buddy tried to imagine what it must be like to have a job like hers and felt a sudden surge of compassion. Golden Manor might have its problems, but whatever they were, they weren't this young woman's fault. "Looks like a high-stress job," Buddy smiled sympathetically at her. "I'm interested in getting some information about one of your residents—who might have moved out recently— and I was wondering if I could speak to your supervisor." He mentally crossed his fingers. It suddenly seemed highly improbable that the right person would be here and would have any time to talk to him. It might have been a huge mistake to just show up like this.

"Let me check," she answered and darted away again. Resigned, Buddy returned to his chair. Outside, a large van had pulled up. Apparently, the occupants of the wheelchairs were being taken somewhere. There was a flurry of activity as doors opened and several staff members suddenly appeared.

The minutes dragged by. Buddy watched as the wheelchairs were efficiently wheeled up a ramp and secured inside the van. None of the residents made a sound during the process; Buddy had the strange feeling that the van was a delivery truck picking up a load of supplies from a loading dock. Doors slammed, and the van pulled away, its suspension creaking as one wheel bumped over the edge of the curb. The nursing home staff disappeared and silence descended on the lobby. The phone had even stopped ringing. Buddy glanced at his watch, willing himself to be patient. Another ten minutes went by and suddenly the receptionist flitted in again.

"Mrs. Briggs can see you at eleven oh eight," she announced, looking in Buddy's direction.

Why such a precise time? Buddy wondered. He looked at his watch again; it was a few minutes before ten. Another hour of sitting in this chair. He sighed inwardly. *I can do this, I can do this*, he repeated to himself. "Thanks, that would be great. Thanks a lot," he said a little too brightly, forcing himself to sound calm and appreciative. "Is it okay if I wait here?"

"You can sit in the visitors' lounge if you want to," she offered. "The chairs are more comfortable in there, and it's usually empty in the mornings."

The visitors' lounge was in fact a huge improvement, although the upholstery had seen better days and there were some odd-colored stains on the carpet. The receptionist, whose name was Kayla he learned, even brought him a cup of coffee in a white Styrofoam cup— not the freshest, but Buddy could feel the caffeine from his morning coffee starting to wear off and he gratefully sipped the tepid black liquid. He stared at the faded reproductions of impressionist paintings decorating the walls and reflected on the winding journey that had brought him to this room. He felt strangely hopeful: *Mouse might be sitting in the lounge watching TV right this minute, just a few feet away*. Something gave him the feeling that his quest was coming to an end. He stood up and paced restlessly back and forth in the empty room, still turning over possible cover stories in his mind.

At precisely 11:08, a trim, middle-aged woman with short graying hair strode into the room. "Hello, I'm Tracy Briggs. What can I do for you? I'm afraid I only have about fifteen minutes," she said without preamble.

Buddy turned from staring out the window. A huge magnolia tree was bursting into glorious color in the center of the overgrown lawn. "Thank you for taking the time to see me. My name is Buddy Kowalski. I'll try not to take too much of your time." Buddy paused, still unsure what to say. On an impulse, he decided to try the truth. "For the past few weeks, I've been trying to find my freshman roommate, back from my college days over thirty years ago. Somehow, we lost touch—mostly my fault, or maybe completely my fault. But I keep hitting brick walls. And I don't know why but something won't let me give up. Once I started it became kind of an obsession almost. Then I found out he was here, in New Jersey, minutes from where I live, and I couldn't believe it. I had no idea he was so close, and I was excited, and also felt terrible at the same time. All those years, I could have been here for him and I blew it. I didn't even know his health was going downhill. Maybe it's a kind of guilt trip, I don't know. At this point I just want to find him." Buddy stopped. *God, I sound like an idiot*, he thought. He stared at the floor, and felt his face getting hot. "I know I'm not family, so maybe you can't tell me anything. I don't even know if he has any family left around here, except for maybe one cousin."

He stopped again and looked up. Mrs. Briggs was looking at him sympathetically. "What's your friend's name?" she asked.

"Darnell Richards. Some people just call him Richards. He used to play in the NFL. Do you know him? Is he here?"

Mrs. Briggs's eyes lit up and she smiled. "Darnell Richards? Our gentle giant? Of course I knew him. Everyone knew Darnell. He's not the kind of person you can get away with not knowing." Her voice petered out.

"From what you're saying, I guess he must not be here anymore. Do you know where he went? I'm not going to give up until I find him."

Mrs. Briggs looked Buddy in the eyes and said slowly, "No, he's not here anymore." She paused again. There was kindness and grief in her eyes as she went on. "Mr. Kowalski, I'm afraid your search has come to an end, but not in the way you had hoped. Darnell passed away about a month ago. I'm so sorry. He was a special person. We all miss him."

Buddy slowly sank into the nearest chair, his face frozen in shock. "Dead? Mouse is dead?" He stared blankly at Mrs. Briggs. "He can't be dead. I just found him."

Mrs. Briggs sat down in a nearby chair. For a moment, Buddy thought she might reach over and take his hand in hers. Instead, she said softly, "He was a good man, Mr. Kowalski, much loved by everyone. CTE can make people mean, but Darnell was one of the sweetest people I've ever met. His memory was just about gone when he got here, but no matter who he saw he always smiled at them like they were his best friend that he had known all his life."

Buddy buried his head in his arms and stared blindly at the stains on the carpet. Fighting back tears he asked, "What happened? Why did he die?"

"I'm not a medical person, but from what I could see, it seemed like his brain just started shutting down. When we went in one morning to get him up for breakfast, he was gone. But there was a smile on his face, like no one could be any happier than he was. I had stopped by his room the previous afternoon—we all knew he was failing. He looked at me with that big smile and didn't say a word, but as I was leaving, I could hear him softly humming one of his favorite hymns. That's how I'll remember him: smiling and humming that hymn." Buddy thought Mrs. Briggs might be choking up too.

"He had an amazing voice," said Buddy, his voice muffled.

"Oh my, yes. From the day he got here, he was always singing. At first, it was mainly in the Sunday worship services, but as his dementia got worse, he would suddenly start singing at any time of day or night. Sometimes at two in the morning if he woke up for some reason. And it was loud! But no one ever complained. Most of the people here don't hear too well anyway. I remember once, though, we couldn't get him to stop. He sang the same verse of the same hymn about twenty times in a row. Finally, we all started singing with him—we didn't know what else to do, and by then we had learned the words by heart." She stopped and sang softly, "*It is well, it is well . . .*" There was a faraway look in her eyes, and Buddy thought she had finished speaking. But then she went on. "He looked so surprised, and then he got this huge grin on his face and laid down and went to sleep." She smiled at the memory. "We all miss him, Mr. Kowalski. I think everyone here is still grieving that he's gone."

Buddy saw Mrs. Briggs glance at her watch. He cleared his throat. "Thank you for everything you've shared, Mrs. Briggs. It means a lot to me. I wish I could have been here once to hear him sing." Buddy's voice gave out for a moment. "I know you have a busy day, lots of other people to take care of. Just one more thing, if you don't mind: would you be able to tell me where he's buried?"

She stood up. "Of course. That should be in his file. I'll ask Kayla to look it up for you." She stood looking down at Buddy reflectively. "Thank you for coming. I don't think any of us will ever forget Darnell. Don't be too hard on yourself. He had a big family here who truly loved him. Take care." She walked briskly from the room.

Buddy couldn't remember driving home. He felt numb. *Oh Mouse, Mouse, my friend, why wasn't I there for you?* He tried to remember Mouse as he had known him so many years ago, but the image that kept coming to his mind was Mrs. Briggs's description: a gentle giant happily singing to anyone who would listen. *Mouse, Mouse, my friend, if only I had remembered you sooner*, he kept repeating to himself. *Mouse, Mouse, my friend.*

As he pulled into the driveway, he was surprised to see the garage door open with Bunny's car pulled up in front. The back seat was full of boxes. He walked in the front door and collapsed heavily into his favorite recliner in the den. A moment later he heard the door from the garage slam and Bunny appeared in the doorway.

"Oh, you're here. What a surprise," she said. "I thought I was going to miss you, but maybe it's just as well." She looked at him thoughtfully. "I guess you couldn't change your plans on Friday after all."

"Are you going somewhere?" asked Buddy dully, his mind still swirling with a confused mix of grief and guilt.

"Yes, as a matter of fact I am," replied Bunny. "And this time it's a one-way trip with no return. Except to get the rest of my stuff," she added after a pause.

Buddy was having a hard time processing what she was saying. "What do you mean? Why wouldn't you come back again?"

"Do you remember the deal we had? That you would never see her again and I would give you one more chance?"

"Yeah, I remember," Buddy sighed.

"Well, I believe you have been breaking your side of the deal. A little bird whispered it in my ear at a certain party not too long ago." Surprisingly, Bunny didn't sound particularly angry. Neutral. Or maybe even wistful. "Am I right?"

Buddy tried the truth for the second time that day. "Yeah, you're right," he admitted.

"I thought so." She looked around the room, her gaze ending up on Buddy still reclining in his lounge chair. "Well, it's been quite a run, Buddy." She looked at him with a trace of sadness in her eyes. "I wish it could have ended differently. But it didn't. You'll be getting the papers from my lawyer in a day or two. I still need to get some more of my stuff, but I've got what I need for now. Goodbye, Buddy."

She turned and started to leave but then stopped and looked back at him one last time. "Somehow—I don't know why—I've never been able to tell you this." She paused and furrowed her brow. "I've always hated being called Bunny. My name, in case you've forgotten, is Berenice." She turned her back and her heels clicked on the kitchen tiles as she walked back through the kitchen and into the garage. A few minutes later he heard her car start up and drive away.

Buddy still hadn't moved from his spot in the chair. A terrible emptiness washed over him. First Mouse and now Bunny. "How did I get here?" he whispered to himself. He gazed back over the wreckage of his life and saw a long trail of evasions, lies, and deception, always one step ahead of disaster, always somehow finding a way to survive for another day, always pretending he was having fun. But not this time, not anymore. This time there was no clever escape plan. He felt exhausted and drained.

As if from a great distance, he heard his phone ringing. He pulled it out of his pocket and saw multiple missed calls from Frank. It was Frank who was calling him now. He watched it ring. Frank . . . should he answer? A sense of dread gripped him. But fate seemed to have him firmly in its grip. Reluctantly, he let the current take him and pressed the answer button. "Hello, Frank. What's up? Sorry I missed your calls."

"Buddy, I've been trying to get hold of you since yesterday. Is everything okay?" Buddy thought Frank sounded tense, but it could have been his own emotions playing tricks on him.

"I dunno—it's been a rough day, but I'm here now. What's up?" he repeated.

"Tomorrow's our first Phillies game. I was afraid you'd forgotten. Can you still make it?"

Buddy's heart sank. The last thing he wanted to do right now was go to a Phillies game. "I don't know, Frank, it's not a great time for me. Maybe we should skip this one."

"But Buddy, you said you could make it. Remember, we talked about it at the party? Has your schedule changed? Are you traveling again?"

The lie was automatically rising to his lips when he remembered his new-found experimentation with the truth. "No, I'm still free," he replied. He thought about Frank. He thought about his empty house. He sighed again. "Okay, yeah, let's do it. What time should we meet?"

"Great! Let's meet at our usual place at seven." Frank sounded relieved.

"Sure. See you tomorrow." Buddy hung up the phone and stared at it. He felt a dull ache settle over him. What else did fate have in store for him?

FOURTEEN

After Frank had relieved her at the stakeout, Catherine drove home and tried to catch up on some reports she hadn't had time to finish before leaving school that afternoon. But she couldn't focus. Feeling restless, she went into the kitchen and made herself a salad for dinner, assuming that Frank might not be home for hours. The lettuce tasted like stale cardboard and she pushed the plate away. The stakeout experience had been unsettling. She kept reliving in her mind the moment she thought she had seen Becky and Ricky. What if it *had* been them? In her heart of hearts, she couldn't believe that Becky would lie to her, but how well did she really know her daughter?

And what about Ricky? She tried to remember everything she could about him, but the truth was she hadn't paid that much attention to any of Becky's friends. Especially not Ricky. Why not? Why had Becky's escape with Ricky in particular been such a shock? (She cringed; why had she used the word *escape*? Becky was not escaping, she was . . . she was . . . exercising her freedom of choice as an adult?) Catherine forced herself to confront a painful truth: had she assumed Becky would never be serious about a black man? Was that the reason? She had been so glad to have her back home again; she had never questioned if Becky was glad to be home—or how she had felt when her parents had ignored one of her best friends. *Oh Becky*, she pleaded, staring out the window. *Please come home again. I miss you. We can make a fresh start.*

She was about to go outside and sit on the deck when she heard her phone ringing in the den where she had left it next to her school papers. Thinking it might be Frank with news from the stakeout, she rushed through the kitchen, ran into the den, and dove for her phone seconds before it went to voicemail. It was Becky.

"Hi, sweetie! I was just thinking about you!" said Catherine happily.

"Mom, I'm calling with some good news!" Catherine could hear music and voices in the background. "Ricky's made it through all the preliminary interviews and he's one of three finalists for the job! There were fifteen people in the last round and he made it to the final three!" Becky's voice sparkled with excitement and pride.

"Wow, that's great sweetie. What happens next? When will he find out if he gets it?"

"Each of the final candidates has to make a huge presentation to the senior executives about their ten-year vision for the company. It's a big deal—very high stress. But Ricky is super great with things like that. I think the presentations are next Friday—is that right, honey?" Becky raised her voice above the music. Catherine could hear an indistinct voice in the background.

"Yes, that's right, next Friday. Sorry about the music— we're having a little celebration with our friends."

"You mean Ricky is there with you, right now?" Catherine asked.

"Yes, of course, why wouldn't he be, Mom?" Becky sounded puzzled.

"Yes, you're right, why wouldn't he be—that was a silly question." Catherine laughed. Either Frank would come home late and very grumpy, or he would catch some Russian hackers. But Ricky would not be showing up at the Gran Dorado that night.

"And, oh Mom, thanks so much for the cash donation in PayPal. It was a lifesaver. Jim and Allie have been buying food for us, so it was really great timing."

"Good, I'm sorry it wasn't much. I was worried about how you were surviving." Catherine hesitated, choosing her words carefully. "I suppose Ricky must have had some money saved up?"

Becky laughed. "Ricky have money? Nope, not this Ricky. Hey, Ricky, what's your net worth these days? My mom wants to know."

Catherine was embarrassed. "Sweetie, I didn't mean to pry, never mind ..." She could hear laughter in the background.

"He says a dollar eighty-seven, but that's probably an exaggeration." Becky was still laughing.

"Well, how did you manage to get to San Francisco then? We thought Ricky must have paid for it." Catherine bit her lip nervously.

"Remember Amanda, my roommate at Ithaca? She was from Phoenix and her parents were constantly flying her home for holidays and weekends. She had millions of frequent flier miles and got both of our tickets for us."

"Oh, wasn't that nice of her." A wave of relief washed over Catherine. "I wish I had asked you that a lot sooner," she said under her breath.

"What was that, Mom? The music is kind of loud."

"Never mind, sweetie."

"Mom, I can't talk any more right now ... we're going out to a bar to celebrate. Say hi to Dad for me."

"I will." Catherine paused. "And tell Ricky he'll be in our thoughts and prayers this week. We're so happy about the interview. I'm sure he'll do a great job."

"Thanks, Mom." Was Catherine imagining it, or did Becky sound surprised? "That means a lot to me. I'll tell Ricky. Bye for now."

Catherine put her phone in her pocket and went through the kitchen out onto the deck, grabbing a towel to wipe off the wet deck chairs. The line of thunderstorms had faded into the east and the sun was breaking through the clouds. It was turning into a pleasant spring evening: the air fresh and cool, the sun low in the sky, slanting through the buds on the dripping tree branches and creating long dappled shadows on the ragged new grass. She would need to do the first mowing of the season soon. It looked like her favorite azalea bush was starting to bud already. She wondered idly where Fred was—probably curled up on the dining room chair as usual, waiting for Frank to get home and feed him. Should she text Frank that Ricky was definitely not in New Jersey? No, it was better not to interrupt the stakeout. Besides, he would still want to see if anyone else showed up. She still felt tense thinking about Frank sitting in the hotel lobby; could he actually be in danger? The credit card had definitely been hacked by someone. She sighed and tried to think about something else. If Ricky got the job, they would presumably move into their own apartment and maybe she could fly out and visit them. Would Frank be willing to go with her?

I hate being an empty nester, she thought with sudden bitterness. She remembered again the day they dropped Becky off at Ithaca, a day forever etched in her memory as the beginning of the end of motherhood. Other images flashed into her mind: crying her eyes out the first time Becky clambered up the huge steps of the kindergarten bus with her Little Mermaid backpack proudly strapped on her back; the first time they dropped Becky off at a week-long sleepover summer camp when she was twelve (Becky had been begging to go to that camp for two years, and Catherine had kept resisting, arguing that Becky was too young, that it would be too traumatic for her—*Too traumatic for* me, thought Catherine ruefully); Frank letting Becky drive the family car to the Jersey Shore with some friends when she was seventeen, and her not getting back until midnight.

Each of these times had been gut-wrenching, terrifying, a feeling in the pit of her stomach that life was changing, that her little girl was growing up. *Which one was the worst?* wondered Catherine as she watched a squirrel launch itself into the air from the edge of the roof and land gracefully on the maple branch above the deck, scattering drops of water on her head. *I hope that squirrel's mother isn't watching,* thought Catherine. It suddenly struck her that all of those moments had felt exactly the same: leaving Becky at the kindergarten bus stop had felt just like leaving her at college—equally terrifying, equally gut-wrenching, equally disorienting. And now California. Ricky. The same feeling all over again. Would it never end? Is this what it meant to be a parent? The slow death of always saying goodbye?

The last rays of the setting sun angled through the branches of the maple. She caught another glimpse of the squirrel, now high in the topmost branches of the tree, bounding with apparent abandon along small branches that swayed wildly each time it flung its body across the abyss below. *Don't you realize that one false step and you could fall fifty feet and die?* Catherine wanted to shout at it. *Didn't your mother teach you not to go on those tiny branches?* Then she realized how ridiculous that was. Squirrels were designed to leap and climb in trees; its mother had *taught* it to do that—leaping on tiny branches brought it joy, not fear.

That thought made something click in her mind and other images flooded in: Becky getting off that same kindergarten bus every afternoon, always excited and thrilled to tell Catherine about her day; picking Becky up at the summer camp and seeing her hug her new best friends goodbye, excitedly showing Catherine and Frank the crafts she had made; Becky proudly giving them a tour of the Ithaca campus that first parents' weekend, introducing them to her professors, showing them the coffee shop where she had gotten a part-time job.

Joy, thought Catherine. *Her joy must be my joy. Let her leap, let her fly, let me be amazed, let me cheer her on. It might sometimes be terrifying, but I must learn to grow up with her. But please let me be with her, not shut out of her life, not a passing stage of childhood, not watching from a distance for the rest of my life.*

The front door slammed, interrupting her reverie. Was Frank already home from the stakeout? She jumped up anxiously and looked through the glass patio door. She saw him come into the kitchen, look around, and then yank on the sliding door, almost pulling it off its tracks. Frank was not the kind to let his emotions show, but this time they were showing. She had never seen his face twisted in anger like that. "Frank, what happened? What's wrong?"

"It was Buddy," he snarled. "Buddy and his lover, Lori—she's the one who helped him with the prank. Mary Smith from HR." He practically spat out her name.

"Oh Frank, what do you mean? What did he do?"

"Buddy is the hacker, that's what I mean. He walked in as brazen as a fricking rat and said, 'Hello, my name is Frank O'Donnell'—and Lori was sitting there waiting for him."

"Frank, I can't believe it! Buddy is the hacker? I thought he was out of town!"

"Well, it turns out you can't trust everything Buddy says." Frank stopped, his eyes flashing with anger. "I need to think . . . I'm going on a walk." Abruptly he turned and went back out the way he had come. Catherine heard the front door slam again.

Buddy was the hacker? Catherine was stunned. How could Buddy be the hacker? He had just organized a birthday party for Frank—and the whole time he was stealing from him? And cheating on Bunny? Her mind was spinning. Frank was going to take this hard; they had been friends for such a long time—for that matter, Buddy was her friend too. She went down the steps off the deck and wandered aimlessly around the back yard, mindlessly picking up sticks and prickly sweetgum balls that had fallen down over the winter.

She heard the side gate screech open and footsteps crunching on the gravel path. Was that Frank already? Why was he coming around the outside of the house? She walked across the yard to a point where she could see down the side of the house. Yes, it was Frank. He was walking slowly and carrying something in his arms. She moved toward him to see what it was and caught a glimpse of a familiar tail. It was Fred.

"Frank, what's wrong? Did something happen to Fred?"

"I found him on the side of the street, around the corner on Maplewood." Frank's voice was strangely calm.

Catherine felt a stab of fear. "Is he hurt? Do we need to call the vet?"

"It's too late for that. He must have been there a couple of hours already; he's already stiff. He looks so peaceful, just like when he's sleeping on the dining room chair. Not a mark on him—just one spot of blood below his ear." Fred gently stroked Fred's soft, silky fur.

"Oh Frank, no, not Fred, how could this happen?" She could feel tears welling up as she spoke.

"People always drive too fast around that corner. Can you find me something to put him in?"

Catherine ran to the shed and dumped tools and garden supplies out of a carboard box. By the time she came back, Frank was up on the deck, still cradling Fred in his arms. Catherine grabbed the towel she had used to dry the chairs, carefully folded it, and placed it in the box on the table. Frank gently laid Fred on the towel. *Frank was right*, thought Catherine tearfully, *he looks just like he's sleeping*. "It must have been sudden," she said. "It doesn't look like he suffered too much."

She put an arm around Frank's shoulder. For a moment he was still, and then she felt huge sobs starting to shudder through his body. She wrapped both of her arms tightly around him, pressing her head against his chest, feeling his gasping breaths and thumping heart against her tear-streaked face. Together they stood without speaking, clinging to one another, as the waves of grief washed over them. Frank's sobs seemed to grow in intensity and Catherine began to sense that this was more than just Fred, that a dam was breaking inside of Frank. Her neck was twisted at a strange angle and her back was starting to ache. "Frank, honey, let's sit down," she said gently, pulling him toward the steps. They sat on the top step, side by side, Catherine's arm still holding him tight, her head now pressed against his shoulder.

Slowly Frank's sobs subsided. "My life is a wreck," he said, staring out across the yard into the gathering dusk. Catherine was quiet and waited for him to go on. His anger seemed to have drained away, his voice low and empty sounding. "How could my best friend be lying to me and stealing from me? You know what I thought of while I was walking, before I found Fred? The whole surprise party was probably charged to that credit card."

Catherine nodded. "Yeah, that occurred to me too."

"And the whole time I was blaming Ricky. I'm such an idiot. Buddy could easily have gotten my social security number somehow—he's been at our house hundreds of times over the years. But obviously I trusted him."

"By the way, Becky called right before you got home. She said to say hi to you. She was all excited because Ricky is a finalist to get the job—I could hear him talking in the background. I asked her about how she paid for her ticket and she said she used her roommate's frequent flyer miles, for both of them. I should have just called and asked her that sooner."

They were both silent for a while. A whiff of onion grass drifted up from the damp lawn.

Frank continued, his voice still low and expressionless. "It's not just being screwed by Buddy. Other than him, I don't even really have any friends. Just a few acquaintances—no one who would miss me if I disappeared. My job stinks. I've been stuck there my whole life, doing the same pointless things over and over again. For a company that does what? Manages parking lots, for God's sake. And now Rupert's fudging the numbers. What am I supposed to do about that? And our daughter ran away from us." Frank glanced at the box beside him. "And now Fred. Why did Fred have to die?" Catherine could feel him choking back tears again.

Catherine squeezed him tighter. "In thirty years, I've never heard you cry like that."

Frank's voice was almost a whisper. "There was one other time—but you never heard me." He was quiet for a moment, his gaze still fixed on the dim outline of the oak tree behind the shed. "The time I left you at the hospital."

Catherine continued to hold him tightly. Twice over the years she had tried to ask him about that terrible night, and twice he had turned away and changed the subject—

the second time had been more than ten years ago. She had resigned herself to letting it stay buried, but she had never seen Frank this broken before. She took a deep breath and said softly, "What happened that night, honey?"

This time the silence lasted so long that Catherine concluded Frank was not going to answer. But then he began to speak, the words tumbling out of him faster and faster. "I've never told anyone this before. That day Julie died on the beach, I lied to my parents. I told them I hadn't heard the lifeguards warning us to get off the beach. But I *had* heard them, more than once. They were screaming at us, but I pretended not to hear because I was having fun and I didn't want the day to be ruined. I thought I was smarter than them—grownups are always warning you about things that never happen. Or maybe I thought Julie would be safe under the umbrella, I don't know. When the lightning struck the umbrella pole, I was about ten yards away. The police said I probably would have been killed too if I hadn't been wearing my flip flops—I had just put them on because the sand was so hot. Even so, the blast stunned me and knocked me off my feet. When I got up Julie was lying on the sand, not moving. The pole was smoking. I couldn't see her face. I'm glad I couldn't see her face."

"Frank, no one is going to blame an eleven-year-old for what happened on the beach that day. I teach eleven-year-olds—I know what they're capable of; half of them forget to put their underwear on in the morning. Julie's death was a freak accident. That's what a freak accident is— something that no one expects and no one can do anything about." Catherine's heart ached for what Frank must have gone through.

"That's not what my eleven-year-old mind thought. I convinced myself that I could have saved her. One day I even went to the playground when no one was around and paced off how far I thought it was to the boardwalk, and then I timed myself, imagining I was grabbing Julie and sprinting up the beach. And in my mind, I proved to myself that I could have saved her. That's what I thought, but I never told anyone. And no one talked about something else either, but it was an open secret that my parents' divorce was somehow connected to Julie's death—even a kid could figure that out. In my mind, all of these things were connected: me lying, Julie's death, my parents' divorce. It was all my fault."

Frank paused for a moment. "And somehow all of that got connected to you and our baby that night at the hospital. I was so afraid; I didn't know what to do. I kind of panicked, like an anxiety attack I suppose. All I could think of was, babies can die, kids can die, and I couldn't live with the thought of going through that again. I had seen what happened to my mom—she didn't deal with it too well, and I was caught in the middle of all that. And so I ran away from you, thinking in some twisted way that it would be better not to even risk having kids, or even be married. But then I was so ashamed of leaving you there when you needed me. I was supposed to be the strong one, and I fell apart. What kind of a husband abandons his wife in the hospital?" Frank stopped. "I almost didn't come back," he whispered.

"But you did come back," Catherine said gently. "And Becky was born two years later."

"Yeah, I've gone over this in my mind a million times. In a strange way, I think that night forced me to face my fears, I guess, for the first time, going all the way back to that day on the beach. You know, I never slept that night—I just walked and walked; I must have walked twenty miles. In the end, I knew I had to make a choice." For the first time since they had sat down on the steps, Frank turned and looked at Catherine. "And I chose you."

Now tears started trickling down Catherine's face. "Oh Frank, I'm so glad you chose me. I love you. I don't care what happened on that beach forty years ago. I don't even care about that night at the hospital. It hurt that you wouldn't talk about it, but that's okay. I'm glad you told me now; it means so much to me. I'm just so happy you came back."

They clung to one another, sitting on the top step of the deck. Frank didn't speak, but Catherine could feel the tension in his body ebb away. There was still a smudge of light in the west, but the yard was dark. In a couple of months there would be fireflies. Tonight the darkness enveloped them like a thick, soft blanket.

"What am I going to do about Buddy?" said Frank at last in a dull voice.

"You have to talk to him," said Catherine.

"No. I'm not going to do that. I don't want anything to do with him," Frank shot back, his voice rising. Catherine could hear and feel the anger returning. "I just want him to get the fuck out of my life."

"Frank, you have to. Look at me." Catherine turned to face him in the dim light coming from the kitchen window. "I'm pissed at him too. How could anyone treat a friend like that? He's a jerk—no, worse than a jerk, he's a ... a ... I don't even know what to call him—a backstabber, a traitor. But you said a few minutes ago you don't have many friends. You're right, you don't. But maybe it's partly because you always bury everything. Or run away, like you did to me. I don't know what the answer is. Maybe this *is* the end of your friendship. You have every right to walk away—shoot, you have every right to call the cops. But don't do it without talking to him. That's all I'm saying." Catherine's voice was gentle but passionate.

"No. No way. I don't owe him anything. I don't think he really is my friend. I'm not sure I even know him. Sure, we were college roommates, and we hang out at baseball games and drink beer. But this is not college anymore. This is not just one of his stupid pranks. This time he went too far." Frank jumped up and started pacing back and forth on the deck.

"Maybe you're right. Maybe you don't really know him like you thought you did. But he is your friend. I don't know what to do either, but I don't think it's too late. Look at us, Frank. It took us over twenty years to talk about that terrible night at the hospital. But that's okay, I'm so glad you did, and I still love you. And we probably still have more to learn about each other, even after all these years. But that's okay too. We're in this together."

Frank looked at her. There was just enough light to glint off the streaks of tears on her face. "I don't know, Catherine. I just don't know. I think it is too late." He sighed, his eye catching the dark oblong shadow on the table. "I need to do something about Fred." He looked sadly at the box and stopped pacing to gently stroke his old friend's head again.

"Can't you wait till tomorrow? You can put him in the shed overnight."

"No, I have to do it now."

Frank found a floodlight in the shed and rigged it up with an extension cord so that Catherine could hold it while he dug a grave for Fred behind the shed. There were two other Freds buried there, but both of them had died of old age. The first one had already been getting along in years when they were married. When they were dating, Catherine hadn't had the heart to tell Frank that she hated cats, but she was glad she hadn't because she'd grown to love them almost as much as he did.

When the hole was deep enough, Frank placed Fred's food dish in the box with him; he always buried his beloved pets with something they had loved, and for this Fred he chose his food dish. Then he closed the top of the box and carefully placed it in the bottom of the hole. Catherine waited patiently, knowing how important this ritual of farewell was for Frank. First, they bowed their heads for a moment of silence to honor Fred's life. Then they each shared some of their favorite memories. Frank remembered how Fred loved to climb the maple tree in the back yard and stretch along the thick branch that overhung the deck, watching whatever was going on below. Sometimes he would doze off and almost fall before catching himself, much to his embarrassment. Catherine shared how Fred always waited for Frank to be the one to feed him, whether morning or evening. He was funny that way; he really didn't like it when someone else fed him, which created problems when Frank was away or came home late. They laughed remembering the time Fred had gotten stuck behind the washing machine and couldn't seem to figure out how to turn around or back out. They had had to disconnect the hoses and move the washing machine away from the wall to rescue him.

Finally, Frank sprinkled several handfuls of dirt into the hole with his hands, and then began to use the shovel to fill it in the rest of the way. Later, he would inscribe a small wooden plaque with Fred's name and the dates of his birth and death and place it next to the other two plaques already hanging on the fence above the graves. This Fred would be Fred VI.

Catherine was feeling chilled and propped the light up in a branch of a tree so she could go into the house. In the kitchen, she filled the kettle with water to make some tea. She shivered. *What a day*, she thought. *Poor Frank. What must he be going through?* As she waited for the water to boil, she stared out the window. She could see Frank's distorted shadow on the lawn in the glare of the floodlight and hear the chunk of the shovel as it bit into the stony soil. *I wonder what is buried below the surface of Frank,* she thought. Even after all these years, she sometimes had a hard time reading him. And tonight he seemed to be edging into new territory. She shivered again.

She saw the light click off, and heard the shed door bang. Moments later, his footsteps thudded across the deck and the door slid open. "I never finished my walk," he said gruffly. "Don't wait up for me." He strode across the kitchen and disappeared into the garage.

"But Frank, aren't you hungry?" she called after him. But he was gone. For an instant, fear gripped her heart, and she wondered if he would be back. She took a deep breath and tried to calm herself. *Frank always comes back,* she reassured herself. But by bedtime he had still not returned, and Catherine eventually went to bed by herself. After what seemed like hours, she fell into a fitful sleep, filled with strange dreams of squirrels and cats leaping across huge gaping chasms.

FIFTEEN

At first, Frank was too upset to think. His mind was blank, emotions racing through him like a flash flood coursing down a ravine, swirling in unpredictable cross currents. When he left the house, he began walking aimlessly, without any destination in mind, turning randomly right or left as he strode through first one neighborhood and then the next. But before long, the neighborhood streets petered out, and he found himself on a busier feeder road, with cars rushing past uncomfortably close and a steady stream of headlights blinding him.

He was about to turn around when he saw a glint of steel reflected in the headlights a short distance down the road and realized an old rail line was embedded across the asphalt. *I don't remember seeing this before,* he thought. *I wonder what road I'm on—no railroad signs or crossing gates, so the tracks must be abandoned.* He moved closer and saw the old track bed looming darkly on either side of the road. *Let's try it*, he decided. But which direction? He looked around and could see the distant lights of Philadelphia glowing on the horizon to his right. *Away from civilization,* he thought. Darting to his left across the road at the first gap in the traffic, he plunged into the darkness.

He felt the crushed rocks of the track ballast crunch beneath his feet. His toe struck one of the old wooden railroad ties and he stumbled, nearly falling. He stopped and let his eyes adjust to the deeper blackness under the overgrown trees along the railbed. At that moment, the moon emerged below a cloud, nearly full but not far above the horizon. The dim light of the moon filtered through the trees and gleamed on the steel tracks disappearing into the distance, no doubt perfectly straight and parallel when last used, but now oddly buckled and distorted. Frank started walking, stepping carefully from one railroad tie to the next. At first it was awkward because the gap between the ties was shorter than the length of his normal stride. But he soon found that if he slowed down and adjusted his pace to match the gap, he could maintain a steady, almost relaxing, rhythm. *I'm not in a rush because I'm not going anywhere*, he said to himself.

When he next glimpsed the moon, it was touching the horizon, and after it had disappeared, the lingering clouds cleared and the stars came out as brilliantly as he had ever seen them in the patchwork suburbs of central Jersey. The temperature dipped, but he did not feel the cold. The slower, rhythmic pace of walking the rails seemed to slow and steady his mind. Unexpectedly, his thoughts first went to Ricky. He cursed himself for connecting dots that never should have been connected. Catherine was right all along, he thought. As upset as she was, she never doubted Becky. And if Becky had chosen Ricky, he needed to accept him. *Who knows, I might wake up tomorrow and find out he's my son-in-law. I have no reason not to like the guy. Hell, I don't even know anything about him. I have to get over my stupid hang-ups and get to know him*, he vowed to himself.

His feet thudded rhythmically on the crossties, echoing the clickety-clack of bygone trains, as he followed the faint glimmer of the buckled rails disappearing into the darkness. At length, he reluctantly turned his thoughts to Buddy. His rage momentarily surged again, but he consciously tried to set his anger aside. *Cool it, cool it—I need to think this through*, he told himself. He forced himself to cast his mind back over the years and tried to remember every interaction he had ever had with Buddy, starting with their sophomore year in college, through graduation, and over the years since they had lived in the same town and seen each other regularly. He thought about Bunny, and Catherine, and other friends. In time, certain patterns began to emerge—and not just on Buddy's part, he had to admit. Buddy, the master deceiver, might skate through life leaving wreckage in his wake, but Frank had his own issues. Catherine was right: his entire life he had buried his feelings, always running from pain, shrinking ever further into a protective shell.

A sense of hopelessness swept over him. *This has to end. Something has to change—but what? How do you break out of lifelong patterns?* As his legs swung rhythmically from tie to tie, the lyrics of a Bruce Springsteen song from their college days flashed into his mind. He knew he had a terrible voice, but there was no one to hear him in the black shadows of the abandoned tracks. In a cracked voice, he started singing: "'Cause the darkness of this house has got the best of us. There's a darkness in this town that's got us too ... so say goodbye, it's Independence Day, it's Independence Day this time." Over and over he repeated the lyrics until they seemed to burn a track into his mind. He knew Springsteen was singing about a son choosing to walk away from a broken relationship with his father, but somehow it seemed to fit. *A fresh start—that's what I need. A fresh start. I need an Independence Day.*

From time to time, the tracks passed behind fences and factory walls, sometimes crossing roads and culverts. Once, he thought he had hit a dead end when the tracks disappeared at an underpass beneath a highway, but then he found the track bed again on the other side. In one section, he glimpsed manicured suburban back yards through the bushes, complete with elaborate children's playsets and swimming pools still covered for the winter. Not long after that, the tracks seemed to enter a wilder stretch, surrounded by dense, tangled undergrowth, although he could not tell how far the forest extended on each side. He heard an owl hooting mournfully close by, and an occasional rustle of leaves from some small nocturnal creature. The darkness under the trees grew thick and impenetrable.

Faintly, in the distance, he could hear a dull roaring that grew steadily louder. At first, he wondered idly if it was the roar of tires on the New Jersey Turnpike, but then something made him glance down and he saw, or more accurately, sensed, empty black space between the railroad ties. He froze midstep. *I'm on a bridge*, he thought in sudden alarm. *That sound is water: rapids? A nearby waterfall?* He stepped tentatively forward to the next railroad tie and tried to peer into the darkness beneath him. The cool air stirring across his face and a certain quality of the sound suggested there was a significant gorge yawning beneath him—how deep he couldn't tell. He carefully knelt, broke off a piece of dried wood from the railroad tie, and dropped it into the void. It disappeared without a sound. How long had it been since someone crossed this bridge, he wondered as he straightened, carefully keeping his balance.

If I fell off this bridge how long would it take them to find me? A dark premonition made him shudder. The damp, murky air swirled up, caressing his face and pulling his eyes down to stare again into the blackness below. He leaned forward imperceptibly, his heart suddenly pounding. *Would anyone even care?* Standing utterly still, suspended above the void, he stared down, half mesmerized by the black gap between the ties. Inexplicably, a tiny detail struck him as odd: it had been nearly pitch-dark under the trees, but now he could see a faint shadow on the rough wood. Slowly, he lifted his head and looked up.

Above him a vast panorama of brilliant stars glittered across the expanse of the sky. He shook his head, as if waking from a dream. Catherine. Catherine would care. Catherine would find him.

Frank slowly exhaled a long shuddering breath and pondered what to do next. Was it safe to cross the bridge? Even with the light of the stars, he could barely see the next tie. For all he knew, there were missing ties, or the entire bridge could have collapsed into the gorge. But he hated the thought of turning around and retracing his steps. *It's a metaphor*, he thought. *In order to cross, I have to step blindly into the unknown and trust I'll land on something solid. Or I can go back. I have to choose.* He looked behind him, and then looked up again at the brilliant stars wheeling overhead. An intense longing for something nameless and indescribable swept over him. He remembered another night of despair when he walked away from a hospital room, and then, just a few hours ago, the feeling of Catherine's arms around him as decades of guilt and pain slipped away into the darkness of a suburban backyard. Another Springsteen song popped into his mind: "Now some guys they just give up living and start dying little by little, piece by piece . . . Tonight my baby and me, we're gonna ride to the sea and wash these sins off our hands."

Then, taking a deep breath and looking straight ahead, Frank squared his shoulders and stepped to the next tie, barely visible as a shadowy outline suspended over the blackness of the empty space below. Step by step, one tie at a time, stretching his arms wide and moving steadily to keep his balance, he strode across the bridge in the darkness. Once, he heard a distinct creak and felt the tie shift as his weight bore down, but he kept going.

Safely on the other side, he paused and took another deep breath. *One step at a time*, he repeated to himself, *one step at a time.*

The eastern sky was glowing when the track came to another road that seemed to be a more major artery. Even at this early hour, a steady trickle of cars whizzed by. Off to the left, he could see the green eye of a traffic light, and beyond that the bright lights of what appeared to be a gas station. He turned toward it and, as he got closer, was delighted to see the familiar sign of a Wawa convenience store. Perfect, he smiled to himself. His legs were aching but his mind was clear, and he knew what he had to do. Catherine was right: he had to talk to Buddy. But not on the phone. He had to meet him face-to-face. He had no idea how Buddy would take it, but he had to try and end this once and for all. He suddenly remembered that, at the party, Buddy had promised to go with him to their first Phillies game of the season on Tuesday—was the party only a week ago? It seemed like something from a different era. *That will work,* he thought, *that will work. I'll call him tomorrow to remind him. I just hope he hasn't forgotten.*

The clerk seemed surprised when he walked into the Wawa. Frank realized it might be because he had suddenly appeared out of nowhere without the help of a car. "Car broken down, mister?" asked the clerk nervously, watching Frank's hand moving toward his pocket. "Not exactly," replied Frank, pulling out his cell phone. "Can you tell me where I am? I need to phone my wife."

BUDDY AND FRANK'S USUAL place to meet for a Phillies game was at the Mike Schmidt statue outside the third base gate of Citizens Bank Park in South Philly. Frank hated driving into the city, so he would take a NJ Transit train into Philadelphia's 30th Street Station where he could connect to the subway to South Philly. The first pitch of the game was usually at 7:10, so Buddy would stay late at his office in Center City, which he often did anyway, and then drive to the park. Then, after the game, they would drive together back to the NJ Transit station where Frank had left his car. Over the years it had become a comfortable routine. They had long ago decided it was worth it to get season tickets, even though they were not the kind of hard-core fans who attended every game, rain or shine.

Although Frank did not like driving into Philadelphia, he did enjoy the experience of being in the city. It was awe-inspiring to descend into the grand concourse of the 30th Street Station with its ninety-five-foot-high ceiling, giant art deco chandeliers, and mammoth columns at either end. Sometimes, instead of catching the subway across the street from the station, he would walk ten blocks down John F. Kennedy Boulevard into Center City, across the Schuylkill River, heading for City Hall, with its iconic statue of William Penn gazing out across the city from its pinnacle. The street was lined with modern skyscrapers and office buildings, pedestrians crowding the sidewalks as the buildings emptied out at the end of the day. There was something energizing about the crowds and the traffic, so different from the dull monotony of the New Jersey suburbs.

However, this time Frank was too distracted to enjoy the urban vibe. He had sensed the reluctance in Buddy's voice on the phone the day before and was half expecting him to call with some excuse for why he couldn't make it—which would be a relief in some ways. The certainty he had felt at the end of his all-night trek had begun to fade now that the reality of seeing Buddy was approaching. This would not be an easy conversation. Would he be able to say what he needed to? How would Buddy respond? Was he doing the right thing? What would Catherine think? *One step at a time*, he kept reminding himself. *One step at a time.*

To make things worse, he was running late. He weaved his way through the crowd inside 30th Street Station as fast as he could, heading directly to the subway entrance on Market Street. At the City Hall station, he had to change to the Broad Street Line, again weaving through the crowds in the narrow connecting tunnel, hoping he would not have to wait long for the next train. He groaned as a train pulled out while he was still fighting his way down the stairs to the platform. Fortunately, another train arrived almost right away, this one an express. As he pushed his way into the car, he could see thickets of Phillies hats and sweatshirts surrounding him, and the train car was filled with an excited buzz of conversation from groups of friends headed to the game—very different from the deathly silent commuter trains that fed into the city from the suburbs.

He arrived at the Mike Schmidt statue at 7:05, out of breath from walking faster than usual from the subway station, which was on the far side of the vast parking lots surrounding the stadium. Buddy wasn't there yet. Frank's heart sank as he scanned the surrounding crowds to make sure he wasn't standing somewhere else—although in all the years they had been coming to games, they had always met at that exact spot. Frank sat down on the base of the statue to catch his breath. Now that he was at the ballpark, his mood had swung again and he was terrified Buddy wouldn't show up. He knew himself too well: if he didn't talk to Buddy that night, he knew he would never have the nerve to try again.

Towering over him, Mike Schmidt was forever frozen at the end of one of his mighty swings, his eyes lifted to the glorious sight of another home run arcing into the stands beyond left field. Frank tended to be a bit cynical about the over-glorification of sports, but Schmidt had been one of his heroes, starting back in fifth grade when he had seen him hit two home runs, one of which had landed two rows in front of where he was sitting with his dad. It was a memory he cherished, and often brought up if he happened to be talking baseball with someone from a younger generation. Some of his favorite memories were going to Phillies games with his dad, and fifth grade had been the high point. The following summer was the accident at the beach, and things were never the same after that—although his dad had still taken him to occasional baseball games even after the divorce. Tonight, sitting in the shadow of Mike Schmidt and with memories of the past stirred up by recent events, Frank felt again that sharp pain of innocence lost. If only he could freeze fifth grade like Schmidt was frozen in glory next to him.

Just then, Frank saw Buddy's familiar head winding through the crowd, wearing the same faded Phillies cap he had worn for as long as Frank could remember. He breathed a sigh of relief. "The Star-Spangled Banner" was already blaring out from the stadium speakers as Buddy reached the statue.

"Sorry, Frank. I forgot what the traffic on Broad Street can be like at this time of day. I think it's getting worse every year." Compared to the night of the party, Frank was surprised to see how tense and drawn his friend's face looked. He looked like he had aged ten years in the space of a week.

"No problem, we'll probably only miss the first couple of pitches." They hurried through security, around to the escalators by first base, and quickly found their seats in section 414 on the terrace deck, high above first. The first couple of years they had bought season tickets they had been one level lower, but there was no cover over that section and it could be brutally hot in the direct sun, or miserably cold when it was wet and windy. These seats were among the highest in the stadium, but they had the protection of a roof above them. Frank liked being up this high and seeing every detail of the whole stadium spread out below them. There was also a decent view of the city skyline. As much as the game itself, Frank loved the experience of being in the stadium: watching the crowds, laughing at the silly traditions and goofy Philly Phanatic mascot, seeing the lights of the city, and, if they were lucky, enjoying a glorious sunset over West Philadelphia.

Buddy, on the other hand, cared more about winning. Tonight, he was already grumbling about the Phillies' losing record so early in the season, with only six wins and nine losses. He wasn't happy with the starting pitcher either. "Why did they even sign this guy? Lannan's never been that great—the only reason he's famous is for pitching *against* us for the Nationals in his first major league game and getting thrown out because he hit two of our batters. He must have been cheap."

Frank smiled. For a moment, he let go of the burdens weighing him down and simply enjoyed being in the stadium with Buddy watching a Phillies game, experiencing all the familiar sights, sounds, and smells. There was nothing like the first game of a new season. But then he remembered with a little lurch of his stomach the real reason for coming tonight. *Not yet*, he said to himself, *later, later—there's plenty of time*. He looked around: there was a scattering of fans around them in little clumps, including one group of twenty-somethings right behind them. All of them were holding beers in what seemed to be super-sized cups. *Ugh*, he thought, remembering one of the downsides of the baseball experience.

The Cincinnati Reds' second batter was already facing Lannan. Lannan had gotten the first batter to ground out to second, but on the third pitch the next batter smashed a line drive down the left field line and made it to second base. After a second groundout, the fourth man up hit another line drive to center field and the Reds had their first run. Lannan's next pitch was wild and the runner on first easily made it to second. "What did I tell you," groaned Buddy. "This is not looking good, and it's only the first inning."

Still keeping his eyes on the pitcher, Buddy said, "Frank, you know how people who don't like baseball always complain it's boring? Well, first of all, it's not true, but even if it was, at least baseball doesn't destroy its players like the NFL does. Do you know anything about CTE?"

"Isn't that related to concussions?" Frank asked.

"Yeah, it's what happens when people get their heads beat to a pulp every weekend for half their life. Do you remember Mouse?"

"Sure, from the U of O, your freshman roommate. Great guy—the guy with the amazing voice."

"Yeah, remember how he pretended to be Old Jackson in the original prank? Well, the whole prank thing got me thinking about people we knew back then. I tried to track Mouse down to find out what happened to him. It wasn't easy—kept hitting dead ends. I finally got hold of Garbo, and the two of them had stayed in touch. Both of them were in Cleveland."

"Garbo . . . I haven't thought about him in years. How'd you find him?"

"That was easy: Facebook. Did you know his real name is Bob? Anyway, Mouse ended up with real bad CTE. In the end, it killed him. And what really gets me is that he died barely ten miles from where we live, and I never knew it. What's wrong with us, Frank? We lose touch with the people we care about. We get so focused on crap that doesn't matter, and the people get left in the dirt. Know what I mean?"

Frank could tell that Buddy's emotions were raw. "Yeah, it's true, friends can be kind of fickle." He glanced sideways at him, stunned at Buddy's obliviousness. *How can he talk to me about friendship*, he thought bitterly. He felt a flash of anger. "That's too bad about Mouse. When did he die?"

"A month ago," Buddy replied glumly. "Man, I wish I could have seen him before he died. If only I'd known he was so close by." He turned his attention back to the game. "You call that pitching?" he shouted derisively at the Phillies' pitcher, three hundred feet away.

Below them, the Phillies had already had their first three outs, a strikeout and two flyballs, and the Reds were up at bat again. The first batter homered on Lannan's third pitch. The second batter almost homered too, but the ball was just short of the wall and the Phillies' left-fielder was there. The third batter hit a double, and the fourth a triple. Lannan was getting hammered.

For the next three innings, Buddy and Frank focused on the game, hoping the Phillies' offense might save the day. But it was not to be. By the end of the fifth inning, the score was eleven to zero and Lannan had allowed fifteen hits. The Phillies had managed just two. "This is hopeless," muttered Buddy. "Why aren't they bringing in a reliever?"

Frank could tell people were starting to trickle out of the stadium. Not only were the Phillies getting killed, but the temperature had dropped sharply once the sun slid behind the horizon—no glorious sunset this time, just a dull orangish red that quickly faded behind a hazy jumble of buildings across the Schuylkill River. Unfortunately, the group behind them seemed to be sticking it out to the bitter end. Their commentary on the game was getting more and more raucous, with the rate of f-words steadily increasing in direct proportion to their blood alcohol level.

"Hey, Buddy, let's go grab a beer." Frank stood up and stretched, trying to signal with a jerk of his chin that he wanted to get away from the revelers behind them. He could feel his stomach muscles tighten with dread thinking about talking to Buddy. Maybe this wasn't a good idea after all: Buddy would be too distracted, there was too much noise, too many people around. *Maybe the ballpark is the wrong place,* he thought. *I'll invite him for a beer on Friday after work, or I'll come up with some excuse to stop by his house.*

Buddy didn't need any arm-twisting about going for a beer. "Sure, why not. Might help lower my blood pressure." He glared at the hapless Phillies scurrying around below, chasing yet another line drive that had just rocketed inches past the mitt of a diving shortstop.

They wound their way through the seats and down to the concession level. There was no line at the beer stand. "I'll take a Yuengling. How about you, Buddy?" Frank asked.

"Sounds good; make that two." The barman efficiently drew off two plastic cups of foaming amber lager from what was advertised as America's oldest brewery, located a couple of hours outside of Philly.

"Give me a pretzel too," Frank said, pointing to the Philly-style soft pretzels hanging in the glass display. "Want one, Buddy?"

"Nah, I ate too much before I came," he answered.

Beers in hand, they headed back to the stands. The crowd was noticeably thinner now. "Let's go somewhere quieter," said Frank. "I'm starting to worry what might land on my head from those idiots behind us." They climbed up to the highest row of their section and then made their way as far to the left as they could. There were no other fans within twenty yards. *Can't find a much more deserted corner of the stadium than this,* thought Frank. *I've just got to do this; it's now or never, no more excuses.*

"Wow," said Buddy, "section four twelve, row sixteen, seat one. This is even higher than our regular seats. Talk about a bird's eye view." He gazed out across the field, but Frank noticed he seemed to be averting his eyes from the latest tally of runs and hits displayed on the giant scoreboard. They sat down and put their feet up on the seats in front of them.

Frank had a sip of beer and took a deep breath. "Buddy, we need to talk. I saw you last Friday at the Gran Dorado with Lori."

"Oh," said Buddy. He kept his eyes glued on the field. "What were you doing there?"

"I found out about the credit card, and I knew there was a reservation in my name that night. So I went there to see who showed up. I was kind of shocked, to say the least."

"Oh," said Buddy. "You found out about the credit card," he repeated in a flat voice.

"Catherine says I always bury everything and run away from my problems. Well, I've thought about this a lot and I'm not running away from anything tonight. Do you have any idea how it feels for your best friend to screw you like that? I'll tell you how it feels. It feels like shit. Pissed, really pissed, that's how I feel. And screwed over, betrayed, kicked in the teeth. What kind of a friend lies to you and robs you blind? And keeps doing it for months, even at the same time he's throwing you a big happy birthday party? Part of me never wants to see you again." Frank's voice was calm, but there was an edge to it. "Not to mention how Bunny would feel if she knew about it."

Buddy turned his head and looked at Frank. There was despair in his eyes. "She does know," he said in a low voice. "She walked out on me yesterday. That's why I didn't want to come tonight. Plus, Mouse. I finally found him, and he was dead. I guess I screwed him over too."

They both stared at the game below with unseeing eyes. "I'm sorry, Buddy. That really stinks," said Frank finally.

"Yeah, it stinks, but I had it coming to me. Bunny had caught Lori and me together another time, last year, and I had promised not to see her again. But I did anyway—actually I never even stopped. And Lori's not the first one—I don't know how much Bunny knew about the others, but she probably had her suspicions."

Buddy was silent for a time. Frank kept his mouth shut and waited. "Frank, the truth is, I'm a sleazy guy. Maybe I always have been. But the last few days . . . I don't know why, but trying to track Mouse down, and then finding he was already gone . . . it really made me think about my life, where it started, where it's ended up. How I got here."

"Maybe we're all sleazy in our own way," said Frank, thinking about his own life.

"It's kind of ironic, though. I didn't even spend the night with Lori that Friday at the Gran Dorado. We had dinner, and she told me she was ending it. Her husband was getting his act together—I guess he wants to try counseling or something. She wanted a fresh start with him. They have kids. I'm glad she ended it; it was just another life I was destroying."

"Maybe that means you can patch things up with Bunny."

"No, I don't think so. It's too late for that. I had my chance and blew it. I don't think I'll see Bunny again, except maybe in court. Berenice. That's the last thing she said, 'My name is Berenice.' What did she mean?"

They were both silent again, sipping their beers, looking down at the game below. The Phillies had managed to get a runner in scoring position and there was a murmur of interest rippling through what remained of the crowd.

"Want some of my pretzel?" Frank broke off a piece of the soft bread and handed it to him. Buddy took the bread, placed it in his mouth, and took another swig of beer.

"I don't know what to say about the credit card," said Buddy in a low voice after he was done chewing. "I'm such a jerk. I don't know what I was thinking; I never meant it to go that far—it was just supposed to be a temporary one-time thing, and I figured you'd never find out. I was pretty desperate for cash, and Lori had expensive tastes. She always wanted to go places and stay in fancy hotels. To be honest, my financial situation isn't that great. I've never been good with money." Buddy paused reflectively, still staring at the tiny figures on the field below. "That's what I meant by saying I was a sleazy guy: my whole life I've done stuff like that and always gotten away with it—always playing the game, figuring out the next move, proud of how much smarter I was than everyone else. I guess it finally caught up with me. I'm really sorry I screwed you like that. I'll make it up to you somehow. I just need a little time to figure out what to do."

"Don't worry about it," said Frank.

Buddy turned and looked at him. "What do you mean, 'Don't worry about it?'"

"The credit card," said Frank. "I took care of it."

"You took care of it?"

"Paid it off. Canceled the card. It's done."

Buddy looked taken aback. "Frank, you can't do that. Give me some time; I can pay it off. It's my problem, not yours."

"Buddy, I don't care about the money. I don't want you to pay me back. I want you back as a friend. I don't want that card hanging over us. Let's just forget about it and let it go. It's better that way. You can pay it forward to someone else if you want."

Buddy sat motionless, his eyes back on Lannan on the mound below. For once, Lannan's fastball was perfect and they could hear the smack of the ball hitting the catcher's mitt as the batter swung and missed. "Wow, you didn't have to do that," he said at last. "I'm blown away. I don't know what to say."

"That's okay," said Frank. "Let's go home."

They didn't talk much in the car on the drive back to New Jersey. But Frank felt like a weight had been lifted off his shoulders. He glanced over at Buddy a couple of times. It was hard to tell what his friend was thinking, but Frank thought he could detect a softening in the lines in his face. When they arrived at the NJ Transit station parking lot, Buddy pulled up next to Frank's car and Frank opened the door and got out. He was about to close the door when Buddy stopped him.

"Frank, I don't know how to say this, but what you just did really means a lot. Actually, I kind of can't get my mind around it." Buddy seemed to be choking up. "But it means more than I can say. I guess all I can say is thank you. Thank you, old pal. It's giving me some hope that I haven't felt in a long time."

Frank reached back into the car and the two friends clasped hands. Then Frank said, "Good night, Buddy. I'll see you around," and closed the door behind him.

Over the roof of the station, he could see the moon low in the clear night sky, just like the night on the tracks. In the trees surrounding the parking lot, white blossoms shimmered in the light of the streetlamps.

SIXTEEN

It was Monday again, and Catherine was exhausted again. The most recent weekend had not been as bad as the previous one, when Frank had called her at six thirty on Saturday morning after walking all night. Her heart had almost stopped when the ringing of the phone had broken into her dreams. His voice had sounded tired but surprisingly calm, and it had ended up being simple to find him. They had often stopped at that Wawa on their way to the Jersey Shore. How exactly he had gotten there still wasn't quite clear to her, but he had greeted her with a huge bear hug as if they had been apart for months. Catherine perceived that the storm raging in his soul had passed, or at least abated.

Frank had fallen into bed and slept for ten hours. When he had emerged for dinner, he told her what he wanted to do. At first, she thought she had misheard him or misunderstood, and she made him explain it again. After it finally sunk in that he planned to forgive Buddy and pay off the credit card, she had been stunned. Eighteen thousand dollars was a lot of money. But when he asked her, "How much is a friend worth?" her heart melted, and she had given him her blessing. And then, when he came back from the Phillies game on Tuesday, his face tired but the tension and despair gone, she had held him in a long hug. It had suddenly struck her that in a completely unexpected—and heart-wrenching—way, Buddy's prank was working: the old Frank was coming back to life.

But now another weekend had passed, and there had been no news from Becky. Catherine had resisted calling her, even though she was dying to know how Ricky's presentation had gone the previous Friday. She had been so happy when Becky had reached out to her with good news the last time, and she wanted to let Becky tell her in her own way again this time. Every time her phone had rung since Friday, she had quickly snatched it up, hoping to see Becky's name on the display. But now it was Monday and Becky hadn't called. Frank had said, "No news is probably bad news," and she hated to admit that he was likely right. *Oh well*, she tried to comfort herself: everyone says you learn more from failing, and Ricky was still young; there must be lots of jobs for people like him. They would be fine. She just needed to stop worrying—but her rationalizations weren't working. She *was* worrying, and she couldn't seem to help it.

Catherine sat down at her desk with a sigh after the last student finally left her classroom. She had not been sleeping well and had felt tired and sluggish all day. The day had not gone particularly well; she knew she had not put enough thought into her lesson plans and she'd had a hard time focusing on her students. Gathering her energy, she stood up, pushed her chair neatly in behind her desk, and grabbed her bag of books and papers on the way out the door. In the car, she kept asking herself the same questions that had been whirling in her mind for weeks: What did Becky see in Ricky? Was this a long-term commitment? Did they really love each other? How much of her fear was because Ricky was black? She knew she wasn't a racist—was she?—but then why did she feel so uncomfortable? Would Ricky ever get a job? What would happen in the meantime? How would they survive without any money? How long could they stay with their friends? Would Becky ever come home? Should she go to San Francisco to see her?

Catherine saw lights flashing red in front of her and jammed on her brakes. Her tires squealed and the car started to skid sideways, stopping inches from the bumper of a tiny gray car in front of her. The driver next to her honked his horn: why? To remind her to stop? Shaken, she tried to clear her mind. While she waited for the light to change, she turned on her favorite classical radio station to find some calming music, but the station was in the middle of a fundraising drive: ". . . ten more calls in the next ten minutes to reach our goal for the hour; the first caller will receive a . . ." She clicked it off in frustration and tried to breathe deeply and focus on the traffic in front of her.

When she unlocked the front door of their house, something seemed different. She frowned. *Where's Fred,* she wondered—before suddenly remembering. *That must be it,* she thought. Poor Fred. She pushed the door closed behind her and dropped her keys in the usual spot next to the phone. No, it wasn't Fred; there was something else that didn't feel right. She cocked her head and looked around the entryway. Everything looked the same as usual: the stacks of old newspapers and broken umbrellas were all in their normal places, the coats on their hooks behind the door hadn't moved, the fingerprints and smudges of dirt around the door knob hadn't disappeared. Wait, the lock . . . that was it. Whenever she left the house in the morning, she always carefully locked both the doorknob and the deadbolt. But just now when she came in, the deadbolt had not been locked. Frank often didn't bother with it—had he come home early? But where was his car? She glanced out the window to make sure his car wasn't there. Or had she just been distracted this morning? Unlikely, but not impossible given her state of mind, she admitted.

Her senses on edge, she walked into the kitchen and looked around. Nothing looked out of order. Still frowning, she dropped her bag in the den and went upstairs to change out of her work clothes. She glanced down the hall as she opened the door to their bedroom. Had Becky's door been closed before? She thought she had left it open so the air would circulate. Annoyed, she walked down the hall and opened Becky's door. In the dim light, she could see a lump under the covers and a patch of blond hair escaping from behind the faded flowers of the bedspread.

"Becky!" Catherine almost screamed. The lump in the bed stirred and emitted a groan. Becky's head emerged, strands of hair covering her groggy-looking eyes. "Becky! You're here!" Catherine couldn't believe her eyes. "Is it really you?"

"Hi, Mom. Sorry, didn't mean to give you a heart attack." Becky rubbed her eyes and sat up. "I caught the red-eye last night—they don't call it that for nothing. Gosh, I was really in a deep sleep." She rubbed her eyes again.

"Becky! You're here! I can't believe it! When did you get here? Can I hug you?"

Becky opened wide her arms and Catherine practically fell into them, wrapping her in the fiercest hug a mother can give. She tried to hold them back, but tears started streaming down her cheeks. Through her tears she kept repeating, "Oh, Becky, Becky, you're here. I can't believe it; I just can't believe it."

At length, Becky was able to disentangle herself from her mother's arms. "Mom, I need to breathe a little here," she said, grinning. "I can't believe it either. It feels so good to be home, back in my own room." She looked around at all the familiar sights: her books haphazardly jammed in every nook and corner, the pictures on the wall, her stuffed animals perched precariously on the shelf over her bed. Reaching up, she took Pooh down and gave him a squeeze. "Hello, Pooh. I've missed you.

"We've been sleeping on a hide-a-bed for weeks. Also, four people, one bathroom. It's been fine, but there's nothing like your own bed. Mom, I needed to go, but I've missed you so much. I'm sorry I left like that. I promise not to do it again."

"Oh Becky, it doesn't matter—all that matters is that you're back. We've missed you too, more than you know. I've been doing some soul-searching since you left and you're right, we have been way too over-protective. But let's not talk about that now. Tell me what's happening. How did Ricky's presentation go? Why did you come back now?" Catherine couldn't resist putting her arm around Becky again, just to prove to herself this was really happening.

"Mom, you're never going to believe this—Ricky got the job! He blew them out of the water, it wasn't even close. But that's not all . . . I have to keep pinching myself." Becky demonstrated by pinching her left forearm. "Ouch. Part of his presentation was that the company needs to have an office on the East Coast, and Ricky made the case for Philadelphia. And they agreed! And they told him that he was going to run the new office, along with another woman. Mom, we're moving to Philadelphia! Can you believe it! And the amount they're going to pay him is mind-boggling, especially after we've been eating ramen and tuna for the past month. I told you Ricky was amazing at stuff like this! It's a really great company." Becky paused to take a breath.

Catherine's eyes filled with tears of joy again. "You're right . . . this must be a dream. Can you pinch me too? Ricky got the job? You're really moving to Philadelphia?"

"It's okay, Mom. You don't have to cry. Sometimes life has happy endings." Becky put her arms around her mother and returned the bear hug Catherine had given her. "Now, can you let me sleep a little longer? I only got here three hours ago and I didn't sleep a wink on the plane. I knew you would be at work so I called my friend Nicole to pick me up." She squirmed out of Catherine's arms and back under her covers. "When does Dad get home?"

Catherine looked at her watch. "Probably in an hour, or an hour and a half . . . you know, I wonder, it might be kind of fun to surprise him. What do you think?"

"Okay, Mom, yes, let's do it!"

"I'll wake you up at six and we'll come up with a plan." She kissed Becky on the forehead and closed the door gently behind her, her heart overflowing with happiness. Becky was home!

CATHERINE HAD TEXTED FRANK on the pretext of asking him to pick something up at the grocery store so she would be able to gauge more accurately when he would get home. Now, expecting him any minute, she was stationed behind the curtain in the living room watching for his car. For once, he wasn't too terribly late. "There he is!" she called out the moment she saw Frank's car pull up to the curb. Becky was in the kitchen waiting for Catherine's signal. She quickly slipped out the back door and went around the side of the house. Catherine returned to the kitchen and pretended to busy herself with dinner preparations. The kitchen table was set with two places for dinner, as usual.

She heard the front door open and close. She counted to three and heard Frank's heavy briefcase thump to the floor exactly as it had done every weekday for the past twenty-five years—Frank was nothing if not predictable. She was not surprised when she heard his steps go into the dining room to greet Fred on his chair. She had been doing the same thing herself, multiple times a day. She felt a pang of grief for Frank; it would take a few more weeks to break that habit. He appeared in the doorway, his face looking glum.

"Hi, Frank. It looks like your Monday was about like mine. So far." Catherine tried to look and sound as gloomy as she could, but wasn't sure she was succeeding; she quickly turned back to the stove and pretended to stir something to hide her face.

"I keep forgetting Fred is gone," said Frank, sounding like he needed a hug. *Hang in there, old friend*, she thought. *There are plenty of hugs coming.*

"Dinner's ready, let's eat," she said. "Just leftovers again, I'm afraid." This was a lie, but Catherine hoped it would add to the gloomy mood. In fact, she had somehow managed to whip together Becky's favorite lasagna.

"Smells pretty good for leftovers," said Frank, washing his hands in the kitchen sink.

Just as they were sitting down, Catherine surreptitiously pressed *send* on a prewritten text message. A second later the doorbell rang. "Who can that be?" said Catherine. "Frank, can you get it? My feet are too tired to get up again."

"Sure," said Frank. "Although it's probably just something about the school board election. They always come right at dinner time. I'll get rid of them."

He pushed back his chair and went to the front door. Catherine could hardly sit still. She heard the door open. A split second later she heard "Daddy!" She jumped up and ran to the front door. All she could see of Becky were two arms wrapped around Frank's back. Catherine couldn't help it; her tears started overflowing for the third time that day. Frank seemed momentarily frozen, and then his arms went around Becky in another huge bear hug, lifting her off the floor. "Becky! It's you!" Finally, he broke loose and turned to look at Catherine. There was a huge smile on his face. "Trickster!" he laughed. "I knew that didn't smell like leftovers!"

Later, sitting around the table, after Frank was all caught up on Becky's news, Catherine asked the question that for some reason no one had thought to ask yet. "Where's Ricky?" she asked. "Did he come with you last night?"

"No," replied Becky, scraping the last bite of lasagna off her plate. "They needed him for meetings this week. There's a lot to figure out, and he'll probably have to go back and forth for a while until things get off the ground. But he's coming on the red-eye this Friday, after work. Can he stay here in our guest room?"

"Sure, sweetie," said Catherine. "We'd love to have him stay with us. We want to get to know him better."

Frank looked at Becky. "I think I owe you an apology," he said. "Not just you, Ricky too. Your mother can tell you that I haven't been very supportive of Ricky these past few weeks, to put it mildly." Frank glanced sheepishly at Catherine, remembering the stakeout. "But I think I might have misjudged him. No, I know I misjudged him, and you too. I want to have a fresh start. So, yes, it would be great to have him stay with us." Catherine's heart felt like bursting; a week ago, she couldn't have imagined Frank ever apologizing to Becky about Ricky. *Please don't let me start crying again*, she thought.

It looked like Becky might have tears in her eyes too. "That's okay, Dad. I haven't handled this too well either. I shouldn't have run off like that. I want a fresh start too."

Becky was still exhausted and went to bed again not long after dinner. After the dishes were cleaned up, Frank came into the den and plopped down on the couch next to Catherine. "Becky's home," he said wonderingly. "I still can't believe it."

"That's what I've been saying all afternoon," agreed Catherine. "It doesn't seem real yet."

"I meant what I said. I want a fresh start. In more ways than one."

They sat quietly together for a while without speaking, each of them thinking their own thoughts. Then Catherine said, "Frank, I have an idea. After Ricky gets here, maybe this weekend, I want to have a little celebration dinner for them. What do you think?"

"Yes," said Frank without hesitation. "Let's do that. And can we invite Buddy? He needs a family right now."

"Sure," said Catherine, still amazed at the change in Frank. "Sure, I would love to invite Buddy."

* * *

BUDDY WAS IN HIS office staring out the window at the Philly skyline when Catherine called to invite him the next day. "Are you sure?" he asked. "I'm not sure Frank wants to . . . uh, I mean, does Frank know you're inviting me?" He realized as he was speaking that he wasn't sure exactly how much Catherine knew about recent events so he decided to play it safe.

"Yes, it was his idea," replied Catherine. "Are you free on Saturday at six?"

"Of course, that sounds great," said Buddy. "I have no travel plans, so I'll definitely be there. Thank you so much." As he hung up, he marveled to himself, *Wow, Frank's idea. I guess he really was serious about a fresh start.*

On Saturday, Buddy arrived punctually at six. He wandered out onto the deck, where Frank was busy grilling steaks. "Hi, Buddy," said Frank. "Don't distract me—this is the critical moment. Timing is everything with steak." Frank was obsessive about getting his steaks done perfectly. He had invested in a sophisticated set of high-end tools, thermometers, and other mysterious devices that had allowed him to approach perfection, but he was never completely satisfied, always striving for that last ineffable frontier known only to him. For normal steak-eating mortals, Frank had achieved perfection long ago. Buddy knew better than to try to talk to Frank when he was in his steak zone, so he quietly retreated back into the kitchen.

Catherine and Becky were busy with last minute preparations in the kitchen and dining room. The dining room was rarely used, but a night like tonight called for the best of everything, including Catherine's china place settings handed down from her great-grandmother. Buddy finally found Ricky in the den. "Hi, I'm Buddy," he said, sticking out his hand.

"Pleased to meet you," said Ricky, looking up from his smartphone and shifting it to his other hand so he could shake Buddy's. "I'm Rachiim. Ricky to friends. Becky's mentioned your name a few times. How do you know Catherine and Frank?"

"We go pretty far back," replied Buddy. "Frank and I were roommates in college. As a matter of fact, I consider myself responsible for them meeting—it's a long story. How about you? How did you meet Becky?"

"My story is actually not very long, although maybe not what you might expect. We met at Ithaca College, but only a week before graduation. It was some kind of party for graduating seniors—I wasn't even supposed to be there because it was for a different department, but I had snuck in to get some free wine and cheese. I met Becky at the cheese table and somehow we started talking. We ended up talking for like three hours, walking all over the campus, recalling memorable experiences that happened in different places. You know, that's the room I failed my econ final in, that kind of thing. Then, when Becky came back here after graduation, she was amazed to find out that I was living in the next town over. I didn't tell her right away that I was supposed to go back home to Pittsburgh, but because of that night we talked, I finagled a place to stay from this other guy at Ithaca I barely knew—but he lived in Jersey, and that's all I cared about. I told my parents that I had a good lead on a future opportunity. They thought I meant a job." Ricky smiled.

"That's incredible! You mean you followed her to New Jersey based on talking to her once, a week before graduation? Talk about love at first sight!" Buddy was impressed.

"Yeah, well, it's true, there was something about her. It was a gamble, but I was trying to take seriously all those older, wiser people who are always saying *carpe diem*, but it seems like they never actually got around to *carpe dieming* themselves. Maybe that's why they're always telling us to do it. So I figured, what the hell. And, yeah, there was something special about her. I got that one right, that's for sure. She's pretty special." Ricky seemed lost in thought, a dreamy look in his eyes, his smartphone temporarily abandoned in his hand.

Buddy cleared his throat. "Ricky, do you mind if I ask you something? It's about your name. I've been thinking a lot about nicknames lately. 'Buddy' is a nickname, as you must have guessed. My real name is Rudolph, Rudolph Kowalski. I can't even remember how I got the nickname Buddy—sometime in junior high I think—but it's stuck with me my whole life. What about you? Why do you use the nickname Ricky?"

Ricky paused before answering and looked at Buddy. "Do you want the honest answer, Mr. Kowalski? I learned the hard way that white people won't hire someone named Rachiim. That's what the real world is like, and that's why I came up with Ricky. I actually don't like it much as a name, but it seems to help get me in the door."

Buddy was taken aback and started to say something, but at that moment, Becky appeared in the door. "Dinner's ready. Gotta come immediately or the steak will lose its extremely perfect perfection. Every second counts." Becky appeared to be rolling her eyes; she had been through the steak drill a few times.

They trooped into the dining room and took their places around the table as directed by Catherine. Then Frank came swooping in carrying a huge platter, muttering curses under his breath, trailing an amazing aroma of grilled meat. Each plate received a massive slab of steaming steak, dripping with mouth-watering juices. Giant baked potatoes with all the trimmings, a green salad, and slices of fresh French bread completed the simple feast. "Dig in, everyone!" Catherine announced.

"Sorry," said Frank, his face sweating and his hair matted and pointing in every direction like a mad scientist. "The steak is terrible. I don't know what happened. I couldn't get the temperature right. If you can't eat it, just put it back on the platter. We have some hot dogs in the freezer I can get out and throw on the grill."

"Dad," said Becky, this time definitely rolling her eyes. "Can you please be quiet and let us enjoy these amazing steaks, that I am willing to bet will make our guests think they have just died and gone to heaven?"

Everyone laughed. And, as usual, Becky was right and the steaks were exquisitely done. Nothing could be heard for a few minutes other than the clink of steak knives and wine glasses. When they had taken the edge off their hunger, Catherine turned to Ricky. "Ricky, congratulations on your new job. Becky says you blew your competitors out of the water. Can you tell us about the job and what you'll be doing?"

Ricky put down his fork. "The company provides software tools and consulting to protect companies from hacking and all kinds of viruses and attacks on their networks—basically, network security. They've developed some really innovative approaches. The recent attacks on big companies that you might have seen in the news are making everyone realize how big a problem this is. Our company happened to be in the right place at exactly the right time. They've been growing like crazy. That's actually a huge challenge I tried to help them see—how to scale up and manage the growth, without getting stretched too thin and then not being able to deliver." Ricky paused to take another bite.

"Is that how Philadelphia fits into the picture?" asked Frank.

"Exactly," said Ricky, trying to swallow. "We have to have offices on the East Coast, probably more places than just Philadelphia. But I was able to sell them on the benefits of Philly—lots of universities like Penn and Drexel that are churning out graduates with the right kinds of skills, great location, reasonable cost of living. Rents are cheap in Philly compared to other big cities. Lots of good office space too. And Philly has cheese steaks." Ricky smiled. "Although, after tonight, I'm not sure they deserve to use the term *steak*."

"Do you have enough experience to run an office?" asked Buddy.

Ricky looked embarrassed. "I think Becky has been exaggerating a little. I'm not running anything—not yet at least. There's a more experienced colleague coming with me who has been with the company for a while, and they'll be hiring more people locally. I think they mainly think I'm good at selling things—and explaining concepts that can be a little technical at times."

Becky was beaming with pride next to Ricky. Buddy turned to her and asked, "What about you, Becky? I seem to remember hearing that you were interested in grad school out in the Bay Area somewhere."

"Well, like Ricky said, there are lots of good universities in Philly too. I'd love to go to Penn, maybe in something like linguistics. So I'll be checking that out, although it's already too late for this fall. I'll probably look for a part-time or temporary job in the short run. Maybe I can even find something at Penn; my former advisor at Ithaca knows some of the professors and said she could introduce me."

There was a contented lull in the conversation. After a moment, Frank cleared his throat and said, "I would like to make a toast." He paused while wine glasses were re-filled. "To Ricky—may he prosper in his new position and find his work enjoyable and challenging." Everyone clinked their glasses. "And to Becky—may she find her true calling and find success in whatever she does." Glasses clinked again. "And to both of them—may they find great joy as they begin this adventure—together." Frank paused slightly before the word *together* and gave it a touch of emphasis. As the glasses clinked yet again, Buddy saw Catherine catch Frank's eye and smile happily.

Then Buddy cleared his throat too and said, "Now it's my turn." The others turned their heads in surprise. "First, let me echo the toasts that Frank has just made by saying three cheers for the amazing power of wine and cheese tables, not to mention *carpe diem*." Frank and Catherine looked puzzled, but Ricky looked at Becky and laughed.

"In all seriousness," Buddy continued, "I have some-thing to say. I would like to make a toast to my best friend, Frank. I don't mind saying that my life has kind of fallen apart in the last week or two. Frank already knows this, but I don't think Catherine does. Bunny and I are getting a divorce. And it's mostly my fault, I'm sorry to say." Catherine raised her eyebrows in surprise.

Buddy looked down, but then gathered his courage. "There've been some other things that Frank has every right to be pissed about, including a debt that I couldn't pay. This is not easy to say, but my finances are not in great shape at the moment." Buddy stopped and looked at Frank. "But for reasons I will never fully understand, Frank has stuck with me. Without even telling me, he stepped in and took care of my debt. He totally didn't have to do it, and it blew me away." Buddy raised his glass and looked at Frank. "And so, here's to Frank—thank you for saving my life." He stopped, and felt himself starting to choke up. The others raised their glasses.

Frank looked at Buddy and then down at his plate. Buddy suspected he might be choking up too. Buddy wasn't sure what to say, and was relieved when Catherine broke the awkward silence. "Buddy, we're so sorry about Bunny. That must be so hard." She paused. "I guess it's my turn now. I have one more toast to make: to our beloved Fred—may you rest in peace. Thank you for all the joy you brought us." She glanced at Frank as she raised her glass; now Buddy knew for sure Frank was choking up.

"Thanks, Catherine," Frank managed to get out. "I miss him a lot." Becky looked like she had tears in her eyes too.

Another awkward pause ensued. This time Ricky, who had put his arm around Becky, took a turn breaking the silence. "I guess lots of changes for all of us. Me too."

"Yeah," said Buddy, regaining his composure, "and something else I haven't told you guys yet. Bunny and I have to sell the house—the lawyers said that was the easiest way to split up the asset. I'm glad. That house was way too big for us; somehow, the kids we imagined never happened. That huge yard is a pain in the butt. I'm ready for a fresh start. Maybe I'll move into Center City, walk to work for a change instead of always fighting the traffic across the bridge. Although, I'm not even sure I want to stay in my job. I've been there a long time, and honestly, it's not my passion anymore. Maybe I'll really start over—but don't worry, I'm not moving to Texas or anything crazy like that."

"What a concept," interjected Frank. "Being passionate about your job . . . I can't really remember that stage of my life. Have I told all of you about Rupert's latest?"

"No," said Buddy, "but if it's Rupert, it's got to be bad. What's he been doing? Did he move you into an even smaller office? Board up your tiny little window to save electricity? Reduce the number of bathroom breaks you're allowed?"

"Much worse," replied Frank. "He's fudging the numbers in his monthly reports. I discovered it a week or two ago. I went back and checked as many months as I could, back to last year. It looks like he started by just rounding up a number here or there, nothing too obvious. But he's steadily been getting bolder. He always tweaks the numbers just enough to make sure he's meeting the monthly goals, or comes close; it's still pretty subtle unless you really know the numbers—like I do."

"What? He could get fired for that, couldn't he?" asked Becky.

"I don't think people like Rupert get fired. He's too cozy with all the top brass," answered Frank.

"What are you going to do about it?" asked Buddy.

Frank looked startled. "*Do* about it? Seriously? Nothing. At most, put something in the file to cover my rear end. Reporting him would be a waste of time. I'm not kidding. I've been at this company long enough to know how things work."

"It seems to me," said Buddy, stroking his chin, "that some kind of poetic justice would be appropriate in a situation like this. And, of course, in the world of poetic justice, the nature of the punishment always fits the nature of the crime."

"Buddy, what are you talking about?" demanded Frank, starting to look seriously alarmed.

"Well, he's obviously doing this to make himself look good in front of his pals. Poetic justice would therefore seek a mechanism for the opposite result."

"You know," said Ricky thoughtfully, "There are people who have certain skills that can be useful in a situation like this. Sometimes, there's a need to hide the traces of certain digital activities . . . if you know what I mean . . . to make sure the agent of poetic justice remains undetected."

Buddy nodded gravely. "Yes, I can see how it would certainly be valuable to have people with those skills on your team. Gentlemen, may I suggest we adjourn to the deck for an after-dinner drink?" He stood up, grabbing his glass and the half-full wine bottle. Ricky and Frank followed him, Frank looking nervously back and forth between the other two.

As they walked through the kitchen, Buddy heard Becky say, "Mom, do you think they're really going to do something to Rupert?" And he heard Catherine laugh as she answered, "With Buddy, anything is possible."

Buddy smiled as he closed the door to the deck behind him.

SEVENTEEN

Frank's eyes burned. He had been in his office staring at his computer screen for what seemed like days—in fact, it had been over two hours since he had taken a break. The go/no-go moment for Operation Poetic Justice was rapidly approaching. The monthly Executive Council meeting was at three o'clock, which meant everything had to be in place by, ideally, quarter of three at the latest. Ricky had said, to be safe, he needed at least thirty minutes for his part, and adding to that the time Frank would need, they had agreed that two o'clock was the cutoff point. "Relax," Buddy had kept telling him. "If it doesn't happen, it doesn't happen. We'll just do it next month. No sweat."

But Frank knew in his heart of hearts that he would lose his nerve if he had to wait another month. As it was, the conspirators had had to work quickly; the monthly Executive Council meetings always took place on the first Friday of the month, which had given them only six days to work out the details of their plan. In fact, Frank had initially argued for waiting a month, but Buddy had persuaded him there was no downside to trying this month, since they could always abort the plan at the last minute without anyone being the wiser—and, Frank suspected,

Buddy had probably guessed Frank's courage would slowly erode if he had to wait that long. Plus, patience had never been Buddy's strong suit.

So here he was, sitting at his desk the Friday after the celebration dinner, staring at a network folder on his screen, waiting for Rupert to copy his PowerPoint presentation into the *meetings* network folder. The conference room computers did not have access to department-level network folders for security reasons, so it was company practice to copy any files needed for a meeting into a company-wide folder prior to the meeting (the IT department had long since banned removable flash drives after they had caused several virus infestations).

The problem was that there was no way of knowing exactly when Rupert would upload his file. To get around this, Ricky had offered to hack directly into Rupert's private folder, but Frank had vetoed that—there were some lines he was unwilling to cross. Besides, they didn't know for sure when Rupert would finish preparing his presentation. Buddy had suggested recruiting Denise to help, but Frank had vetoed that too. He was adamant about not getting Denise into any trouble.

Knowing how Rupert always wanted everything done far in advance of deadlines, Frank had not actually thought this would be a problem at all; Rupert would probably finish his presentation the day before and copy it into the *meetings* folder first thing Friday morning—it was not like him to procrastinate, especially for something important like the Executive Council. For sure, he would do it by noon on the day of the meeting, or by one o'clock at the absolute latest.

Yet now it was 1:57 p.m., and Frank was still staring at an empty *meetings* folder. Something unexpected must have happened. Had Rupert's report been bumped from the agenda for some reason? Could he have decided not to prepare a PowerPoint? *Or been* told *not to*, thought Frank. *They're probably as boring as hell.*

"Come on Rupert, you can do this, you can do this, don't let me down," he kept muttering to himself. His computer clock ticked over to two o'clock—the go/no-go deadline. He'd wait five more minutes; that should still be fine, he decided. The minutes ticked slowly by: 2:05 p.m. "I guess that's it," Frank said to himself. "Better let Ricky know it's a no-go. As usual, Rupert, you screwed me."

At that moment, his phone rang. Frank snatched up the receiver, not sure what he was expecting, but it was just an internal call from someone in sales asking for another copy of a report that Frank had already sent him twice. By the time Frank finally got rid of him, it was already 2:18 p.m. Frank pulled his cell phone out of his pocket to text Ricky, glancing at the meetings folder as he did so. He froze. There it was. Rupert's PowerPoint file was there. Frank rubbed his eyes and checked again. Yes, there was no question: a PowerPoint with today's date and the title "Exec Sales Report" was sitting in the folder. *But now what do I do?* Frank cursed Rupert under his breath. Was there still time? He frantically texted Ricky, "file just got hair, two late?" *Damn the stupid text correcting*, he swore. He started retyping the message but Ricky replied instantly: "Let's try." *At least he understood me*, thought Frank, putting down his phone, his mouth dry and his hands shaking from a sudden adrenaline rush.

Slow down, don't panic, he told himself, carefully copying Rupert's PowerPoint into his own private folder and double-clicking on the file to open it. A message popped up on the screen: "Enter password to open file." "Shit!" said Frank out loud. It had never occurred to any of them that Rupert might password-protect his file. *I'm an idiot*, thought Frank. *I should have known—after all, this is Rupert we're dealing with. I guess we're definitely screwed now.* Disappointed, but slightly relieved at the same time, he picked up his phone and texted Ricky: "urgh we're screwed file pw protected." But Ricky texted back right away: "no prob send me file plus yr new slides." *Seriously?* thought Frank. *Okay, Ricky, if you say so; you're the hacker genius.*

The plan had been for Frank to insert the doctored slides into the presentation, and then send the file to Ricky to add the macros and magically erase all traces of their work. Safely sending the file had been another problem they had had to solve. During their brainstorming session the previous weekend, Frank had assumed he would just email him the file, but Ricky had pointed out that company email was not private, and the first thing a competent IT tech would do would be to check the emails of anyone they suspected. "Yikes," Frank had gulped, "I didn't think of that. I'm definitely going to be a suspect— Rupert just complained to HR about me a couple of weeks ago, and I'm the one he gets his numbers from. Do we have to worry about sending texts too?"

"No, texts are fine," Ricky had reassured him, "as long as it's not a company cell phone—although WhatsApp would be safer. You need to get a smartphone one of these days, Mr. O'Donnell." He went on, "Fortunately, there's an easy solution for safely transferring files." The following Monday, he had called Frank at his office and walked him through setting up a separate encrypted file service through the browser on his work computer, assuring him, "I'll remove this when we're done, and no one will ever detect it—I guarantee it." Ricky had insisted that Frank practice sending and retrieving files several times to make sure there were no hiccups.

Frank was glad they had practiced; even though his hands were still shaking, he was able to quickly upload the files to Ricky. With Rupert's PowerPoint password-protected, Ricky would have to do everything by himself. Would he be able to crack the password, insert the doctored slides, and do the rest of his magic all before quarter of three? It was 2:26 p.m. now.

"This is impossible," groaned Frank.

He couldn't sit still any longer. Gripping his phone in one hand, he started pacing in clockwise circles around his tiny office. Could Ricky really get around a password-protected file? In less than twenty minutes? He tried to comfort himself with Buddy's refrain: *don't sweat, if it doesn't happen it doesn't happen.* Maybe he should just text Ricky to call the whole thing off; maybe this whole idea was crazy. Why had he listened to Buddy? It had seemed so simple when they were sitting on the deck with a bottle of wine. *Note to self: don't plan career-threatening capers after three glasses of wine, especially if someone named Buddy is anywhere nearby.* What if the whole thing backfired and Rupert ended up getting him fired? He looked at his watch for the hundredth time: 2:41 p.m. There was no way. Not even Ricky could pull this off. He tried pacing counterclockwise around his office. On the fifth circuit, his phone buzzed in his hand—the message said, "we're good to go." He looked at this watch: quarter of three on the nose. Incredible.

Frank felt another surge of adrenaline and leaped into his chair. He quickly logged into the file transfer website and carefully followed the steps to download the updated file from Ricky. In a few seconds, there it was: a PowerPoint file sitting innocently in his folder. Frank clicked on the file and right-clicked his mouse to copy it into the *meetings* folder. A message popped up: "The destination already has a file with this name. Replace file?" He stopped and stared at his screen. This was it. He could still change his mind . . . but as soon as he clicked *OK*, there was no going back. He thought about Rupert and the fudged numbers. He thought about poetic justice. He thought about all the years he had dutifully done whatever was asked of him. He looked out the tiny window at the barren parking lot.

He remembered the feeling of stepping into the dark on the railroad bridge and the brilliant stars wheeling overhead.

Frank clicked *OK*.

There was no time to lose. Buddy had called him the night before in a slight panic: it had suddenly occurred to Buddy that Rupert might get to the conference room a few minutes early to have a final check that his presentation was in order. To forestall that possibility, Buddy had insisted that Frank come up with a contingency plan to stall Rupert on his way to the meeting to make sure Rupert got there right when the meeting started, or, even better, a few minutes late. At first, Frank had drawn a blank on what excuse he could use to be in that part of the building. Just loitering by himself in an empty hallway had seemed far too conspicuous. Buddy had suggested that he pretend to tie his shoe. Frank had told him that was ridiculous: how long would he be able to keep that up? What if someone went down the hallway, saw him tying his shoe, and then the same person came back five minutes later and he was still in the same position tying his shoe? They might call security.

But then he had remembered there was a supply room that opened onto the main hallway not far from the executive conference room. It was not the main supply room that he usually went to—it was smaller, intended mainly for restocking the conference rooms and guest offices in that part of the building. But Rupert wouldn't know that, and Frank had figured he could easily come up with an excuse for being there if someone asked.

Frank exited his office and walked toward the executive conference room as quickly as he could without drawing attention to himself. "Just going to get some paper clips," he kept repeating to himself. First, he swung by the door of the conference room. Good: it was still dark and empty. On an impulse, he slipped into the room, located the projector remote, clicked the power button to turn on the projector, and then hid the remote at the back of a drawer in a cabinet on the opposite side of the room. Before leaving, he opened the door a crack to make sure the coast was clear.

The supply room, just a few steps down the hall, was empty too. He picked up a box of paper clips and then pretended to analyze the merits of two different brands of mechanical pencils, positioning himself so he could see out the small window in the door. It wasn't an ideal vantage point, as the angle did not allow him to see very far down the hallway, but it would have to do. It might just have been the adrenaline surge, but Frank's nervousness had vanished. He was starting to enjoy himself. He suddenly remembered Maxwell Smart from *Get Smart* and could imagine the exact tone of his voice: "Of course, Agent Ninety-nine, the old hide-in-the-supply-closet trick . . ." *Careful*, he told himself, *this is not a good time to start laughing.* At first, he had hoped Rupert wouldn't show up early and he could just go back to his desk—now he realized he would be disappointed if the opportunity passed him by.

Frank looked at his watch: 2:50 p.m. Ten minutes to go. No one had arrived for the meeting yet—he guessed that there would be eight to ten of the company's senior executives in attendance. He heard footsteps and saw someone come around the corner of the hallway—his pulse quickened, but it was just Denise. She walked by without seeing Frank lurking in the supply room and went into the conference room. *Ah, she must be there to take notes,* thought Frank. Just like Rupert to make sure *his* assistant was the notetaker, always taking any opportunity to suck up to his superiors. At that moment, he heard more footsteps.

This time it was Rupert. He was early, just as they had feared.

He was walking rapidly with a bundle of folders under his arm. Frank had to act quickly to open the door before he passed by. In his rush, he didn't have time to put down the mechanical pencils. Awkwardly holding one in each hand, he jumped out from the door and called out, "Rupert! Perfect timing—I was just thinking of stopping by your office."

Rupert appeared startled and then looked oddly at the pencils in Frank's hands. "Frank. What can I do for you? I'm in a bit of a rush." He glanced pointedly at his watch.

"Oh, that's right, today's the first Friday of the month. You must be on your way to the Executive Council meeting." Frank nodded knowingly, as if it had just occurred to him that it was Friday. "Big agenda today?"

"The usual. What can I do for you, Frank?" There was a note of impatience in Rupert's voice.

"That's excellent, excellent. It must be so interesting to sit in on those meetings. I've always wanted to be a fly on the wall." Frank gazed at Rupert with admiring eyes, thinking to himself, *especially today, Rupert old pal, especially today*. "Don't worry, I'll only take a minute of your time. I certainly don't want to make you late for such an important meeting. I just wanted to tell you that I think I have some good news. Yes indeed. I might have solved that little problem we were talking about the last time we met."

"What little problem is that, Frank?"

"I'm sure you remember: the extra column on the quarterly report. We were having a hard time fitting it in without making the font too small. You know the guidelines—can't go below ten points on any reports for senior management. Quite a dilemma, actually." Frank shook his head despairingly.

"Uh, Frank, I'm not sure I have time for this now . . ."

Frank ignored the interruption. "Well, I think I may have the solution. An ingenious idea, if I do say so myself. After several hours of research, I've discovered a *different* font which is slightly narrower, so that even if we keep it at ten points, it takes less space horizontally, if you know what I mean." Frank knew Rupert well enough to guess that he would take the bait. He was right.

"Frank, we've been over this many times. The guidelines only allow certain fonts, and we've already tried them all. You can't simply go out and find another font that has not been approved. If you want to use this new font, it will have to go through the Editorial Standards Committee, which only meets once a quarter—and they haven't approved any new fonts for years. I really don't think . . ."

Frank cut him off. "Ah, but that's the ingenious part. This particular font I've discovered, after several hours of work I might add, is *extremely* similar to Times New Roman. In fact, it is so similar to Times New Roman that I defy anyone to tell the difference without a magnifying glass. Now, what was the name of that font? I'm blanking on it at the moment . . . I believe it starts with a *B*, but I could be thinking of Bahnschrift, or was it Leelawadee . . ." Frank scratched his chin and looked up at the ceiling, pretending to be lost in thought.

Rupert seemed to have temporarily forgotten about the meeting, even though several other meeting participants had passed them on the way to the conference room. "No, Frank, we simply cannot do that. It does not matter if it's similar or not. Is it a different font? Then we can't use it. It's as simple as that. There's a reason for the guidelines: can you imagine what would happen if everyone was allowed to pick any font they wanted? It would be chaos. I'm afraid this solution of yours is really a nonstarter, and to be honest, I have to question whether it was worth the hours of time you put into your so-called research. In the future, please consult with me before getting distracted down these rabbit trails that really serve no purpose. No, we will simply have to go back to the report and see if there are any other options, perhaps by exploring acceptable abbreviations in the text columns . . ." He suddenly stopped and looked at his watch again. "Darn it, now I'm going to be late . . . Frank, we will discuss this another time." Rupert abruptly strode away, muttering under his breath.

Mission accomplished, thought Frank happily. *Enjoy your meeting, Rupert: may it be the most memorable of your life.* One final step remained. He returned to his office and texted Ricky when he was back in front of his computer: "operation poetic justice has launched." Ricky was evidently waiting to hear; "congrats stand by for remote login," he texted back. A few seconds later a window popped up on Frank's screen: "Remote access requested. Click *OK* to accept." Frank clicked *OK* and watched his cursor move around the screen like magic as Ricky took remote control, clicking here and there, opening and closing windows, and typing occasional commands. Ricky had explained that he needed to do this to ensure there was no trace of Frank having accessed Rupert's file. In less than three minutes, his screen was back to normal and Ricky had signed out. A few seconds later another text appeared on Frank's phone: "everything is clean, good luck, fingers crossed." Frank texted back a smiley face emoticon. Apparently, Ricky was in touch with Becky, because a text from her appeared next: "let (poetic) justice roll down . . . go DAD!" Frank smiled.

He had decided to leave work early; it would be just as well not to be around if Rupert came looking for him. Besides, there was no way he was going to get any work done. He started gathering papers to fill his briefcase as usual, but the sight of the overstuffed manila folders spilling out pages of tightly-packed numbers and charts suddenly filled him with loathing. He abruptly slammed the briefcase shut and jammed it under his desk out of sight. Without looking back, he closed his office door behind him and exited into the parking lot through the back door of the building. As he climbed into his car, he noticed a missed call from Buddy. He put his phone into speaker mode and pushed the call-back button. Keeping his eyes on the road, he heard Buddy pick up.

"Hey, Frank, how'd it go? Is Rupert toast?"

"It was touch and go—our friend didn't upload his file until like two twenty, and then I hit a huge roadblock we should have thought of: Rupert had password-protected the file."

"Damn. He password-protected it? I guess that means you had to abort the mission?"

"That's what I thought, but Ricky was incredible. He somehow bypassed the password. Buddy, it's scary how much he knows about this stuff. It's a good thing he's on our team."

"Wow, that's amazing. So what happened?"

"You were right—Rupert tried to go to the room early. But let's just say he ran into a little distraction on the way. The meeting is in progress now—he should be enjoying our little surprise any minute, maybe even as we speak."

"Man, I wish I had found a way to video that meeting. If we'd had another week, I would have figured something out. We're missing all the fun." Frank couldn't tell if Buddy was joking or not. Probably not.

"Yeah, I'm not going to know anything until Monday. Unless Rupert figures out who did it and tries to blow up my house. I hope he doesn't know my address."

Buddy laughed. "Don't worry, old pal, he wouldn't have the guts. He'll never be able to prove anything."

"Seriously, Buddy. At the crucial moment, I almost chickened out. I honestly think I could get fired for this. I kept asking myself, is it really worth it?"

"Stop worrying, you're not going to get caught. So what made you go through with it?"

"I guess I decided I don't care if I get fired. I've been there for twenty-five years and I hate the place." Frank paused. "Wow, I think that's the first time I've ever said that out loud. Let me try that again: I really hate my job." He paused again to savor the moment. "Besides, I have to admit, taking Rupert down, if it works, or even if it doesn't, has been kind of fun. So I'm just going to go with the flow and let whatever happens happen. A wise old mentor of mine has been trying to teach me that for a long time."

"You must be talking about someone I don't know. I'm sure not old, and definitely not wise," Buddy laughed. "I have to run—unfortunately, I'm not around this weekend, so I'll give you a call Monday night to get the latest."

"Bye." Frank flipped his phone shut. He rolled down his window and drank in the warm spring air, feeling freer and more relaxed than he had in a very long time.

When he got home, Catherine was waiting at the door to greet him with a kiss. "Have you decided where you want to go for dinner?" she asked.

"Dinner?" said Frank. "Are we going on a date?"

Catherine laughed. "No wonder you fell for Buddy's prank. You don't even remember when it's your *real* birthday. Did you forget that tomorrow is your fiftieth birthday, and we're celebrating tonight—you, me, and the kids?"

Frank laughed sheepishly. "I guess I did kind of forget. After all, I already had a fantastic surprise party—was it only a month ago? Plus, I've been pretty distracted today with Operation Poetic Justice." He gave her a hug. "Notice anything different about me?"

Catherine took a step back and examined him carefully. "New glasses? Haircut? Possibly a few more hairs missing? Nope, everything looks the same to me."

Frank held up both hands. "No briefcase!" He wrapped his arms around her again. "All the better to hug you with."

THE FOUR OF THEM spent a delightful evening together at Frank's favorite Mexican restaurant, mostly talking about Becky and Ricky's plans for the future: imagining where they might live, what school Becky might end up at, where Ricky's job would take him. Catherine was in her element, and Frank enjoyed watching her out of the corner of his eye, her face animated and glowing with joy. Other than a quick report on the day's events, with effusive praise from Frank for Ricky's heroic contribution, they didn't talk about Frank's job or his future. He preferred it that way; he had decided to let Monday worry about itself. After all, it was his birthday.

EIGHTEEN

Although he had succeeded in putting the office out of his mind over the weekend, Frank could feel his stomach muscles tightening with tension when he got to his desk on Monday morning. He opened his inbox, but there was nothing of any significance. He tried to focus on the routine tasks that needed to be completed the first week of the month: checking data submitted by regional offices, verifying bank statements, reviewing reports from junior colleagues. One of the reports had an obvious mistake. Frank groaned, but was able to quickly track it down to a formula that had accidentally been deleted in one of the spreadsheets.

An alert popped up that there was new email. He immediately tabbed over to his inbox, but it was just a question from another office about a bank transfer that hadn't arrived yet; the same person asked the same question every month. *This is my life*, thought Frank. *It's like strip malls*, he mused: if you were blindfolded and dropped into a strip mall on a highway in any US city you would see exactly the same stores and would have a hard time knowing which state you were in. His job was the same: you could transport him in a time machine to the first week of any month over the past twenty-five years and he wouldn't be able to tell what year it was—unless he could see his hairline in the reflection on his computer screen.

It was no good—Frank couldn't focus. *What am I waiting for?* he asked himself. For Rupert to come pounding on his door? For HR to summon him? For the FBI to show up with handcuffs? He needed to find out what had happened on Friday, not just sit there waiting for the sky to fall. What he really wanted to do was talk to Denise; she had been in the meeting. But he was truly afraid of getting her in trouble. If he ended up being a suspect, and she was seen talking to him—plus the fact that she used to be his assistant—could that somehow link her to him? For that matter, Denise might already suspect that he was somehow behind it. The frustrating thing was that he didn't even know if anything had happened on Friday. Maybe Rupert had been quick on his feet and managed to sidestep the whole thing. He was pretty good at weaseling out of tight spots.

Finally, he couldn't stand it anymore. He picked up the phone and dialed Denise's extension. "Uh, hi, Denise, I was wondering if Rupert was around this morning. I have something to drop off for him." Frank was sure he could come up with something to give Rupert that would make this hardly even a white lie. Maybe a sample of the new font.

"Hi, Frank. His light is on, but he's not in his office, so he must have been in early, before I got here. There's nothing on his calendar, so I really don't know where he is. You can give it to me if you want."

"Great, I'll stop by in a few minutes . . . although, actually, I'm expecting an important phone call . . . is there any chance you could swing by my office sometime this morning? If not, that's fine, I can give it to you later." *Okay, that's getting closer to a lie,* Frank admitted to himself, *but it's definitely a white one.* Denise had a cubicle outside

Rupert's office, and there was no way Frank wanted to talk to her in such an exposed location.

"Sure," replied Denise. "I can come right now—I'm not really doing anything anyway."

Frank hung up and quickly found the report he had referred to in his hallway chat with Rupert on Friday. It was true that the layout of one page of the report had been the main agenda item of a meeting that had lasted over an hour. He randomly picked another font that was similar to Times New Roman, adjusted the size slightly so the column would fit, and printed it out. On the top he scrawled with a red pen, "Sample report layout, let's discuss—Frank." *So much for hours of research*, he thought wryly.

A moment later, Denise tapped on his door. She had been one of Frank's favorite assistants; an older woman with many years of experience, she was smart, capable, and always quick to help with whatever needed doing. She was famous for her homemade cupcakes, which reliably appeared in the break room whenever there was a reason to celebrate. Frank was glad to see her warm smile and friendly face as she came through the door. Ironically, the positive performance reviews he had given her had probably been the main reason Rupert had snatched her away at the beginning of the year. HR had yet to hire a replacement. During tax season they had brought in a temp, but she was almost more trouble than she was worth.

"Great to see you, Denise. Thanks for coming by." Frank handed her the printout.

"Sure thing, glad to help. It's always nice to revisit my old stomping grounds."

She was about to turn and leave when Frank said, "Actually, would you mind closing the door? There's something else I wanted to ask you." Denise pulled the door shut and looked at him expectantly. "I . . . uh . . . I heard some . . . uh . . . rumors about the Executive Council meeting on Friday . . . were you there?" he asked cautiously.

Denise moved some books out of the way on the seat of the lone chair in the cramped office and perched on the edge of it. "Oh, my goodness, yes, I was there. The strangest thing happened—I can't even begin to explain it."

"What happened?" asked Frank, feeling butterflies in his stomach.

"It was Rupert's presentation. First, he got there a few minutes late, looking kind of flustered—that's unusual in and of itself. Then, when it was his turn to present, he gives out his handouts, like he always does—he likes to give everyone a printout of his slides, although he's the only one who ever does that—and then he brings up his PowerPoint on the screen. The first few slides are fine—the normal stuff listing some of the highlights of the month. Then he gets to the slide where he always shows a graph with the projected sales and actual sales, you know two lines with the months across the bottom . . ."

Frank nodded, "Yes, I know what you mean." The butterflies were really going to town now.

Denise continued, "So, he says how everything's going great with sales, and he's about to go on when someone asks—I think it was Mr. Ketchum, although it might have been President Freiburger—anyway, someone asks, 'What's that third line, the one zigzagging down below the other two?' Rupert is looking at his printout, not the slide, and he says, 'What line? I'm not sure what you're referring to.' And Mr. Ketchum—yes, I'm pretty sure it was him—goes 'That one, right there,' pointing at the screen. Now Rupert turns and looks at the screen and he sees it too. You can tell he's really surprised. He stares at it, and then he quickly clicks to go to the next slide, but nothing happens."

Frank interrupted, "You mean like the computer was frozen?"

"No, not exactly frozen; it was really weird, because each time he clicked, the bottom line on the graph got brighter and brighter and the legend on the bottom of the slide got bigger. So Mr. Ketchum asks, 'What exactly is the difference between *Actual Actual* and *Wishful Actual?* Which are the real numbers? What are you trying to show here? I hope it's not those *Actual Actual* numbers, because they don't look so good.' Mr. Ketchum kind of laughs, but now everyone is staring at the screen and trying to figure it out. Rupert's face is getting red, and now he's obviously flustered. He keeps clicking and clicking but it just makes it worse. Finally, he gets smart and tries to just close the whole presentation, but then the computer *does* freeze up and he can't even close PowerPoint—the graph is just stuck there on the screen with everyone staring at it, the lower sales line still gradually growing brighter and kind of pulsing, like it's been zapped with lightning—kind of cool looking, actually.

So at this point, Rupert frantically tries to turn off the projector, but you need the remote to do that because the projector is on the ceiling, and he can't find it anywhere— Murphy's law, right? I actually found it later, way at the back of a drawer—who knows how that happened. Everyone is staring at him now, and he says 'There must be some kind of glitch, I don't know what's going on. Someone has obviously tampered with my presentation.' Then there's this awful silence and Rupert finally says, 'I can assure you that we've been meeting our sales targets almost every month since I've been in this position.' Then he just sits down, without even finishing the rest of his report—which is very unusual for him. His face was bright red."

"Wow," said Frank. He was having a hard time keeping a serious and concerned look on his face. "I've never heard of anything like that happening before. How bizarre. What happened next? Did the meeting continue? Did Rupert just sit there?"

"Well, eventually I had to call IT to come and figure out how to reboot the computer. They seemed kind of fascinated by the glowing PowerPoint slide. Oh yeah, by that time it had started beeping too, and the beeping was getting louder. President Freiburger kept looking over at Rupert and clearing his throat—you know how he does that when something's bothering him—and then he finally moved on to the next item on the agenda once the beeping stopped. Everyone tried to keep going, but it was very uncomfortable. A few minutes later, Rupert made some kind of excuse about needing to make a phone call and left the room. He didn't come back. At the end of the meeting, I heard Mr. Ketchum asking Ms. Harris to look into what had happened. That's probably where Rupert is this morning—trying to figure out how his presentation got messed up." Denise looked thoughtfully at Frank. "I suppose they might come and ask you about it, since you would be able to confirm which numbers are correct, wouldn't you?"

"No one's talked to me yet," said Frank, "but yes, I would be able to confirm the numbers. So could you, for that matter—just check his numbers against the reports I send you every month."

Denise frowned. "If they want me to do something, I'm sure they'll ask. Probably better to just wait and see what happens at this point." She paused and then added politely, "Is there anything else you wanted to ask me about?"

"No, no, that's all, thanks a lot," replied Frank hurriedly. "I really appreciate your telling me—have a great rest of the day." Denise nodded her head and left. *Poetic justice*, he thought with satisfaction. He felt a momentary twinge of guilt, but it quickly faded. Rupert had made his own bed; he would have to sleep in it. What now, he wondered? No doubt Rupert is turning over every stone to get to the bottom of this—he probably had a terrible weekend. Frank's initial elation at the success of the prank was being replaced with a growing sense of dread: what had they unleashed? IT would definitely be under intense pressure to find out what had happened— Rupert would make sure of that.

The rest of the morning crept by. Frank was still not able to focus and kept checking his inbox. He decided to go out for a bite to eat just to get a break from the office—unusual for him, since he usually brought a sandwich from home and ate at his desk. When he got back, the first thing he did was check his inbox again, and there it was at last: a new message from Sandra Harris, the HR director. Just like the last time, the message was short and to the point: "Frank, please stop by my office as soon as possible. Sandra."

Frank's stomach muscles tensed up again. He felt slightly nauseous. *That bacon cheeseburger was a mistake,* he thought. *Oh well, whatever happens happens.* He stood up and began the long walk to Sandra's office. *Whatever happens happens, whatever happens happens,* he kept repeating to himself as he walked.

He had a sense of déjà vu as he approached her office. Was it only a month since he had been here the last time? He tapped on the door and opened it. Facing him was the same expanse of mahogany gleaming in the fluorescent light, a single folder centered on the desk, the empty inbox in the corner. Sandra's face was as impassive as ever. "Hello, Frank. Please take a seat."

As soon as Frank had sat down, she began, "Frank, it goes without saying that what I am about to share with you today must remain confidential." Frank nodded. "Something rather unusual happened in the monthly Executive Council meeting that took place last Friday afternoon. When Rupert was making his usual monthly presentation, one of his PowerPoint slides became frozen on the screen. That in itself is not unusual; computers often freeze up, as you know. However, what was unusual was that the slide showed two different sets of sales figures, one set significantly lower than the other. Rupert says he did not make that slide, and he believes his presentation may have been tampered with. I'm inclined to agree with him, as he would have no reason to present both sets of figures." Sandra paused. Frank wasn't sure if he was supposed to say something, so he kept quiet. He hoped the tension on his face was not too obvious.

Sandra went on. "This morning, I asked a member of our internal audit team to review both sets of figures. Unfortunately, the figures in the lower set of numbers were the correct ones. It seems that Rupert has been inflating the numbers—not by a large amount, but to a sufficient degree that, over time, they presented a somewhat misleading account of our sales results. Apparently, he has been doing this consistently since sometime last year. As you can imagine, this reflects rather poorly on Rupert." Sandra paused briefly again before adding, "Over the weekend, I also asked our IT team to investigate the PowerPoint file that Rupert believes was tampered with." Frank's heart beat faster and he noticed that his hands were tightly gripping the arms of his chair.

"I believe our IT experts are reasonably skilled, although I do not know if they would be considered experts in the field of computer forensics. Nonetheless, they have applied their best efforts and so far, have been unable to detect any trace of anyone other than Rupert accessing the file. What they find particularly baffling is that Rupert had password-protected the file. They are not aware of any simple way to bypass such a password. Nor were they able to identify any evidence of external intrusion of our networks."

Sandra paused reflectively again before continuing. "Now, I can only assume that if anyone did want to tamper with Rupert's file, it would have to be someone on our staff. It is hard to imagine an outsider wanting to hack into our system for the sole purpose of making such a specific alteration to a single file, not to mention also having access to the accurate financial data that was presented on the slide. All of this leads me to the following conclusions: either we have someone on our staff with unusually sophisticated skills in computer hacking, which seems unlikely, or, as seems even more unlikely, Rupert himself created that slide for unknown reasons."

Sandra nodded meditatively as she seemingly reflected on these two unlikely and inexplicable scenarios. As he waited for her to continue, Frank silently applauded her excellent, if flawed, logic. He began to feel a glimmer of hope.

"You may be wondering why I called you here to tell you all this." Sandra looked at Frank and seemed to be waiting for a response.

"Uh . . . yes . . . I was kind of wondering about that," he said, hoping she wasn't expecting something more substantive.

"Let me go straight to the bottom line: about an hour ago, Rupert submitted a letter of resignation, a course of action that was strongly advised by President Freiburger. It seems that this recent incident prompted conversations with several other senior staff and, how shall I put it . . ." She paused and added delicately, ". . . a certain *pattern* of behavior began to emerge. Furthermore, I believe the matter of the PowerPoint can be looked at from a different perspective. One of my priorities as the new director of Human Resources has been to put in place a procedure for whistleblowers to report the kind of problems revealed by the PowerPoint, a policy gap I immediately observed upon my arrival. Unfortunately, I have not yet had time to implement such a policy. In light of that gap, I have advised President Freiburger that it might be best to treat the recent PowerPoint incident as a kind of anonymous whistleblower complaint. He has accepted my recommendation. Consequently, there will be no further attempt to investigate exactly how or why the PowerPoint was tampered with, if, in fact, it was tampered with." She narrowed her eyes and looked at Frank, again seeming to expect a response.

"Uh . . . that certainly seems reasonable," he responded cautiously, still nervous about the way Sandra kept looking at him, and hardly daring to believe that Rupert was gone.

"And now we come to the real bottom line," she continued. "I have consulted with other members of the senior executive team, including, of course, President Freiburger, and there is unanimous support for offering Rupert's position to you, effective immediately. Your track record with our company is impeccable and we believe you are far and away the best candidate to step into Rupert's shoes." She stopped and looked at Frank again. It was hard to detect, but he thought the ghost of a smile might have flitted across her face.

Frank was stunned. This was the last thing he had expected. After twenty-five years, they were finally offering him a real promotion! His mind spun. "Uh . . . wow . . . that's very generous . . . I don't know what to say . . ." he stammered.

"The details of the salary and benefit package are included with the offer letter in this envelope. I'm sure you will find them satisfactory." She removed a white envelope from the folder on her desk and slid it across the gleaming desk. He picked it up and stared at it, but did not open it. After twenty-five years, the promotion he had often dreamed of would be his, the promotion he knew he deserved, the job he knew he was capable of. He would probably even get Denise back as his assistant. The salary increase would be significant too. This was what he had been waiting for all these years.

He could feel Sandra's eyes boring into his skull. "Would you like to sleep on it?" she suggested. "Perhaps talk it over with your wife?"

Frank was not sure why he was hesitating. "Uh . . . yeah . . . maybe I should do that . . ." But as he stalled, he could feel something rising up inside him like water bubbling up from a hole in the ground after a pick strikes a buried pipeline. Distorted images of overflowing in-boxes, PowerPoint bullets, and meeting minutes in three-ring binders flashed through his mind. He remembered the faint shadow of starlight on a splintered railroad tie and the feeling of warm spring air blowing in his face through an open car window. He thought about stepping into Rupert's shoes. Spontaneously, hardly knowing what he was going to say, he began to speak.

"Ms. Harris, I'm deeply honored to be offered the position. I do agree that I am ready for it. In many ways, it's the obvious next step for me, something I've even imagined stepping into." Sandra was nodding her head, ever so slightly. "So there's a strange irony in what I am about to say. The truth is, I came here today planning to submit *my* resignation. You may not be aware of this, but next month will mark my twenty-fifth year with the company. I feel that I am at a point in my life that I need to move on to new horizons. My decision does not reflect at all on how the company has treated me, or on any of my colleagues here. It has much more to do with some personal changes going on in my life and with my family." He stopped.

Sandra's face was as inscrutable as ever. At length she said, "If I understand you correctly, you are saying that you wish to decline our offer and resign from the company. Is that correct?"

"Yes," said Frank, his heart pounding, but feeling strangely light at the same time. "Of course, I would give whatever notice is required, or appropriate, for the transition to my successor."

"I see," said Sandra. "In that case, may I have the envelope back?" Frank had forgotten he was still holding the white envelope, still unopened, and now slightly wrinkled.

"Oh, sure, of course." He handed it back, feeling foolish, and she carefully opened the folder, placed the letter inside it, and closed the folder again.

"Thank you, Frank. One of my staff will follow up with you about next steps. I wish you all the best."

Frank knew the meeting was over. He walked out, closing the door gently behind him.

What did I just do? he said to himself as he stumbled down the hallway in a daze. *What did I just do?*

NINETEEN

uddy had been stopping by Frank and Catherine's house once or twice a week ever since the celebration dinner, sometimes to join them for a meal, sometimes just to hang out. Today, he had left work early to try to beat the Friday afternoon traffic heading out of Philly, but by the time he pulled into their driveway it was already after five. He knew the side door was usually unlocked and, no longer feeling the need to knock, he opened the door and walked into the kitchen. There was no one there, and the rooms he could see also looked empty. "Anybody home?" he called out. He heard a muffled voice from the deck, and then through the glass door saw an arm waving above the back of a deck chair facing the other direction. Buddy grabbed three wine glasses in one hand from a cabinet in the kitchen and, using his elbow to slide the door open, went out onto the deck. It was a lovely, warm late afternoon, the temperature still hovering in the upper seventies.

"Hey Frank, it's me," he said to the back of the chair. "Where's everyone else?" Buddy was carrying a huge bottle of champagne in his other hand. He carefully set the glasses and champagne on the table.

Frank put down the *New York Times* crossword puzzle he was working on. "Catherine and Becky went out shopping for stuff for Becky and Ricky's new apartment. They should be back soon. Ricky must not be back from work yet. Hey, what's with the champagne? Are we going to toast my new status of being unemployed? I'm not sure Catherine's quite ready for that."

"How *did* Catherine take it?" he asked.

"She started to cry, of course—it seems like there've been a lot of tears around here lately," Frank replied. "But, in all seriousness, she wasn't crying because she was upset. She's seen how that job has been grinding me into the dirt over the last few years, and she seems thrilled that I quit, so I guess they were tears of joy. I was kind of surprised at her reaction, actually. So maybe she would join us in a toast after all." He added, "Becky, on the other hand, was like 'Duh . . . what took you so long?' with a full eyeball roll."

"The wisdom of youth," said Buddy. "Actually, this champagne is not for you, although maybe it is indirectly. It's for me."

"For you? For breaking the record of ordering the most pizzas in a row without missing a day?" Frank joked.

"Hey, give me a break—I eat a salad for lunch almost every day," replied Buddy with a wounded look. There was a loud pop as the champagne cork shot into the air and landed out in the grass. Buddy sloshed some champagne into two of the glasses and handed one to Frank. He lifted his glass. "A toast to me, for following the example of my wise old mentor and experiencing the joy and freedom of unemployment."

Frank had just started to take a sip but suddenly spluttered and almost choked. Buddy pounded him on the back until he stopped coughing. "Are you serious? You quit your job?" he said in a strangled-sounding voice, staring at his friend in shock.

"Yep," said Buddy. "Just walked into Carol's office this afternoon and said, 'I quit.' What an amazing feeling." He took another big swallow of champagne. "When I woke up on Tuesday morning, after you had called me Monday night and told me what you'd done, I said to myself, 'If Frank can do it, I can do it.' And there was no going back after that—I just had to wait until Carol was back in the office, which was today. I wanted to do it to her face." He lifted his glass again. "So, this champagne really is for you too. For both of us. To Frank, for inspiring me to do what I should have done five years ago." He took another swig of champagne.

"You could knock me over with a feather," said Frank. "I thought you loved your job."

"I used to," replied Buddy, sitting down. "But honestly, just like you, I think I've been there too long. I was just going through the motions, doing the same things over and over again. Maybe that's the curse of corporate jobs at these big companies. After a while, they just wear you down with all the stupid crap that goes on, and there's no more fun, no more challenge, no more passion. But even though you don't care anymore, you don't dare do anything about it because you're pulling in the big bucks." He paused. "Remember how I told you about Mouse? That had something to do with it too, I guess. Put things into perspective, or something. I know it doesn't make sense, but that was definitely part of it."

"Makes perfect sense to me," said Frank. "Congratulations. Welcome to my world—can I get you a crossword puzzle? Here, top up my glass."

Buddy laughed and stretched out his legs. The two friends sat in silence, sipping champagne, both lost in their own thoughts. The maple tree was in full leaf now, the leaves still tender and bright spring green. The azalea bushes had already finished blooming and the flower beds that Catherine had been working on were full of fresh green shoots and leaves. Ricky had volunteered to mow the previous weekend, and the grass was filling in and starting to look almost summer-like. Even the dandelions were hardly noticeable.

"The question is," said Frank eventually, "what do we do now? I'm sure not ready to retire."

"Me neither. I've been thinking about that question a lot the past few days, ever since Tuesday morning, in fact. We both just turned fifty. Forget what everyone says about being over the hill. When you're in your fifties, you're at your peak. You finally know what you're good at, you've got all kinds of experience and connections, you know what you want to do, you've still got energy, health, even money. Think about that, Frank: we're at our peak. We've got twenty or thirty years to do whatever the hell we want. The world is our oyster."

Frank laughed. "Yeah, right, look as us—I don't know about the energy part. You say you know what you want to do? That's news to me. Please do tell."

"Well, I don't know exactly what it is, but I know that I want to make some kind of a difference—pardon the cliché. I want to do my own thing, get away from huge corporations that suck the life out of you. Do something that *I* want to do."

"Yeah, that does sound good," agreed Frank. "Sign me up." A quiet silence descended on the deck again, broken only by a pair of robins in the maple tree sharing their joy with the world.

After a time, Buddy said, "I don't know how they measure it, but I recently heard on WHYY that Philadelphia is the poorest big city in America. Once you get out of Center City, I can believe it. Have you ever driven around North Philly?"

"Only a couple of times," replied Frank. "I try to avoid it. It's scary."

"The thing is," continued Buddy, "there are tons of organizations doing good things in places like North Philly, but it's hard to see the impact. And it seems like a lot of them are doing the same thing. Or maybe I just don't know enough about it."

Frank set down his glass. "I hear what you're saying, but what can *we* do about it? How are two old white guys going to fix Philadelphia's problems?"

"Yeah, I know." Buddy was lost in thought. Frank was content to sit quietly and enjoy the pleasant evening. A few minutes later, Buddy went on. "The thing is, I bet there are a lot of people like me; people who care about the city, and would help if they could, but don't know where to start, or how to go about it."

"That sounds like a job for the Internet," said a voice from behind them.

Buddy and Frank both jumped and twisted around in their chairs. "Ricky!" said Frank. "When did you get here?"

"About five minutes ago," said Ricky, standing in the open sliding glass door and leaning against the doorframe. "Someone left the door open, so I guess you didn't hear me."

"Come over here and have a seat, fellow partner in justice," said Buddy. "I still can't figure out how you managed to get around the password on Rupert's Power-Point in, what was it, thirty seconds flat? That must be some kind of a record." Buddy grabbed an empty glass and sloshed some champagne into it. "Here, you deserve this."

"A college degree has to be good for something, I guess," said Ricky modestly, taking a sip.

"Somehow I doubt you learned that in college," laughed Frank. "But maybe it's better we don't know too much about your secret powers. What did you mean that this is a job for the Internet?"

"You know, connecting things, connecting people. I heard you say there are a lot of organizations all doing the same thing, and a lot of people who want to help but don't know how. You don't have to fix Philadelphia's problems yourselves—just connect the people who want to help with the organizations who know what to do but don't have enough resources. That's what I meant." Ricky tilted his chair back against the railing and stretched out his back. He looked tired but his body still radiated a kind of quiet energy.

"Someone must already be doing that, don't you think?" asked Buddy.

"I'm new in town," said Ricky, "so I'm probably not the best person to ask. I bet there are directories and lists of organizations, but actually coordinating them and making things happen? I doubt it. That takes money and hard work."

"Hmm," said Buddy. "This is an intriguing idea. You might be onto something. I have tons of connections with corporations in Philly, and most of them have some kind of budget for social responsibility or local philanthropy. I wonder how effectively they're using that money. But it's not just about money—people really do want to volunteer and make a difference, and it's often hard to figure out how to do it in a meaningful way. I wonder if the right kind of organization could figure out how to connect all the pieces and really make a significant difference. I'm going to look into this some more. I know a guy who's on the board of one of Philly's big nonprofits. I'll give him a call and pick his brain."

Frank turned and looked at Buddy. When he spoke, his voice had lost its joking tone. "Look, Buddy," he said.

"I'm with you—I definitely do not want to go back to work in the accounting department of another big company that will drain me dry again. I'm done with that. But accounting is the only thing I know. If you're serious about starting something up, I would love to be the guy behind the scenes who handles the money and takes care of the business side. You can be the up-front schmoozer and idea guy, and I'll be the guy who actually gets stuff done."

"I'm not trying to sound like a broken record," said Ricky, "but you have to build this as a web-based enterprise from day one. It also has to be very social media savvy. That's how the world works now. Otherwise, it'll just be another tiny well-meaning nonprofit added to the list, always scrounging for money and only able to help a handful of people. Look, this sounds like a really great idea that I would love to have a hand in. I'm too busy to get involved on a day-to-day basis, but I can help put you in touch with the right kind of people and act as a tech advisor. Plus, my company is just getting started in Philly so we want to make a good impression by getting involved in stuff like this. I can probably persuade my colleagues to be supportive."

Buddy was sitting up in his chair, feeling newly re-energized. "Wow, I've been unemployed for less than two hours and I'm already the founder and codirector of a new organization. We just need a name and some start-up capital. And one thing I'm good at is getting people to part with their money for a good cause." He grabbed the half-empty champagne bottle and topped up their glasses. "It's time for another toast: to two old white guys and one young black guy making the world a better place!" They clinked their glasses.

There was a sudden commotion in the kitchen behind them. Ricky jumped up and disappeared into the house. They could hear Becky's excited voice, and a few minutes later she and Ricky appeared on the deck, followed soon after by Catherine.

"Where have you two been?" asked Frank.

"Shopping!" answered Becky, her face flushed with excitement. "Mom helped me find the perfect curtains for our living room. Plus a bunch of other stuff we needed, mostly for the kitchen. She talked me out of a bread machine that was half off. But I'll probably sneak out later tonight and buy it anyway. Hello, Mr. Kowalski," she added. "It's great that we're practically going to be neighbors. Fishtown is an awesome neighborhood."

"Yes," replied Buddy. "I can't wait to move into the city and say goodbye to the Ben Franklin Bridge."

"Hi, Buddy," said Catherine. "How's life?"

"Couldn't be better. I quit my job this afternoon, inspired by your husband, and in the last half hour, the three of us have come up with a brilliant new idea to make the world a better place." Ricky was still holding his glass, and the three men clinked their glasses together again.

"That sounds lovely," said Catherine, obviously not believing him. "Will you be solving world hunger too?"

"He's not kidding," said Frank. "He really did quit his job, and we really are thinking about starting a new organization together."

Catherine sat down. "That's what I get for leaving the three of you alone for a couple of hours. Good thing at least one person is still bringing home a paycheck." But Buddy could tell she was brimming with happiness. The tension he had noticed in her face and voice back at the birthday party had completely disappeared ever since the celebration dinner with Becky and Ricky. Having Becky back had clearly returned order to her world.

"Where did Ricky go?" said Becky. "Oh, there he is." Ricky reappeared with two more glasses in his hand.

"I have another toast," he said, "since that seems to be a thing in this family." He gave glasses to Becky and Catherine and then filled each glass with a half an inch of champagne from the dwindling supply. "This wasn't planned," he said, "but it won't be a surprise to anyone, least of all Becky." He reached into his pocket and pulled out a small, bright orange, plastic egg. After twisting it open, he walked over to Becky. "Hold out your hand, my love." Becky looked confused, but she held up her hand with the palm up. Ricky dumped the contents of the egg into her hand. "A toast to the woman I love," he said, "and to my future wife."

"Um," said Becky, still looking confused, "this is very sweet, but I thought you had ordered something a bit more . . ." she hesitated, "a bit more . . . I mean, with more diamonds. This looks kind of like a ring from a bubblegum machine."

"It is, my love, it is," said Ricky. "When I was at the 7-11 today, I randomly put a quarter in the gum machine and out came a gold ring—or at least a gold-colored ring. So I said to myself, 'What kind of omen is that?' And here we are all together, celebrating like a family, and there's still champagne in the bottle, so I figured, why not a pre-engagement to the engagement?"

"Don't worry," he quickly added to Becky, "the real one has been ordered."

"Well then," said Becky with exaggerated solemnity, "please at least place the ring on my finger, so I don't have to do it myself." Ricky picked up the ring from her hand and slipped it on her finger, but it was much too loose so he took it off again and carefully squished it to make it smaller. This time it fit, and Becky threw her arms around him and kissed him. "I do," she announced. The three witnesses cheered and clinked their glasses.

"To love and to cherish until death do us part," said Ricky, adding with a grin, "just practicing."

"Uh-oh," said Buddy. "I sense more tears coming. It's like Niagara Falls around here lately." A trickle of tears was already winding its way down Catherine's cheek. Frank, looking like he might be choking up too, put his arm around her.

Buddy picked up the champagne bottle, which still had a half inch of very warm, flat champagne. He dribbled a few more drops into everyone's glass until at last the bottle was empty.

"As the oldest person here," he said, "I get the last toast." He raised his glass. Becky and Ricky disentangled themselves and picked up their glasses. When all five glasses were raised, his voice cracking slightly, Buddy pronounced the final blessing: "To old friends . . . and new families." In the warm summer evening, the sound of the glasses clinking went out across the lawn like the pealing of bells.

EPILOGUE

Buddy had insisted on an early start, and it was a few minutes after eight in the morning when he pulled into Frank and Catherine's driveway. It was a typical spring morning in New Jersey, mist drifting along the street and the temperature hovering in the low forties. Frank must have been looking out the window watching for him because the front door opened right away, and Frank appeared in the doorway holding a steaming travel mug. He awkwardly tried to close the door while blocking the opening with his leg, but a dark shadow darted out the door. Buddy chuckled as Frank set his mug down on the step, knocked it over, picked it up, then kneeled in front of a bush next to the door before finally lying flat on his stomach and reaching under the bush. When he stood up, he was holding a small gray cat by the scruff of its neck. He gently tossed it into the house and slammed the door shut.

"Hey, Buddy," Frank said as he dusted himself off and climbed into the car. "Thanks for picking me up. Sorry for the delay—that stupid cat is always getting out and we're afraid he'll run out into the street."

"Sure thing, glad you could come. Fred, I presume?"

"Yes. Fred the seventh, to be precise."

Buddy was not in the mood for chatting, and neither of them spoke as he expertly navigated the back streets of the neighborhood and turned south on Route 41. Frank quietly sipped his coffee. The traffic was minimal this early on a Saturday morning, and in less than half an hour Buddy was swinging into a tree-lined driveway, gravel crunching under the tires as they passed under an arch with large, slightly rusted metal letters announcing they had arrived at Cherrywood Memorial Park.

Buddy parked the car in the empty parking lot. "I like to get here early so I can be by myself," he said, opening his door. He led the way down a winding brick path that had fresh green weeds already starting to emerge in the cracks. Gravestones were scattered on either side without any apparent logic or pattern, many of them crumbling or slanted at odd angles. Occasionally, a larger obelisk or statue could be seen looming indistinctly through the mist. Abruptly, he turned off the path and wove his way through the headstones, walking quickly on his long legs, his shoes getting soaked by the wet grass. More space began to open up between the tombstones, and there was evidence of recent graves as they approached the edge of the vast cemetery. Behind him, Frank struggled to keep up.

Buddy slowed and then stopped. "This is it," he said, pointing at a modest granite gravestone in front of him. Smaller matching stones enclosed a small flowerbed in front of the headstone. It looked neatly tended, and a clump of cheerful yellow daffodils with darker orange centers was in full bloom. The green blades of tulips were beginning to emerge around them.

Frank bent over and read the inscription out loud:

Darnell Richards
February 17, 1963 – April 5, 2013
A Big Man with a Big Heart
Micah 6:8

"A big man with a big heart," he repeated. "Who chose the epitaph, do you know?"

"No," said Buddy. "I did finally manage to connect with his New Jersey relative, but we only had one brief phone call. I assume it must have been her. I'm not even sure she still lives in the area. I wish I could have gone to the funeral, but I found him too late. By about two days." Buddy sighed.

"The grave looks well cared for," remarked Frank. "Is that thanks to you?"

"Yeah." Buddy stared at the grave somberly. "This became my thoughtful spot last year after Bunny left. You know, like Winnie the Pooh. I came here a lot. Not so much lately though, now that I'm living in Philly."

Frank looked around the cemetery. It had clearly been there for a long time; tall trees and overgrown shrubs were scattered among the gravestones, many of which had been faded by weather to near illegibility. "I guess if you ignore all the graves, this place easily could be the Hundred-Acre Wood. Have you ever noticed Eeyore munching on thistles or Piglet gathering haycorns?"

"No," Buddy said with a smile, "but it is kind of magical and timeless here. I suppose I did have a few Eeyore kind of days—and a few bouncy Tigger ones, too. Another thing I like about this place is that it has benches. Come with me." Frank followed him around a large shrub, and there on a low hillock below an ancient-looking oak was a wooden bench that had seen better days but still looked solid enough. Buddy took a dingy handkerchief out of his pocket and brushed off the leaves.

"It might be kind of damp," he apologized. The two men sat down and gazed out across the tombstones. The mist was lifting and it looked like the sun was trying to break through.

"A lot has happened in the past year," said Frank. "If you had told me a year ago that I would quit my job and that the two of us would be running a new nonprofit we started, I would have said you were crazy. Frank O'Donnell doesn't do that kind of thing. It had never occurred to me that I could just quit my job and do something I wanted to do."

"That was the old Frank O'Donnell," said Buddy. "But it's the same for me; I never expected any of this. Our new venture is going really great, don't you think? I love the name Catherine came up with, Shoulder-to-Shoulder. Did I tell you that our latest grant application looks like it will be approved? I told them you would be in touch with the updated financial info. I bet this idea will work in other cities too. I'm going to talk to Garbo and find out about the situation in Cleveland."

"Even Becky has helped out a bit. Did you know the concept for the new logo was her idea?"

"No," said Buddy, "but I'm not surprised; she's one smart cookie." He pulled out his wallet, pulled out a business card, and handed it to Frank. "Check out the new card. Hot off the press. The logo came out great."

"Nice," said Frank, examining the card. "*Rudolph Kowalski*?" He glanced at Buddy with raised eyebrows. "What happened to *Buddy*?"

"I dunno. I'm getting kind of tired of that old nickname, I guess. Thought I'd try out my real name for a while and see how it grabs me."

"Well, don't expect me to get used to that for at least another fifty years. But I get where you're coming from."

Buddy gazed out across the gravestones, a few of the taller ones now tipped with sunlight, a contented look on his face.

"We couldn't have done any of this without Ricky," said Frank. "And to think that a year ago I hated the guy and thought he was a criminal. Now he's going to be my son-in-law. He really is the perfect match for Becky. Moral of the story: fathers can be blind and clueless idiots, or at least this one was. The wedding is coming up soon, in June. Catherine's in her element. Next project—grandkids."

"Frank, I want to start a college scholarship fund named after Mouse. Can we do that? I'll raise the money."

"Sure, I have no objection. But who will it be for? Athletes?"

"That's the problem. I do want to help athletes, but Mouse always hated the way kids believed that sports were their ticket out of the ghetto, and how they always looked at him as some kind of proof. But even though football did pay off for him, at least money-wise, he said it chained him down at the same time, and never gave him the chance to do what he really wanted to do. Which was sing. Plus, the number of kids who make it in sports is tiny. It's a fool's dream for most of them. Not to mention destroying their bodies, like it did for Mouse."

"We could call it the Darnell Richards Fund to Rescue Wannabe Athletes From a Fate Worse Than Death," suggested Frank.

"Ha," said Buddy, "I know you're joking, but it's not far off the truth. I want to give kids in those poor neighborhoods something to dream about other than sports. They can play sports for fun—sure, that's great—but they need money to go to college for a real reason. I'm serious about this, Frank."

"It's a good idea, Buddy. We should do it. We can ask Catherine to come up with the name."

The sun was definitely breaking through the mist now, and as it rose above the trees the sunlight caught huge banks of tangled forsythia bushes along the edge of the cemetery that were just coming into bloom. The brilliant yellow blossoms bursting in the sunlight were almost blinding in contrast with the earlier mist. The sun seemed to have awakened the birds as well, and their chattering songs echoed cheerfully among the trees and gravestones.

"Aren't you glad we got here early?" asked Buddy.

"You know what I just realized?" said Frank. "Today is the day of my surprise birthday party last year, April fifth. That means Mouse died the same day as the party."

"That's funny—I never made that connection before. It's strange to think about, isn't it? It was because of the party that I started looking for Mouse."

"I know. Catherine and I were discussing this the other day. When you think about it, that party had incredible ripple effects."

"What do you mean?" asked Buddy.

"Well, to begin with, that's how I found out about the credit card."

"Ugh. Did you have to remind me of that?" said Buddy with a groan. "But I suppose that whole screwup was part of my hitting bottom, which ended up turning me in a new direction."

"And the party is also what tipped me off about Rupert. Denise was there and made some kind of comment about the sales figures, and one thing led to another. And the whole Rupert thing is why I ended up quitting."

"Here's another one," said Buddy. "It was at the party that Bunny heard that other guy from your office—was it Dave?—talking about how Lori helped with the prank. So

I guess you could say the party is what triggered Bunny leaving me. Although not the reason for it, of course," he added quickly.

"That one was too bad," Frank said. He hesitated, and then went on. "You said once that you thought it was too late by then to patch things up with Bunny. But the divorce happened so fast . . . do you think things could have turned out differently somehow? Do you miss her?"

Buddy furrowed his brow and said, "Yeah, I do miss her. A lot, actually. We had been friends for such a long time. And then, bam, it's over, she's gone from my life. But, no, I don't think there was anything I could have done at that point, sorry to say. I had already messed it up too bad."

"That stinks," said Frank. "And now it turns out that Mouse died the very same day of the party."

"I was just trying to throw a surprise party to cheer you up," said Buddy. "Something made me start thinking about that prank back at the U of O." They fell silent, pondering the mysteries of fate.

The sun had risen high enough to reach the bench with its warming rays. As it touched the grass, the dew sparkled in the light. A squirrel ran along one of the branches above them, chattering angrily at their intrusion on his day.

"Was that a Bible verse on Mouse's gravestone?" asked Frank after a while. "Was it Matthew something?"

"No," replied Buddy. "Micah 6:8."

"I'm going to look it up," said Frank, pulling out his new smartphone.

"No need," said Buddy. "I memorized it long ago." He cleared his throat. "'He has showed you, O man, what is good; and what does the Lord require of you but to do justice, and to love kindness, and to walk humbly with your God.'"

Frank nodded his head thoughtfully. "Good words to live by," he said.

"Yes," said Buddy, "very good words."

The two old friends sat for a while on the bench and let the sun warm them. Then, without speaking, they stood up, passed by Mouse's grave one more time, and walked back to the car together.

Acknowledgements

This book would not exist without the love, inspiration, and encouragement of my wife Janet, truly my best and oldest friend. Writing a novel has been on my bucket list for almost as long as I can remember. In 2020, when the pandemic lockdown hit me hard, Janet said, "Now's the time." When I didn't know where to start, she enrolled me in a MasterClass taught by Margaret Atwood, one of my favorite authors. Then, as the chapters of *Old Friends* began to emerge, she read each one and kept encouraging me, offering insightful comments from her counseling experience, and not letting me stop until the final (fifth) draft was completed over two years later. So, thank you, Janet, for believing in me!

I also greatly appreciated the encouragement and thoughtful comments from those who read the "First Edition," including family and friends, with a special shout-out to the old friends at the Gary Brasor Princeton Area Book Club.

Vini Libassi was a lifesaver, finishing the cover design with a masterful touch when last-minute glitches had stalled the project.

Finally, I would like to acknowledge the helpful editing team at 2Nimble: Audrey Hoisington, Sarah Knapp, and Christy Woods.

Gloria Deo.

www.ingramcontent.com/pod-product-compliance
Lightning Source LLC
Chambersburg PA
CBHW020138310726
48970CB00006B/1930